DATE DUE

THE DEVIL IN ME

BOOKS OF POETRY BY J.D. CARPENTER

Nightfall, Ferryland Head (1976)
Swimming at Twelve Mile (1979)
Lakeview (1990)
Compassionate Travel (1994)

THE DEVIL IN ME

A CAMPBELL YOUNG MYSTERY

J. D. CARPENTER

National Library of Canada Cataloguing in Publication Data

Carpenter, J.D.
The devil in me

"A Campbell Young mystery".
ISBN 0-7710-1922-X

I. Title.

PS8555.A7616D48 2001   C813'.54   C00-933015-1
PR9199.3.C37D48 2001

We acknowledge the financial support of the Government of Canada through the Book Publishing Industry Development Program for our publishing activities. We further acknowledge the support of the Canada Council for the Arts and the Ontario Arts Council for our publishing program.

Lyrics from "Night Moves" written by Bob Seger, copyright © 1976 Gear Publishing 6 (ASCAP), are reprinted by permission.

Typeset in Janson by M&S, Toronto
Printed and bound in Canada

McClelland & Stewart Ltd.
The Canadian Publishers
481 University Avenue
Toronto, Ontario
M5G 2E9
www.mcclelland.com

1 2 3 4 5   05 04 03 02 01

For D.C.C.

"Farewell the tranquil mind; farewell content!"

– Othello, III, iii

PART ONE

Tuesday, October 6, 1992

THE MORE GRUESOME the crime the more you smoke, so when I see the entrance to apartment 412 choked with smoking men, I pretty much know what to expect.

"Find out who the M.E. is," I say to Wheeler, and as she heads inside I exchange pleasantries with Silliphant from HQ and the black guy with red hair whose name I can never remember. "Who do you like?" I ask Silliphant.

He doesn't even blink. "Oakland in six. Rusty here likes Toronto."

I nod. "I like Toronto in six myself."

I'm just lighting a cigarette when Wheeler comes back out.

"Cronish wants to talk to you," she says.

"Cronish, great," I say, and make a face. Silliphant and Rusty smile.

Inside the living room, one whole wall is books and the other three are paintings, like in a store.

The half-glasses Elliot Cronish wears make him look Chinese. He's sitting on the sofa flipping through his notes.

"What have you got?" I ask him.

He gives me his inscrutable look. I feel like reminding him he's Jewish, not Chinese, so why does he try to look like Fu Manchu, but I hold my tongue.

"You better take a look," Cronish says, "before Forensics fucks it up."

"Where is it?"

The angle of Cronish's head doesn't change, but his eyes swivel up like a lizard's so he's looking at me over the top of his glasses. "You're the detective. Detect."

It's in the bathroom, kneeling bare-assed in front of the toilet with its head in the bowl. Wrists bound together behind its back with silver duct tape. This is not a fresh kill: for one thing, there's the smell – ripe as bad bologna; that, and the buttocks and thighs are grey-blue. It's the width of the hips tells me it's a woman. That and the pink sweatpants down around the ankles. I step forward. The head is upside down in the brown water. I can't see the face. I step back and look around. No sign of a struggle. Shampoo still standing on the edge of the bathtub. Towels neatly folded on their racks. I hear someone come in behind me.

"Jesus," Wheeler says.

After she takes notes for a minute or two, I say, "Come on, we've seen enough."

Back in the living room, Cronish stands up.

"What can you tell me?" I ask him.

"Not much till the autopsy. She's been dead awhile."

"No shit. My dog could tell me that."

Cronish looks at me. "Four or five days, judging from the lividity. Blunt trauma to the back of the head, but she may have drowned."

"How long till you know?"

"Two days."

"Who found her?"

"Her sister." Cronish gestures towards the bathroom. "Are you done, Young? Can I tell them to get her out of there?"

"How'd the sister get in?"

"I don't know. I'm the coroner, remember? Ask your patrolman. Can I tell them to get started?"

"Yeah, go ahead."

Across the room, a uniform is standing by the window. It's Barkas. His olive complexion isn't olive. It's tzatziki. I walk over to him. "You all right?"

He looks at me. "Cocksucker drowned her in the toilet, Sarge."

I let out a breath. "You're first officer, right?"

"Yeah, me and Big Urmson."

"How'd the sister get in?"

"She has her own key. They were going shoppin' for their mother's birthday."

"Where is she?"

Barkas looks confused. "In the bathroom?"

"The sister."

"Oh. She's gone. Big Urmson took her home. She wasn't in no state for any questions."

"You should have kept her here."

He looks worried. "She was flippin' out, Sarge. She was high-sterical."

"Anything else?"

"Well . . ." He hesitates. "It might not be important, but the spare room has a photocopier in it, and a lot of other equipment, like maybe she ran some kind of business."

I tell Barkas to grab a cup of coffee, then I stick my head into the spare bedroom. There's a photocopier, a computer and printer, a stamping machine and rolls of address stickers. Piles of magazines. I'm thinking maybe porn, so I flip through a couple, but there's no pictures.

Cronish is in the kitchen, peeling off his rubber gloves.

"Let me know what else you find," I say. "I'll be in tomorrow."

"Yes, Your Highness," he says.

Wheeler is waiting by the door. I say so long to Silliphant and what's-his-name, we let the body-bag boys through, and then we get on the elevator. Downstairs in the lobby we nod to a couple of uniforms, and I make a boogie face at a couple of kids hiding behind a potted plant. Outside, we walk along the curved driveway that leads from the building's entrance past about ten police vehicles – unmarkeds, black-and-whites, a rescue truck – to the street where we left our cruiser. It's a cool morning, leaves falling like a bomb's gone off.

Parked behind our car is an old Toyota. I point at it and say, "What do you think?"

Wheeler studies the car for a few seconds. "What do I think about what?"

"Look at the bumper stickers."

She reads them. "So?"

"So, appearances can be deceiving. Man buys a used car, like this old shitbox with 'We're Proud of Our Gay and Lesbian Children' and 'I Heart Highland Dancing' on the bumper, and he might hate faggots and he might not know Scotland from Siberia, but he just never got around to scraping off the previous guy's politics."

Wheeler's staring at me.

I inhale deeply. I see the body again. Naked and bound. I survey the blue and cloudless sky. Maybe an explanation will appear – like a marriage proposal behind a Cessna.

"What's your problem?" Wheeler says.

I exhale, long and slow. I lean against the roof of the Toyota. "I don't know. Gay bumper stickers. That's my problem."

"You're homophobic."

I'm about to turn away when something yellow inside the Toyota catches my eye, and when I look more closely I see about a million parking tickets on the passenger-side floor. Then I hear somebody shouting my name. I turn around, and here comes Silliphant chugging along the sidewalk.

"Cronish thought you oughta know . . . ," he says, panting, when he reaches us.

"What?" I say.

He can hardly talk he's puffing so much. ". . . they got her out of the toilet . . ."

"Whoop-de-doo," I say.

". . . and her mouth was wide open . . ."

"Yeah, and . . . ?"

". . . and there was something inside."

"Something inside her mouth?"

"Yeah," he puffs. "A tennis ball . . . a brand-new, lime-green Slazenger. Crammed inside her mouth."

Wheeler got bumped up to detective last March. When she was assigned to Homicide and introduced to her partner – me – she was thrilled. She told me so, our second day together. We were in the cruiser, and she said, "Sergeant, I like your size." She asked how tall I was. When I told her, she said, "You're as big as Randy Johnson!"

"Don't know him," I said.

"Pitcher with the Seattle Mariners?"

"Oh, *that* Randy Johnson," I said. "No, *Street & Smith's* has him six-ten. He's got a couple of inches on me, though I've probably got seventy-five pounds on him. He's a skinny son of a bitch."

She looked at me with pure admiration. "You know your base-ball," she said.

Nothing much happened the first few weeks. Considering how large it is, Toronto's pretty quiet. We average about seventy homicides a year. By comparison, a small place like Gary, Indiana, has forty times as many. So me and Wheeler did other stuff. Checked into a few suicides, a few accidentals. And when we had time for ourselves – in a coffee shop, or when we were driving – we talked about the really important things in life: baseball and dogs and movies.

"Sarge, did you watch cop movies when you were a kid?" she asked me once. We were sitting at a light on Mount Pleasant, and I'd just popped a Bob Seger tape into the cassette. We were halfway back to HQ from a botched suicide. We'd just taken the kid home to his father. Watching that little reunion was better than TV.

"Sure. *Dog Day Afternoon. Bullitt. French Connection.* Gene Hackman played Popeye Doyle."

"Do you ever imagine a movie being made about you?"

"Me?"

"Yeah, you and me, say."

"I don't recall us busting any major drug rings in the past three weeks."

She frowned and looked out the window. The lights changed. "Who would play you?"

"You mean what actor?"

"Yes."

"Harvey Keitel."

"You *have* thought about it."

I gave her a look, but she just stared back at me, big-eyed. You never know which eye to look at with Wheeler, because one of them's black-coffee brown, and the other's light blue. The brown one's like a button, you can't see into it, but the blue one's like a pool – you could fall right in if you got too close.

"But you're wrong, Sarge."

"About what?"

"Harvey Keitel. I mean, he's wicked in *Reservoir Dogs*, but he's not big enough."

"Well, that's true. So who?"

"Brian Dennehy."

I nodded. "Yeah, I can see that. And who plays you?"

"Who do you suggest?"

I think for a minute. "Sally Field."

"Never heard of her. Is she an older actress?"

"You've never heard of Sally Field?" I glanced away from the traffic long enough to see she was smiling at me.

"Just teasing, Sarge. I was thinking more along the lines of Bridget Fonda or Jennifer Jason Leigh."

And so on. This was the way we talked to each other – relaxed, kidding. Even though I was fifteen years older, and even though we hardly ever socialized off-hours, and even though I never talked about my personal life – despite her prodding – we became good partners.

Until one hot night in June.

We were driving up Yonge Street through the downtown section of video parlours, arcades, adult bookstores, fast-food outlets, table-dancing emporiums. The street itself was jammed with muscle cars and Volvo station wagons crammed with tourists. The sidewalks were crowded – street people selling jewellery; well-dressed black families from Buffalo and Detroit walking up the main street of the safest big city in North America; kids down from the 'burbs for a weekend of walking on the wild side; skinheads and dopers and bums. The air was full of rock 'n' roll from the bars and car radios and music stores, and smells coming off the sausage carts like cartoon aromas. It was just that type of evening – quiet, easygoing – that makes me nervous, and when Wheeler, who was driving, pulled alongside a Tim Hortons for coffee, I said, "Not here. Go on up to Coffee Time."

But I hadn't been fast enough. As she started to pull away, she glanced into the window, saw what was going on, and hit the brakes.

"Assault!" she yelled, and pulled her billy out with one hand as she opened her door with the other.

I radioed Dispatch, then followed her into the restaurant, where she already had a kid in a Bulls jacket face-first over the counter. I used the phone beside the cash register to call an ambulance for the bloody-faced counterman, cleared the place of everyone who claimed not to know anything, and began to take statements from those who claimed they did. It was only later, driving back to HQ with Dennis Rodman, or whoever he thought he was, cuffed and trash-talking in the back seat, it dawned on me that Wheeler was seriously pissed at me.

"Good work in there," I said, but she wasn't talking.

I went back to my notes for a few minutes, and then she suddenly blurted out, "Why did you tell me to drive away from there?"

I looked out the side window at the passing parade. "Coffee's better at Coffee Time."

"Don't give me that! You saw what was going on in there before I even pulled up. Didn't you? And another thing. I was alone in there for a good thirty seconds before you arrived. How come?" She was glaring at me. "Answer me." And she pounded the steering wheel with her fist.

"All right," I said, turning towards her. "Yeah, I saw what was going on in there. Another goddamn doper making a withdrawal."

She was shocked into silence. She looked into the rearview mirror at Dennis Rodman, then back at the road ahead.

"I'm three years from retirement," I said quietly. "Three years and a few months."

She said nothing.

"I can practically taste it, and I'm not going to get myself carved up by some crackhead nignog."

She paused for a moment, deciding whether or not to say what was on her mind. Didn't take her very long. "Not only are you a coward, you're a racist coward. I'll put in for a new partner tomorrow. Or maybe you'd better do it. It would look better coming from you. Personality differences or something. But I don't want to ride with you any more."

Of course I never put in the request for transfer – I could have done a lot worse than her – and she, learning the ropes, knew better than to finger a respected nineteen-year man for dereliction. Career suicide. Calling me a racist burned, though. It wasn't true, despite what I'd said. Before Wheeler arrived on the scene, Artie Trick and I had been partners, and he's as black as Bill Cosby. Me and him were tight. We knew each other's moves like we knew our own. But after we'd been together ten years, Staff Inspector Bateman split us up. "You're too comfortable with Trick," he said. "You're losing your edge. I want you working with someone younger." Maybe he was right, but I wish Trick still was my partner, and if I thought there was any chance we could get back together, I'd put in for it. For the first five years we were together – before my marriage went belly-up – Trick was over at my house all the time. We used to watch the Bills games on Sunday afternoons and knock back a few beers. He loved the Bills. And my daughter Debi loved him. Still loves him. Uncle Artie. So what I'm saying is sometimes I say things I shouldn't, but I'm no racist.

Anyway, from that time on my relationship with Wheeler was kind of stiff. She didn't look up to me any more, like she did at the beginning. Just like marriage. When they stop admiring you, when they stop thinking you're the cat's ass, you're basically done. You might as well crawl into a hole.

"Homophobic! What the fuck is homophobic?" I'm lighting a cigarette, and we're both watching Silliphant huff and puff back towards the apartment building.

"It means you're afraid of men," Wheeler says.

I look at her. "I'm afraid of men?"

She looks up into the sky. "We don't have time for this," she says.

"What do you mean I'm afraid of men?"

She pulls her gaze back down from the sky and turns it on me. "Maybe it didn't sink in, but there's a dead woman up there."

I'm not moving. "How can I be afraid of men? Look at the size of me. I'm not afraid of anything."

Wheeler has this trick she does with her eyes. If she's being sweet to you, she somehow makes you look at the blue eye, the one you could fall right into, but if she's pissed at you, she makes you look at the other one – the brown one. Right now I'm looking at the brown one.

"Homophobic," she says in the slow, patient tone you'd use with a child, "means you hate gay men because you're trying to hide the feminine side of your own personality."

"Oh really," I say. "What feminine side would that be?"

"Like maybe you enjoy certain things that are usually associated with women, like cooking or decorating or knitting. Maybe you like to dress up."

"Maybe you're lucky you're a woman or I'd crush your skull like a beer can."

We're at the cruiser. "Who's driving?" she says.

"You've got the keys," I say. Wheeler walks around to the other side of the car. Over the roof I say to her, "The reason I hate fags is because they fuck each other up the ass. I don't believe in the big picture men were *intended* to fuck each other up the ass."

Wheeler's unlocking the driver's door. "It's not a manly thing to do?"

"Forget it," I say. "Come on. I'll buy you a coffee and a donut. I know how you love them raised vanillas."

She's inside now, and my door unlocks with a click.

"How about an orange twist or a double chocolate?" I ask her. "How about a *cruller*?" Most days Wheeler would die for a cruller.

She turns the key in the ignition and then she looks at me. "A woman's been murdered. She was raped first, and then she was murdered. Me, I'm going back to Homicide, and I'm going to get to work. I'm going to figure out why the killer crammed a tennis ball in her mouth. You can come with me or you can go to Coffee Time. I personally don't care, but make up your mind." She moves the gearshift into drive. "What's it gonna be?"

CHAPTER 2

Wednesday, October 7

CLOSE TO MY EAR someone's telling me the Blue Jays' championship series against the Oakland A's begins tonight. I open my eyes and look across the room at Debi staring back at me from her picture on the dresser. My wife insisted on the spelling. Not Deborah. Not even Debbie. I thought it was stupid then and I think so now. Maybe if we'd spelled it the normal way she wouldn't be so screwed-up. Right now she's got a crewcut. But at least it isn't pink or green. It's her natural colour – white blonde. When she was growing up, my friends enjoyed making mailman jokes about her. Especially Trick. "So, let me get this straight, Camp. Your wife's got straight brown hair, your daughter's got straight blonde hair, and your hair's kinky as mine and red as a baboon's asshole. Wicary in Fingerprinting says he's the daddy, but so does Sven the caterer. All I know is it ain't me. What's the real truth?"

Debi dropped out of high school after grade ten and right now she's walking hots and grooming horses at Caledonia Downs for a public trainer named Shorty Rogers, an old drinking buddy of mine.

Debi doesn't think before she does anything. She's reckless, impatient, short-tempered, and she's also got quite the mouth on her. In other words, she takes after me. She was cute when she was little, but she's turned out kind of plain, despite the blonde hair. She can blame that on my ugly mug. And she's big as a linebacker, which she can blame on me as well. Her mother may have been a bitch, but she was a good-looking bitch. When she was sixteen Debi ran away from home with her boyfriend – a pizza deliveryman who happened to own a Honda Nighthawk and a dream of joining the Hells Angels in California. She phoned me from Field, British Columbia, a week later, and I sent her money for the bus trip back to T.O. She settled back down, but then a friend of hers named Kelly did a swan dive off the Bloor viaduct into rush-hour traffic, and Debi lost it again. She was in hospital for a few weeks, then she was out, and then she was back in again. Then she was pregnant. And then she had an abortion – she never did tell me who the father was. Now she's twenty-one and she's got a three-year-old half-black baby boy named Jamal – a cute little guy, but I can barely even stand to say his name inside my head let alone out loud – a bad apartment in a bad part of the west end, and a job at the racetrack. No sign of Jamal's pappy. Maybe he was the abortion's pappy, too. She also has a tattoo of a tulip on her ankle and another below her left collarbone that says "DOLL PARTS." I have a tattoo of my own, a simple heart on my left arm: written through it is the word "DEBI."

I reach across to the bedside table and tap the kill button on the radio. I sit up and rub my fingers through my hair. Me and Wheeler are on days, which means I'll be able to watch the ballgame tonight.

My bulldog, Reggie, pads into the room and noses under my elbow. "Yes, girl," I say, and massage behind her ears. "Yes, you fat pup." She pants with enjoyment. "Nice breath this morning," I say. "Let me take a whiz, and we'll fix us some breakfast."

I crack my toes, stand up, and head for the bathroom. The toilet seat is up – it's usually up, unlike the old days with women in the house – and as I lean one hand against the wall above the toilet and let go my bladder, I close my eyes, and there she is again: wrists taped together behind her back, short dark hair floating like an oil slick.

I open my eyes to watch what I'm doing. We Aim To Please. You Aim Too Please. One of those wooden novelty plaques we had on the walls at the cottage. Before the breakup. Buckhorn Lake. Debi on the dock in her orange life preserver. A light breeze lifting her blonde hair. Me in the boat, lowering the red metal gas tank into position. Picnic on Gull Island.

There had been a second tattoo, on my right arm. "TANYA," it said. A few years ago Tanya gave me an ultimatum: quit the force or quit the house. I left her in a minute. Back then I *was* the force. I loved my work and my colleagues and the danger and the Friday nights at McCully's. I didn't have any time for my family. So she kicked me out, and I moved into a walk-up over a Greek restaurant on the Danforth. When Debi came to visit the first time, she cried. All I had was the La-Z-Boy, a frying pan, one set of dishes, and a dozen knives, forks, and spoons, about twenty-seven ashtrays, and the Ken Danby print of the goalie, which I hung over the artificial fireplace. The walls were mauve, the carpet was orange shag, the mirror in the bathroom was cracked like somebody's forehead had hit it, and the shower curtain smelled like piss. "Goddamn," Debi said. "Who lived here before you did, Daddy? Megadeth?"

Eventually I moved to where I'm living now. It's a second-floor apartment in a duplex. Two bedrooms, so it's bigger than the old place. Kitchenette. Living-room window overlooks the street. It has a balcony out back, which is real nice, with stairs down to a little yard where Reg can do her business. The view isn't great – all you can see is a parking lot and an alley and the backyards of the small houses the next street over. One guy keeps a goat in his yard. Another guy has an old DeSoto he works on all the time. I was sitting out there one evening last week, listening to the ballgame on the radio, Reg asleep under my lawnchair, and I did an inventory of all the stuff on the balcony. Three dozen red bricks. A Moffat Synchromatic Range in need of some serious repair. An empty jar of Bick's Hot Banana Peppers I use for an ashtray. A skinny old sideboard from the cottage with glass windows in the door. Inside you can see Scattergories, Pictionary, Balderdash, Probe, Pit.

Anyway, the divorce proceedings went ahead. Debi began to get in trouble, Tanya wouldn't talk to me, and my love for the job began to die. And where the TANYA tattoo used to be there's an ugly rectangle of raised red skin, which I hide with long-sleeved shirts.

I have my shower, get dressed, let Reg out, feed myself, fix Reg's breakfast – Purina dry, a charcoal Milk-Bone for the breath, a slice of bread, and the milk left over from my Grape-Nuts – let her back in and let myself out.

While we were together, one of the many things me and Tanya argued about was air conditioning. She wanted it everywhere – in the house, in the car, in the backyard if she could get it – and I didn't want it anywhere. So now, as I drive down Woodbine towards the Danforth, I have my left arm resting comfortably through the open window of my robin's-egg-blue 1978 Plymouth Volare. Despite the disintegrating ceiling – you can pull the material off in strips, like skin off a burn victim – and the rust around the wheel wells and a subpar tape deck, I love the car. It dates back to family life, maybe that's why. The only thing I would really change about the car has to do with smoking. Tanya had always objected to me smoking in the car – or in the house; anywhere, for that matter – and since the divorce, I've been a smokaholic. What the car lacks are those little no-draft windows you can open to just the right angle to flick your ashes through. I spent my youth in such cars and miss those little no-draft windows. When I mentioned this to Debi one Saturday afternoon as I was picking her up at the track, she said, "What can I say, Daddy? They don't make things like they used to," and I was once again reminded about the age fence, and how I was on the other side of it.

—〰—

As I pull into the parking lot at HQ, I see Wheeler getting out of her Suzuki. She has her windbreaker zipped to the neck against the cold.

"Morning, Wheeler," I call, and she gives me a nod. "Morris versus Stewart tonight. Should be a wild one."

"Whatever," she says. "Let's see what they found out about the dead woman."

The walls of my office are not walls at all, but those soundproof dividers that are about as soundproof as a tent. I'm not complaining. Except for Staff Inspector Bateman, everyone else is in the same boat as me. So my working conditions leave something to be desired. A few years earlier I loved the noise, the hustle and bustle. Music to my ears. But back then my adrenalin was pumping full-time. Now I can hardly stand the sound of a pen dropping.

Used to be you could put anything you wanted on the walls of your cubicle. Within reason. Naked women were out, of course, but semi-naked women were okay. So every January I would begin pinning up the daily Sunshine Girl from the paper; by the end of March I would have run out of space and would have to take them all down and start over. Someone made a sign, CAMP'S *GAL*-LERY, and no one objected. Not even the recruits, not even the girls with their nineties ideas about women's rights. Not even Wheeler, until the spot of trouble we had at the Tim Hortons. About a week later, after I had successfully done nothing about her demand for a new partner, I got a memo from Bateman himself: "SORRY CAMP, NO MORE SUNSHINE GIRLS! DON'T ASK."

While I was taking them down, Trick told me he saw Wheeler in Bateman's office earlier that morning with one of my Sunshine Girls in her hand; he said she'd balled it up in her fist and whipped it at one of the glass windows that separates the staff inspector from the rest of us. I said, "Well, fuck that shit," and Trick said, "She's got a good arm, you know. We should try her at second," and I said, "Big Urmson plays second," and Trick, who's tall and lean and looks a lot like Denzel Washington, and plays centre field on our slo-pitch team a lot like Devon White plays centre field for the Blue Jays, said, "Big Urmson's well named, Camp. He's a fat cow, he's a tub of shit. The only reason you keep him on the team is because he's been around forever, and he's always played second. He averages a dozen errors a game!" and I said, "Game is the key word, pal, it's just a game," and Trick said, "If it's just a game, how come you went after Jack Talsky of 51 that time over at Thorncliffe?" and I said, "He was out by a mile but he still threw himself at me like Pete Rose did to Ray Fosse, and besides, that was years ago. You won't catch me doing that sort of thing any more."

The upshot of it was that I let Wheeler have her way about the Sunshine Girls, and after that the only items that graced my walls were baseball and hockey schedules, cartoons I'd cut out of the newspaper, an eight-by-ten of Debi in the winner's circle holding the bridle of one of Shorty Rogers's valiant claimers, and another of Reg with a Santa hat on her head.

Barry Estabrooks leans his head over the top of one of my partitions like a giraffe, and waits till I notice him. He's almost as tall as I am. Well, not really. Six-four, maybe. Left fielder. Kind of goofy. Borderline stupid. Thinks he's a hit with the ladies. Thinks he's Ted Danson. In his fourth or fifth year and, since Wheeler's arrival, Trick's new partner. Probationary.

"Yes, Estabrooks," I say, and he comes into the opening of my cubicle. Jacket over one arm, file folder in his hand.

"Thought I'd deliver this before I went home," he says. "Dope on your victim."

"Thanks," I say, and for an instant I feel the old excitement. Clues. Pieces of the puzzle.

Estabrooks says, "I hate nights."

"Look at it this way, Estabrooks. Tonight when you wake up, you can catch game one before coming in."

"Oh yeah," he says, nodding. "I'd forgotten about the game. That'll be good."

When he's gone I clear my desk and open the folder.

```
Joanne Jane Stevenson
830 Berton Street,
Apartment 412
Toronto, Ontario M4T 2P9
Age: 29
Marital Status: Single
Occupation: Journalist
Criminal Record: None

Next Of Kin:
Parents:  Thomas and Edith Stevenson
          26 Victory Arch Avenue, Toronto
          M7R 5J8

Brothers: James George Stevenson
          354 Baldwin Street, London, Ontario
          L8H 1W3
          Michael Andrew Stevenson
          Apartment 1004, 19 Queen's Walk,
          Toronto M6K 7Y7

Sister:   Vanessa June Murphy
          88 Clocktower Road, Toronto M4R 5B2

B. Estabrooks
```

I close the folder and carry it around to the south end of Homicide where Wheeler has her cubbyhole. When she got bumped up, I told her she could have the desk opposite mine, but she said she preferred to be off by herself, so I said okay. She's off by herself, all right. Next to the Coke machine. Back when we were friends she used to complain to me about the sound the cans made as they fell. "Like railway cars being coupled," she said once. "Even the sound of the coins bugs me." And like an idiot I said, "Like railway cars coupling?" and laughed, but she just frowned and shook her head at me.

I do the giraffe thing over the top of her cubicle. "Wheeler," I say, "this is the file on the Stevenson girl. It ain't much, but it's –"

"Thanks," she says. Without even looking, she reaches up and takes the folder from my hand.

"As I was saying, it ain't much. In fact, my dog could have dug up more. Read it over and check with Cronish. We should have the autopsy results sometime today. See what he found out: cause of death, what other injuries she suffered, what was under her fingernails. And I want to know everything about her: how old her brothers are, what they do for a living, what does her father do, working or retired? What kind of journalism did she do? What kind of car did she drive? Who did she —"

"I get the picture," Wheeler says, finally looking up. No smile or anything, plus she's giving me the brown-eye treatment.

I have other fish to fry, including two cold cases: the murder of a hospital janitor in 1986 and the killing a year later of a used-car dealer who had, among other things, a sophisticated rollback mileage scam, a monster house in the suburbs, and an enormous debt to a loan shark with a propensity for violent collection. Small potatoes next to a fresh murder, no argument, but I'm close on both and I have a feeling the Stevenson case will soon be taking up all my time.

"Right," I say, getting in the last word. "Okay then." I turn around and walk away.

At four o'clock Wheeler comes by. "I've got what you want," she says.

I have a cute little headache right behind each eyeball. Too many reports. Too much staring into computer screens. "Would you mind reading it to me? My eyes kill. Sit down." As I rotate my fingertips into my temples, I can sense her hesitating. "Wheeler, it's not like I'm asking you to make a pot of coffee, for fucksake."

Finally she sits down and starts reading. "Her father is an investment manager with the CIBC. Her mother is a housewife. Does volunteer work twice a week at the Institute for the Blind. Her brothers are thirty-one and twenty-two. The older one sells steel in London, Ontario. The younger one is a student at York University.

Her sister is twenty-seven, married with two kids. Elementary-school secretary. Husband's a musician."

"What's he play?" I ask.

"French horn. For the past two years he's been in the pit with *The Phantom of the Opera*."

"Go on."

"Joanne herself was not a journalist, as Barry's report stated. She was the editor of a quarterly magazine called *Good Return*."

"Never heard of it."

"It's a literary magazine. Short stories, poetry, book reviews."

"Who owns it?"

"She did. She ran it from her apartment."

"That would explain all the equipment. Any hobbies?"

"What equipment?"

"The photocopier in her spare room. The address stickers. Any hobbies?"

Wheeler looks back at her notes. "She was quiet. Her sister says she played the harp. And she liked dancing."

"The harp? No shit. Friends?"

Wheeler shakes her head. "She kept to herself."

"Did she make enough from the magazine to get by? It's a nice apartment."

Wheeler looks up from her notes. Her brown eye gives nothing away, but the blue one's worried. "I'm not sure," she says.

I think for a moment. "What did Cronish have to say?"

She takes a breath. "The autopsy won't be ready till Friday, likely, but they can confirm blunt-instrument trauma to the back of her head. At least three blows. Fingernails are clean."

My eyebrows must have gone up like flags, because Wheeler says, "What?"

"Nothing under the fingernails. No sign of a struggle. No chairs knocked over or dishes broken. Shampoo still standing on the edge of the tub. No forced entry, right?"

Wheeler nods.

"She knew him. She let him in. He was able to talk his way into her apartment. He was able to get close to her without scaring her. Fingerprints?"

"Several sets. So far, we've identified her own. The sister's coming down tomorrow morning to give us hers. There are at least four other sets of clear prints."

"What does the computer say about the other sets?"

"Nothing yet. Probably relatives."

"Well," I say, leaning back and stretching, "you've done good work, Wheeler." I glance up at the clock on the wall. "Fuck, it's already past four. That's enough for one day. Time to go home and get ready for the first pitch."

"What about interviewing the neighbours? Someone might have heard something or seen something."

"Tomorrow."

She stands up and lays her notes on the seat of her chair. "I think we may have a developing serial killer here," she says, and I can tell she's getting pissed at me. "He shows all the signs – he came to her apartment prepared, equipped, then there's the ritualized death, and the fact that he left a clue, a *tennis* ball, for God's sake, like some kind of personal mark or seal. And how did he get a tennis ball into her mouth? A tennis ball's bigger than you think. Maybe a man's mouth, maybe *your* mouth, but a woman's? I'm telling you, if we wait too long the trail will be cold. And he's going to kill again. I can feel it."

"One murder does not make him a serial killer," I tell her. "Relax. Tomorrow, we'll find out more." I stand up. I'm about to take her arm to steer her towards the stairs, but she pulls away, turns on her heel, and stomps off, her blonde pageboy bouncing off the blue shoulders of her shirt.

"Should be a wild one," I call after her.

—◊◊◊—

It *is* a wild one. Winfield and Borders homer for the Jays, but it's not enough. Oakland beats us 4–3 with a ninth-inning tater by Harold Baines. I drink nine beers, four or five shots of Jack Daniel's, and eat a large pizza all by myself, except for the crusts, which I give to Reg. I'm not sure whether it was the loss or the booze or the food, but when I take Reg out for her constitutional about eleven, I feel like shit. We're on the balcony, and I'm bending over to clip her leash to her collar when I see the ball. It's the old tennis ball I used to bounce off the wall in the little yard down below when she was younger. She loved it. She could field one-hoppers as smooth as Tony Fernandez. I stand up and hold the ball in front of my face. I open my mouth. Wheeler's right. The ball's too big. And if it's too big for my huge yawp, it must have been *way* too big for Ms. Stevenson's.

Unless he broke her jaw.

CHAPTER 3

Thursday, October 8

I DON'T FEEL much better this morning. Estabrooks is off, so I send Wheeler and Trick to talk to Joanne Stevenson's neighbours, and I tell Wicary in Fingerprinting to let me know what he knows as soon as he knows anything about Vanessa Murphy's fingerprints. She promised to arrive before ten.

Just before noon, he calls me.

"Well?" I say.

"Well, nothing. Her prints match about 10 per cent of the prints taken at the apartment, but the computer says nothing. She's got no record."

"No problem, she's a long shot at best. She didn't do it. What per cent of the prints are unaccounted for?"

"Let's see." There's a thirty-second silence. Wicary is a very fussy guy. He always wants to make sure what he says is dead-on. That's his business, after all, so I'm used to his pauses. After he was hired three or four years ago, I dealt with him on the phone for two or three months before I actually met him – at Staff Inspector Bateman's barbecue last June. I felt I had a pretty good idea of what he was like. I expected this medium-sized guy with thick glasses who raised goldfish or collected stamps or something. Turns out he's short, balding, and totally into line dancing. He wore cowboy boots and a Stetson to the barbecue. "Three other sets, accounting for seven, four, and three per cent. The victim herself accounts for about seventy and is probably responsible for most of the unreadables."

"Check out the rest of the family – the parents, the brothers. Print them all."

"Will do."

"One last thing, Dave. How did she seem to you?"

"Huh?"

"Well, you know, did she seem nervous or angry or . . . ?"

"I just take their prints, Sarge, I –"

"Yeah, I know, but just give me your impression. I should have come down there myself and questioned her, but I got busy."

"She did wonder if she was going to be questioned. She asked me who the lead detective was."

"What did you tell her."

"I said I didn't know."

"Okay then. That's fine. Let me know what you find out about the rest of the family."

"I'd say heartbroken."

"What?"

"She wasn't angry or nervous. I'd say she was heartbroken."

Trick comes back. We go to Subway for lunch, which we always did at least twice a week when we were partners. I guess you could say Trick's my best friend. If you're partners for ten years with someone, you're basically brothers. He let me camp at his place when Tanya kicked me out. I stayed there for about a week, which wasn't easy on him because, like Wicary, he's real fussy, everything's neat as a pin in his apartment, and I'm a total slob. Felix and Oscar. But I'm good to him, too. I looked after him when his mother died. He doesn't have any brothers or sisters, never knew his father. Even though he's had two or three girlfriends – *nice* ones – he's still a bachelor. But he's never lonely. "I'm a citizen of the world," he'll tell me. "I got all the brothers and sisters I need." We've looked after each other on the job, too. Couple of medals each. Commendations. One time Trick comes around the corner of an alley with a flashlight and sees this dealer with a steak knife to my throat. Bastard had come up behind me and I was helpless, hands in the air. Trick unholsters his Glock, drops to one knee, aims and says, "Drop it." Dealer says, "Drop it yourself, motherfucker, or I'll slit his throat." Trick waits maybe two seconds, then fires. End of drug dealer.

We get our sandwiches and find an empty booth. Trick tells me none of the neighbours he talked to heard anything. Hardly anybody even knew her, he says, although the old lady next door said she often heard music – sometimes harp music, sometimes bagpipe music – and at other times she heard some sort of machinery working late at night. Through the walls.

"The photocopier," I say. I ask if Wheeler came back with him.

No, he says, she's still going door to door.

Did the dead girl have any regular visitors? I ask.

"I don't know," Trick says. "Like I said, nobody knew anything about her."

"How long had she lived there?"

"Six years," says Trick.

We shake our heads and pick up our subs and start eating.

When we get back from lunch, Staff Inspector Bateman's waiting for me at my desk. "This just in," he says, and hands me a photocopy of what looks like a crumpled eight-and-a-half-by-eleven with typing on one side that somebody's flattened with the side of his hand. I sit down and read it.

When I'm finished, I look up at Bateman. "Where did this come from?"

"Cronish. It was inside the tennis ball."

I phone Cronish. "My partner's not convinced a tennis ball will fit inside a woman's mouth," I tell him, "and, frankly, neither am I. Did he break her jaw?"

Cronish laughs. "You underestimate the ingenuity of our clever friend. What he did was *slice* the tennis ball almost in half. He killed two birds with one stone – *three*, if you include Ms. Stevenson: by slicing the ball open he was able to put the note inside, and he was also able to crush the ball enough to stuff it inside her mouth."

"Okay, but why a tennis ball?"

He laughs again. "I'm flattered you think I might know the answer to that question, but, sadly, I don't. That's your job."

"What do you know about a magazine called *Good Return*?"

Daniel Curry clears his throat. "It does me good, Campbell, to learn that you've finally accepted the existence of literature."

"Poetry sucks," I tell him. "In your heart you know it's true." Daniel is the only person in the world who can tease me about my lack of culture. The first time he called me a philistine, I had to look it up. "Just answer the question," I say.

"Okay, but first you have to answer one for me." He pauses, and I quickly switch the telephone receiver from my left ear to my right so I can retrieve the bag of Hawkins Cheezies hiding in the bottom drawer of my desk. "Don't you hate it," he goes on, "when we outhit them and they outscore us?"

"Yes," I agree, "I hate it. And I hate it when we out*homer* them and they outscore us. But that's all right because Cone's on the mound tonight –"

"And all will be right with the world," Daniel finishes.

"Exactly."

Daniel and I have been friends since we played defensive half and defensive tackle for the best high-school football team in the city. We were pretty close in those days, and people used to do double-takes when we walked by in our maroon-and-gold jackets, OLD YORK BULLDOGS across the back, our numbers, 21 and 66, on the sleeves, Daniel slim and quick and sharp, and me huge and awkward beside him, a foot taller, a hundred pounds heavier. Like most high-school friends, we eventually went our separate ways, but we kept in touch, a beer once in a while, a Jays game. He did his undergraduate work at the University of Toronto and then a Ph.D. in Modern American Literature. He's a college professor, and he writes poetry, and he's husband to a wife who still loves him, and father to two grown children who both won university scholarships – Harvard and McGill. He's a lot of things I'm not.

From his office at Seneca College – the walls covered with diplomas instead of all-points-bulletins and glossies of crime scenes – he says, "It's a small-press literary journal, a quarterly, with a huge reputation. Any aspiring or, for that matter, any aspired writer of poetry or fiction would be happy to have his or her work appear in the pages of *Good Return*."

"Ever hear of a woman named Joanne Stevenson?"

"Sure. I've met her. Editor and sole proprietor."

"Not any more," I say.

Daniel is silent on the other end of the line.

"She was found dead in her apartment," I tell him. "Yesterday."

"Good God," he says.

"I need your help," I say. "I'm going to read something to you. I need to know where it came from."

Daniel's voice is subdued. "Go ahead."

"'We are men, my liege.'

'Ay, in the catalogue ye go for men;

As hounds and greyhounds, mongrels, spaniels, curs,

Shoughs, water-rugs, and demi-wolves, are clept

All by the name of dogs –'"

Daniel interrupts me: "It's pronounced 'shuff,' not 'shug.' Just for your information. Go on."

"'– the valu'd file

Distinguishes the swift, the slow, the subtle,

The housekeeper, the hunter, every one

According to the gift which bounteous nature

Hath in him clos'd; whereby he does receive

Particular addition, from the bill

That writes them all alike: and so of men.'"

I stop. "Well?"

"Shakespeare isn't my specialty, as you may be aware," Daniel says. "But I remember that speech all right. It's from *Macbeth*. Somewhere in Act three."

"What's it mean?"

"Macbeth is telling one of the murderers he's conscripted to kill the king that even though he – the murderer – may look like a man, he's not really one, any more than a mongrel's a greyhound."

"Even though they're both dogs."

"That's right. What does this have to do with Joanne?"

"It was written on a piece of paper that was found inside a tennis ball that was inside her mouth."

"Good God!"

"If you can stomach it, I should tell you the rest. Describe how she died, I mean. The murder scene. My partner thinks we may have a budding serial killer on our hands."

Daniel says, "I have a class in a few minutes, but they can wait."

I tell him everything I know, from the posture of the body to the room full of office equipment to the reactions of the neighbours.

When I'm finished, I say, "Are you still there?"

"Do you have any leads?" he asks.

"No. You knew her. What do you think? Ex-boyfriend, maybe?"

"I knew her, but not well. As far as I know, there was no man in her life. She was quiet. I would see her occasionally at book launches or readings, but she rarely hung around afterwards for the socializing. One drink, maybe."

He pauses.

"What?" I say.

"Well, there are plenty of lunatics on the literary scene. Maybe you should look for someone who submitted poems or stories to the magazine."

"Good," I say, making a note.

"Especially poems or stories she rejected."

"Good," I say again. "Listen. One last question. What do you make of the tennis ball?"

He's quiet. I can almost hear him shaking his head. "I don't know. I'll get back to you."

At a quarter to four I'm doing the giraffe thing at Wheeler's cubicle. "How's that profile coming?"

As part of her detective training, Wheeler spent two weeks with the FBI in Quantico, Virginia, learning how to work up profiles of crime suspects. Profiles are especially important with serial-killer cases because you want to stop them before they kill again, and since that's what Wheeler thinks this killer is – or is about to become – she's working up a profile. To be able to do this, she had to study character types, the differences between psychopaths and psychotics, and she had to learn how to interpret crime-scene evidence.

Her eyes still glued to the blue screen of her computer, Wheeler says, "Almost done. Give me a minute."

According to Wheeler, 90 per cent of serial killers are white and male, between twenty-five and thirty-five years of age, and all of them are what she calls inadequate personalities, usually sexually inadequate, but also inadequate in general. Wayne Williams was an exception. He was the Atlanta child-killer. He was black, as were all his victims. Serial killers don't usually cross colour lines. Aside from his race, Wayne Williams was a typical serial killer – a loser, a failure.

A wannabe music producer living at home with his retired school-teacher parents. Light-skinned, soft hands. All serial killers want to be powerful. They wish they could be cops or soldiers. They want to carry weapons and make people afraid of them. Wayne Williams drove a second-hand cop car.

"They're into control and dominance," Wheeler told me once. "Most of them have been turned down by the armed forces or police departments. Some get into the military, but they don't usually last long. The guy who went around Buffalo a few years ago randomly shooting black men was a white soldier on furlough from Fort Benning, Georgia. When they do cross colour lines, the crimes are racial as opposed to sexual, although sex does sometimes figure in as a form of defilement."

I tip my hat to Wheeler, learning all of this state-of-the-art detection stuff. I wish they had it around when I was young, when I was a keener. Sometimes Wheeler makes me feel like a dinosaur.

"Okay," she says, and as she swivels around on her chair, she pulls a sheet of paper from the tray of her printer. Then she clears her throat. "This is how I see him. Based on my training," and she gestures with one hand towards the stack of Profile Manuals on her desk. "He's typical in some ways, atypical in others. He's male, obviously, he's white, he's detached emotionally – it's unlikely that there's a woman in his life, a wife or girlfriend – and he's organized. He came to the apartment prepared to rape and kill. From the crime-scene evidence, this was not an opportunity situation, but rather one that was planned. He brought duct tape. He brought a sliced-open tennis ball and a note. He brought the still-missing murder weapon, a hammer or something. The rape was consistent with the idea that he was organized. A disorganized killer, or one who just stumbles onto a situation – a janitor or a repairman – would leave more of a mess, and probably would have tried to stage the scene to look like a break-and-enter. Except for the bathroom, you'd never know a crime had been committed. Nothing was disturbed. Not in the kitchen – the first room an unprepared killer will search for a weapon – not even in the bedroom, where most rapes take place. And the awkward posing of Joanne – kneeling, bound, helpless, humiliated – tells us that he hates women, probably because they threaten him. Most serial killers of women were abused as children, sexually or psychologically, by their mothers or some other female authority figure. That, or they come from homes where the mother was despised by the father, and they grow up with the same attitude."

While she pauses for a breath I tell her what Daniel Curry told me – that we should be looking for someone whose poems or stories she rejected.

Wheeler nods, blue eye sparkling. "That makes sense, because what makes him atypical is that he's probably very bright – Shakespeare isn't for blockheads, after all – so the anger he's feeling may have an intellectual rather than a sexual source."

"So it's not like he tried to ask her out and she said no."

"No, he wasn't romantically interested in her. My guess is he raped her after he killed her, which would tell me he was just adding insult to injury. If he raped her first, I might think he wanted some kind of interaction with her, some kind of response. The autopsy will straighten that out. But the most important thing is the Shakespeare, because it tells us he deliberately planned and left a clue for us to find. To him this is a game. And it's only just started." She pauses and looks up at me. I'm still leaning on my arms over the top of her partition. "Remember," she says, "this is all conjecture. But I feel pretty confident about it."

"That's all right," I say. "That's what you're paid for. Did you find out anything more about how much Ms. Stevenson made?"

Wheeler nods. "Her parents are reasonably well off, but she had a second source of income – an invested inheritance from her grand-mother. She lived off that, primarily, and a few grants."

"Grants?"

"Government subsidies. For artists or artistic projects that aren't likely to make any money."

"Must be nice being an artist. Did you find out if she owned a car?"

"She drove a car owned by her mother."

"Has it been brought in yet?"

"No. We can't find it. She had a parking space in the under-ground garage, but when Barry and I went to check it out, there was another car there. So we traced that car – a new Mustang – to another resident in the building. Man and wife, matching Mustangs, but only one parking space, so they rented Joanne's."

"Why didn't she use it herself?"

"He didn't know – the husband, apartment 708 – so we talked to the super, and he said Joanne was terrified of being attacked in the underground garage, so she parked on the street. He said she was always getting tickets, but she didn't care."

"What kind of car did she drive?"

Wheeler checks her notes. "A blue Corolla, 1982."

A Toyota, I say to myself, something vaguely stirring. A blue Toyota. "Wheeler," I say, "do you remember when we were first on the scene, when we were walking back to our cruiser?"

Wheeler frowns. "What about it?"

"Do you remember the car with the bumper stickers?"

She nods. "'We're proud of our gay and lesbian children.'"

"Right –"

"'I love . . .' something or other."

"'Scottish dancing.'"

"'*Highland* dancing'!"

"One of her hobbies was dancing, right?"

"And the neighbour heard bagpipe music!"

"And the floor on the passenger side was ankle-deep in parking tickets. Shit! Find Barkas or Big Urmson. Tell whichever to haul ass over to Berton Street and see if the car's still there. I've got twenty bucks says it's not. I've got twenty bucks says it's probably in Mexico by now, along with the killer. But who knows, maybe we'll come up with something. Is there an APB on it?"

"As soon as we got the make and licence."

"Well, it's too late anyway. He's had since Friday to get wherever he wanted to go." I pause and scratch my ear. "And the other bumper sticker – find out if she was a dyke, or if either of her brothers was queer. And find out if the super has a record of any kind. He'd have a key to her apartment."

"I'll get Barkas moving," Wheeler says. "Urmson's already gone home. Then maybe you and I should start searching her files."

"No," I say, glancing at the clock on the wall. "Save it for tomorrow. We've done good work, but it's past four, and I've got a date for the ballgame. You're beat. You should go home and relax, watch the game. Moore against Cone."

"But the files –"

"The files ain't going anywhere, Wheeler. It's a secure location. They'll be there in the morning."

Trick is my date, and we are off-duty and nicely settled at McCully's by seven bells, quaffing pints of Labatt's Blue and waiting for the first pitch. And that's when Daniel gets back to me. Trick and I are just finishing up some wings, wiping our fingers on those little towelettes, when the bartender, Dexter, calls me over to the phone.

"Young," I say into the receiver.

Daniel's voice says, "Can't teach an old dog new tricks."

"What are you talking about?"

"You've been drinking there since the creation of man, or am I wrong?"

"Is that how you found me?"

"Yup. Just a hunch."

There's a small commotion – raised voices – and I look over at Trick. He sees me and smiles and points at the waitress, Jessy, who's standing with her hands on her hips, talking to two men at the table next to ours.

"So, what have you got?" I say to Daniel. "You'd better make it quick because there's a fight about to break out here, involving Jessy the super-waitress and a couple of sorry drunks."

"Are you there to watch the game?" Daniel asks.

"Indeed I am."

"Ten bucks says Oakland takes it."

"You want to bet *against* David Cone?"

"Ten bucks," he repeats.

"You're on," I say. "Now what's the dope?"

"I found out about the tennis ball."

I turn away from the disturbance and stare down into an ashtray beside the phone. "Yeah? Go ahead."

"'Good Return' is a tennis term. According to Rule 22 of the *Official Tennis Yearbook and Guide*, a good return occurs when the ball is driven accurately back into the opponent's court."

"That's it?"

"I can't find any other meaning for it."

"I can see it as a title for a tennis magazine, but why would anyone use it for a poetry magazine?"

"Well," says Daniel, "I never did ask Joanne where she got the title. The only thing I can figure is that she felt the magazine provided a good return on the subscriber's investment, or on the efforts of the writers who submitted their work to it. I'm not sure."

"At least the tennis ball in her mouth makes sense now. Sort of. Anything else?"

"No, but I've got a feeling there's more to the *Macbeth* quotation than meets the eye. I just haven't figured out what it could be."

"Let me know."

By the time I get back to the table, Jessy is really into it with the two drunks.

"We just want you to sit down for a few minutes," one of them is saying, "and let us buy you a drink."

Her hands still on her hips, Jessy leans forward as if she's speaking to a child. "I've told you three times already, I'm working, and even if I wasn't working I wouldn't sit down with you. Now, can I get you something – a beer, something to eat, a therapist?"

Jessy has red hair to her shoulders, as red as mine, fiery green eyes, and a pot belly. She's been at McCully's for three years or so, and she's a particular favourite of me and Trick's. She's young, around twenty-five, and twice a year her and a few of her girlfriends fly to Vegas for some gambling and shows and whatever. We're drinkers, she told us once. Our idea of a good time is a week of drinking and gambling. And never having to go outside.

"I just want you to sit down for a minute or two," the drunk says.

Jessy looks at the other drunk, "Take your friend home," she says. She turns and shouts towards the bar, "Dex, eighty-six these two."

I sit back down beside Trick.

"Jessy," Trick calls, "could you come here for a second?"

She glares for another don't-mess-with-the-messer moment at the two drunks, then turns towards our table and glares at us. "What is it?"

"These little towelettes you gave us aren't moist. They're dry. It says on the package 'Moist Towelette,' but these ones aren't moist."

"We think we should get our money back," I say.

"Because the little towelettes aren't moist," Trick repeats.

At first, Jessy's eyes narrow, but then she nods and gives us the smallest of smiles. "Very funny." She looks at Trick's half-empty glass. "Ready for another?"

"Oh, all right," says Trick.

She turns to me. "What about you, big guy?"

"Might as well bring us four," I tell her.

As she walks away I notice the bar's starting to fill up.

I begin to get antsy. I know what it is, too.

After half an inning and half my beer, I lean over towards Trick. "I gotta go."

"What?" he says. "The game's just started!"

"I know, but there's something important I gotta do."

"What could be more important than baseball?"

"I have to do some reading."

"*Reading?* What the hell?"

"Poetry," I say. "Haven't you ever heard of poetry? What are you, a philistine?"

I drive back to HQ, requisition a few copies of *Good Return* from Properties, and drive home. For the next hour I sit in the La-Z-Boy and watch the game with the sound turned down and read poetry. For a good hour I read poetry. I even like some of it. Then when I see the seventh inning is over, I reward myself with a beer and watch the Jays score one in the eighth and Henke nail down the save in the ninth for a 3–1 victory. All is right with the world, as Daniel would say, and then I notice the *TV Guide* face down and open on the floor beside my chair. And there's the dead girl again, face down in the toilet.

I need some air, so I get my jacket and the leash, and me and Reg walk down to the corner, where I tie her to a parking meter outside the Busy Bee Variety. The first thing I see inside is the headline of *The Standard*: KILLER SOUGHT IN EDITOR'S SLAYING. The by-line, Andy Bartle, is well known to me. He's an asshole. And now that he's covering the Stevenson killing, it's only a matter of time till he comes sniffing around my door.

The guy behind the counter has the radio on, and as I return from the cooler with a two-litre bottle of Mountain Dew, I hear a voice saying, "So far, police have no suspects in their search for the killer or killers of twenty-nine-year-old Joanne Stevenson." From the rack beside the cash register I take a program for tomorrow night's harness-racing card at Mohawk. When the time comes I'll probably be too tired to go, but that's all right, I still like to pick them. See how they did in the paper the next day. One program or one copy of the *Racing Form* or *Sport of Kings* and I've got bathroom reading for a week. Besides, the harness programs have this great smell, like peppermint, like Tiger Balm.

When I get back outside, Reg is lying down beside the parking meter. When she sees me, she gets to her feet and makes a little growl to tell me I took too long.

CHAPTER 4

Friday, October 9

I'M SITTING IN MY breakfast nook eating Grape-Nuts when the phone rings. I lower my cereal bowl to the floor for Reggie. A guy on TV said too much milk could give a dog the shits, so I don't overdo it.

It's Daniel on the phone. "You still in your nightie?"

"You owe me ten bucks," I tell him.

"This is true, this is true, but the bet doubles next time Cone pitches, game five or whatever, okay?"

"Beautiful," I say. "Music to my ears."

"Now listen, I came up with a couple of ideas, and I wanted to catch you before you headed off to the donut shop."

I grab a pad and pencil. "Shoot."

"As I told you before, the quotation from *Macbeth* is about how murderers may look like men but really aren't. It's about how murderers are cowards. Your killer is educated, Campbell, and he's also aware that what he's doing is wrong. He just doesn't care. I'm no shrink, but he sounds like a psychopath. Your partner's serial-killer theory may be a good one."

"What's the second thing?"

"He's giving you a clue. You can find his name if you look hard enough. If you look in the right spot."

"Where's the right spot?"

"From the quotation: 'The valu'd file / Distinguishes the swift, the slow, the subtle . . .'"

"'The valu'd file.'"

"I think Joanne may have kept a file with all her correspondence in it. She may even have a 'reject' file. Also, she may have kept copies of replies she sent to submitters. What do you think?"

"I think you're a fucking genius."

Just past the lights at Donlands and Mortimer on my way to work I see a woman standing at a bus stop. I know her, but she doesn't know me. I've seen her hundreds of times, but she's never seen me. I've driven the same route to work, basically, for more than fifteen years, and at least once a week – when I'm on days, anyway – I see this woman walking from her house to the bus stop. Or I see her husband walking their daughter to school. The mother is always dressed smartly and looks professional. The husband still sports the ponytail and beard he's had since I first laid eyes on him. He always wears jeans. I figure he works at home. Computers or something. Maybe he doesn't work at all. Maybe he's a retired rock star. But sometimes I see him jogging along O'Connor, so I figure if he's industrious enough to do that, he must work at something.

Over the years I've watched the little girl become a teenager. She doesn't hold her father's hand any more, and she wears glasses just like her mother's. I've watched the mom put on weight, I've watched her hair go grey. She carries herself with pride, but there's something disappointed about the way she stands at the bus stop, head up, hoping for sunshine. Her husband's hair is still black and full, and even though he's got a bit of a gut, he looks ten years younger than she does.

But they've stayed together. They've kept their little family together, which is more than me and Tanya can say. When Debi was in high school, I would drop her off on my way to work, and sometimes we would pass the woman at the bus stop or the man walking with the girl, so Debi got to know the family, too. "There they are," I'd say, pointing. "Father and daughter, on their way to school. Just like us." But Debi would always make some smartass comment: "Doesn't he know the sixties are over?" or "I'll bet they've brought the kid up vegetarian. She has no idea how goddamn good a cheeseburger tastes." Once, when we passed the mother at the bus stop, Debi said, "I can't believe how frumpy she's got."

And here she is this morning, and while I'm sure her life isn't perfect, her family's still intact. She's worked hard to keep it that way. I slow down as I pass her, but she's looking up at the sky.

It's always strange going back to a crime scene a few days after the event. The place has been cleaned up, and all the smoking cops with their black humour are gone, and what you have left are the details of a victim's life: leftover carrot, raisin, and peanut salad in the fridge; a half-full laundry hamper; photos of relatives on the mantel; the *TV Guide* open to Friday, October 2; a giant stuffed panda in the bedroom; the harp in its place of honour in the living room. In the bathroom, there's still a brown line of blood circling the toilet bowl.

Wheeler says, "When's the family coming in to pack up her stuff?"

"Funeral's tomorrow," I say. "I expect they'll be in on Monday. Bateman gave them the okay for then. I want you there tomorrow."

"At the funeral? I'll be there."

"I want you watching everything."

"No problem. Will you be there?"

"Of course I'll be there."

"Okay," she says, "so back to business. I've gone through the kitchen, but I didn't find anything unusual."

"Like you said yesterday, whatever he used he brought with him. And took with him when he left. He used duct tape to bind her, and she doesn't seem the type to own any herself."

"Did you find anything?"

"It's what I didn't find that's interesting," I say. "The drawer of her bedside table, for instance. Aspirin, eyeglasses, loose change, paper clips, bankbooks, that sort of stuff."

Wheeler looks at me. "Why is that interesting?"

I shrug. "That's all there was."

"What did you expect, condoms and a vibrator?"

When she says this I have to look away. "Yeah," I say. "Something like that."

She shakes her head. "Joanne was a quiet person. No boyfriend. No singles bars or one-night stands."

"Do you think she was a dyke?" I ask.

She sighs. "Not everybody's as . . . as sexual as you make them out to be."

It gives me a small charge when she says "sexual." "So you don't think she was a lesbo?"

She shakes her head in exasperation.

We're standing in the living room having this conversation when I notice the *TV Guide* again on the coffee table. I pick it up. "Did Cronish give us a time of death?"

"He said she'd been dead too long to guess with any accuracy, but he figured last Thursday or Friday. We should get the full report this afternoon. Why?"

"*Guide*'s open to Friday."

"Yeah, but she could have been browsing through it Thursday night to see what was on the next night. That's what I do."

She says this plainly, and I see her sitting at home in the evenings in her pyjamas, a cup of tea on the coffee table, the remote in her hand. A cat nearby. But she's making me nervous the way she relates to the dead girl. Calling her by her first name. She's been trained not to identify with victims.

"Oh, by the way," Wheeler says, "Estabrooks checked the street. You were right: her car's gone."

"What else you find out?"

"The super's clean. He's been here twenty years. No record. Good reputation. The worst anyone would say about him is he likes a drink."

"Big deal. I like a drink myself."

"That's what I thought you would say."

"Anything else?"

"Yes, one more thing. Joanne's younger brother is a gay activist at York University."

"Well, there you go," I say. "Sometimes bumper stickers *do* have tales to tell. Not that her faggot brother or her Scottish dancing would tell us anything about her death, but at least we'd have the car and whatever's inside it."

There's a few seconds of silence before Wheeler says, "So, now what?"

"Come on," I say. "Let's check her files. My friend the professor phoned me last night and again this morning. He thinks your serial-killer notion makes sense."

"What does he know about serial killers?"

"Fucked if I know, but he's a smart guy. He also said we should be looking for guys she said no to."

Wheeler narrows her eyes. "You mean guys who came on to her? I told you, Joanne wasn't the type to –"

"No," I say, lifting my hands. "Guys whose poems or whatever she rejected. Jesus, take a pill, Wheeler. And for fucksake stop calling her Joanne."

—ɷ—

It doesn't take long to find what we're looking for. Ms. Stevenson was a very organized person. Meticulous, Wheeler says. Although we can't find any copies of rejection letters she may have sent to writers, we do find the letters they sent her, filed by month. As well, we find page proofs of the Winter issue of *Good Return*, including the table of contents. We're able to eliminate as suspects eleven poets and four short-story writers who have written to her and whose work is scheduled to appear. We're sure our killer isn't a woman, so we can eliminate another eighty-seven female submitters whose cover letters we find and whose names do not appear on the table of contents.

When the crime scene was first examined, the Forensic Identification guys noted that nothing out of the ordinary had taken place in the office. So if the killer was a rejected writer, it seems he wasn't interested in reclaiming any evidence. In fact, as Daniel pointed out, just the opposite seems to have been the case. Rather than cover his tracks, he pointed them out – 'the valu'd file.' I was hoping we might find poems or short stories that would point the finger at someone, but when I mentioned this to Daniel, he said that editors always return rejected manuscripts, that it's unethical to take copies. The whole time we're going through the drawers of the six file cabinets in the office, I keep glancing over at Ms. Stevenson's computer.

"There's a ton of information in there," Wheeler says, following my gaze. "It's an old machine – an IBM P.S. 2, Model 30 – but useful enough for her purposes. She's probably got mailing lists for subscribers and submitters in there, but I've tried and we can't get in without a password, and we don't know what it was, or what file names she used. If we need to, later on, we can do a search, but we need some kind of password. For the time being, we're better off just going through these."

"Besides," I say, "that's what the killer told us to do."

Eventually, we have our list. It contains the names and addresses of sixty-two male writers (a few names, like Pat Bridges and Bobby Bradshaw, could be male or female, and another nine use initials –

F.R. Bender, for example – all of these are kept on the list) who submitted work for the Winter issue which Ms. Stevenson rejected.

The autopsy report is on my desk when we get back. The best Cronish can do on the time of death is last Thursday or Friday. Cause of death is drowning. The contusions on Ms. Stevenson's head, most likely made with a hammer, might have stunned her, but didn't kill her. Her lungs were full of water. And as Wheeler predicted, she was raped *after* death. At no point during her ordeal did she struggle – there was nothing under her fingernails, no trauma to her hands or arms. The tennis ball was forced into her mouth after death.

My name comes over the intercom. "Sergeant Young, line four."

It's Wicary in Fingerprinting. "Yes, Dave," I say.

"We've done as much as we can. Most of the prints are hers or her sister's. One brother has a few. And the parents. That's it."

"He must have worn gloves. He didn't want to make it too easy for us."

"The careful type," says Wicary.

"Maybe he has a record," I say, and hang up.

Estabrooks is hanging his head over my partition.

"What have you got?" I ask him.

"We found the car."

"Yes, and . . . ?"

"It's in the police compound on Eastern Avenue. Tow truck took it away last Saturday. Unpaid parking offences, seventy-seven of them."

I lean my forehead into my hands and rub my thumbs into my temples. "Well, that's seventy-seven parking offences that never *will* be paid. Get Forensics to go over the car. The killer didn't steal it, but he may have ridden in it."

—◊—

I ask Staff Inspector Bateman for some help, and he pulls Barkas off the beat, so I've got Barkas and Wheeler, and Estabrooks and Trick, who both agree to a shift change, poring through the phone books, making calls to literary magazines and small presses all over North America. By six o'clock, we've done all the names on the list. Nothing. We check them against our master file of previous convictions, and although we come up with a petty theft and a driving under the influence – both convictions are ancient, both resulted in probation – and some outstanding traffic summonses, everybody's clean. Nobody smells. But what puzzles me is a few come up empty of any information at all.

Trick's got a real date, so he's no use to me. It's an off-day for baseball, the teams are flying to Oakland for game three tomorrow, so there's nothing on TV. So where am I this Friday night? McCully's, of course, propped on a stool and talking to Dexter about the important things in life, like dogs and movies and baseball and horseracing, when who should walk in the door, brushing the rain from the shoulders of his corduroy jacket, but Daniel Curry.

"In the flesh," I say, as he climbs aboard the stool beside me.

"I phoned your apartment. Reg said you were here."

I nodded. "One of the great things about dogs. Totally dependable. Leave them with a job to do, like pass on messages, and they do it."

"Right," says Daniel and turns to Dexter, who's waiting. "Johnny Walker Black. Double. On the rocks, thank you."

"And they never complain," I continue. "Another great thing about dogs. They never tell you to put out the garbage or get your feet off the coffee table."

"How long have you been here?" Daniel says.

"Not long. Me and Dex've been discussing the mysteries of life, haven't we, Dex?" I reach for a cigarette from my pack on the bar.

Daniel shakes his head. "You still smoking those?"

For the past thirty years my brand's been Export "A," a short strong cigarette favoured by truck drivers and other tough guys. I light one, inhale deeply, and exhale heavenward with great pleasure. I can feel Daniel still shaking his head. He's always hated it when I smoke. I even smoked when I was playing football. Daniel, being an intellectual, smokes a pipe, which he claims not to inhale.

"The other great thing about dogs," I continue, "is they don't care what you do. You can walk around the apartment naked, or not wash for a week. You can visit the fridge forty times a day and all they'll do is lift their head – maybe not even their whole head, just their *eyes* – and stare at you for a couple of seconds to make sure you aren't going anywhere without them, because they hate that, they absolutely hate that. But otherwise, they don't give a shit. Just as long as you're nearby and you pet them once in a while. And give them the occasional cheesie."

Daniel is settled now, sipping his drink and looking at me. "Campbell," he says. "Buddy. What have you found out?"

Suddenly I'm not drunk any longer. It was like I was playing at being drunk, and suddenly all the fun goes out of me. I rub my hands over my face. "Nothing. We checked out most of the sixty-two names of male submitters whose work was rejected. Nothing. The only thing that bothers me is there's a few who not only don't have a record, we couldn't find anything else about them either. Not even a social insurance number."

"How many?"

"Five or six."

"They're probably pseudonyms."

"Pseudo-what?"

"Pseudonyms. Pen names. It's not uncommon. I could try to check them out for you."

"That'd be good," I say, "but I don't have them here."

"When can you get them to me?"

"Have you got your car?"

"Yes."

"We'll have one more drink and we'll go get them. They're on my desk at work."

"Your colleagues won't be too thrilled to see you in your present condition."

"Is it that obvious?"

He just looks at me.

"Not to worry," I say. "When I have to, I'm very good at disguising my true state of mind. Dex, another Black for my friend and another Blue for me, with a little Jack alongside for company."

In fact, there are seven names: Grant Brito, Tim Virgin, Lennox Ross, James Clay Ryan, James L. Lee, Brock Beattie, and someone who simply signs himself or herself Oracle. Daniel writes them down on a piece of paper. We're in and out in two minutes, and nobody gives us a second glance, except maybe Gallagher, the desk sergeant, who I know pretty well. He likes the horses, too. A ripple goes across his forehead, like, what the fuck are you doing here at this time of night? But even though I'm three sheets to the wind, he don't say diddly, we're out of there, and Daniel drives me home.

As I'm getting out of his car, he says, "I'll let you know what I come up with."

"Much appreciated."

"Good night," he says. "And Campbell?"

"What?"

"There's someone waiting for you."

"Beg your pardon?"

He says nothing, but nods towards the living-room window of my second-floor apartment, where the silhouette of a bulldog is clearly outlined against the background lighting. She's up on the back of the sofa, front paws on the windowsill. Although I can't see it, I know with complete certainty – like the surest of sure things – that her little stump of a tail's jerking back and forth like a thumb.

CHAPTER 5

Saturday, October 10

WE'RE SITTING IN A rear pew of St. Clement's United Church. From what the minister says in his eulogy it's clear he knew Ms. Stevenson well. Wheeler leans over and whispers, "Joanne attended church regularly." Me and Wheeler look like a married couple, a middle-aged man with his younger – as in second – wife.

When the minister is finished, Ms. Stevenson's father, a tall, distinguished-looking bald guy in a brown suit, stands up and speaks briefly about the effect the murder has had on his family and about how he prays the person responsible for his daughter's death will be brought to "swift justice." All around me I can hear people crying. "The only pure and natural straight line in nature," he says, "is the sunbeam, and that's what Joanne was – pure and natural and as unwavering in her morality and ethics as a sunbeam is unwavering in its path to the earth." He breaks down for a few seconds, and around me the weeping gets louder. Beside me,

Wheeler sits with her head up, the tears flowing freely down her cheeks.

Outside, there's frost on the ground, and the sky's grey.

Grey. I remember one time me and Trick were doing paperwork on a corpse somebody found in the trunk of a car, and for hair colour Trick wrote *gray*. I told him he spelled it wrong, it should be *grey*. He told me both spellings were okay and to mind my own business. He said, "Don't try and fool me on the subject of spelling. What you know about spelling wouldn't fill a thimble!" That was two years ago, but I've always remembered it because I like his spelling better. It's happier somehow: the old gray mare; the grey face of the dead girl.

From the look of them, a lot of the mourners are writers or artists of some kind: the men have shoulder-length hair, leather jackets, earrings, and thick glasses; the women, some of them, are as slim as ballet dancers, with the same thin faces, hardly any make-up, while others are overweight and all business, moving through the crowd like parade marshals.

Trick and Wheeler stand among them. Estabrooks is writing down licence-plate numbers, and Barkas, out of uniform for the occasion, looks like a grieving cousin – a grieving cousin with a video camera.

The camera is Wheeler's idea. She says certain types of killer – serial killers included – want to see what effect their crime has had on the victim's loved ones, so they follow the media attention closely, and will even show up at funerals or fundraisers or memorial services. Sometimes they'll even visit the cop shop to offer a few suggestions. Those are the stupid ones, she says. The smart ones know the more visible they make themselves, the more likely they are to get caught.

People are standing in small groups, huddled against the cold. A couple of workmen in lumberjack shirts and down vests stand at a distance; farther away there's a yellow backhoe waiting to finish up.

On our way back to Homicide, we stop at Allan Gardens, which is a botanical garden with a lot of benches the rummies sleep on. Me and Wheeler try to visit at least once a week – to check up on the clientele, especially in winter, when it's cold enough to kill them – but also to find out if anyone has any useful information. If we're on nights, we shine our flashlights on faces that are usually only half visible under their blankets of newspapers. The faces are amazing: red with drink or frost; scarred or bruised or both. White faces, black faces, native faces. Hardly any orientals. If it's a nice afternoon when we stop, we get into conversations, especially with the men we know: Lefty, Pete, Beans. There's lots more. Women, too, with all their worldly belongings bundled up in shopping carts: Annie, Lucy-in-the-Sky, Queenie. They're getting used to me being with Wheeler instead of Trick, but sometimes she can come on too strong, like a sociologist or something. One time she said to Queenie, "Where did you grow up, Queenie? Where did you come from?" and Queenie – with her face like leather, like one of those apple dolls – just glared at her and said, "It don't matter where I come from."

All of these people have known better times, but it doesn't take much to move a person from a home in the suburbs, a family, a job, to living on the streets. All you need to do is make the people who love you give up on you, because you can't stop doing whatever it is that's ruining you: gambling, drugs, women. There's other ways of hitting bottom, but the main one is caring more about something else than you do about your family. It doesn't even have to be booze or the horses or whatever. It can be work. That's what it was with me. But I landed more or less on my feet. Sometimes having a big ego comes in handy. Even though one half of you's a worthless piece of shit, the other half's firmly convinced he's a solid citizen. You're two people, basically – one might fuck around on the wife, but the other would throw himself in front of a train to save her.

Not that I fucked around on *my* wife. I didn't. If anything along those lines took place, I would bet the farm she fucked around on me – probably with that coke-snorting Nissan dealer she worked for. My crime was I was married to my job, not to her. When she kicked me out, there were times when I felt like claiming one of those benches in Allan Gardens for myself. I could have become a real serious drinker. I still could. When she kicked me out, I just didn't realize how fucked-up I was. A typical day was ten hours working, three hours drinking, then home at eleven to a dinner in the micro and the wife and daughter asleep. The only one who would wake up for me was Reg, and I'd take her for her walk – I never missed; she can't look after herself, after all – even if I was so drunk I was stumbling. The thing is, nobody ever told me I was out of line – except Tanya, of course, but I didn't listen to her. Trick never said a word, and although I can't blame him I wish he'd said something. Even, "How's Tanya? How's Debi? They still recognize you?" But I guess he figured it was none of his business. Besides, he's a bachelor, so what the fuck does he know about anything?

Still, if a man shows up for work, and his button-down collar isn't buttoned, wouldn't you mention it? Wouldn't you step up to him and do up a button for him? Wouldn't you at least say, "Hey, shithead, your collar's unbuttoned"? Well, nobody did that for me.

So, like I say, after the funeral me and Wheeler coast by Allan Gardens till she pulls over to the curb near the entrance to the arboretum. We sit there a minute, and then I say, "Well, are we going in, talk to buddy, see what's up?"

"If it's okay with you," Wheeler says, "I don't feel like going in. That funeral kind of took the wind out of my sails. Let's just call it a day."

"Suits me. Drop me by McCully's if you don't mind."

"What about your car?"

"Fuck my car."

"Sprague to Alomar to Olerud," I say. "Beautiful."

"Five, four, three," says Trick.

"I don't get it," says Jessy, who's standing beside my chair. "Is it a code?"

"Yeah, it's a code," says Trick. "So you can score the game. The shortstop's six."

"I don't know what you're talking about," Jessy says. She has a dishcloth in one hand and a plastic bottle of spray for wiping the tables in the other. The bar's almost empty, and me and Trick are drunk. We've watched every pitch of every inning of the Blue Jays' 7–5 victory over Oakland in game three, and now we're watching the highlights on the late late sports. "You two laugh and ooh and aah at the same time," says Jessy. "I'm watching as careful as I can and I don't see what's so amazing."

"You're young," Trick says, his eyes focused on the screen above the bar. "We forgive you."

I say, "You're from the generation when all the girls had to be named Melissa or Samantha or Jennifer or Jessica – like you – and all the boys had to be named Jason. There was legislation passed to that effect. Isn't that right, Trick?"

"Right on, brother."

I glance up at Jessy.

She makes a sour face. She looks like she's about to swat me. Instead she says, "How long you been drinking here, big guy?"

I consider the question. "Since about seven."

"No, in years."

"Oh, in *years*." I think as carefully as I can. "I'm proud to say that I am a fourth-generation patron at this establishment. I drank here when it was nothing but a draft room with a salt-cellar for every ashtray, and beer was twenty-five cents a glass. In those days it was called the Wallace House. I drank here when it was upgraded to a strip bar, the Runway. It didn't last long as a strip bar. Too middle-class a neighbourhood, I guess. I even drank here when it was a singles bar."

"What was it called then?" Jessy asks. She squats down beside my chair, one hand on the edge of our table for balance.

"I can't remember. I think it was a plural – something like Friends. No, that wasn't it. Neighbours? Connections? Some stupid name like that. Maybe it was called Losers. Or Assholes. Didn't last any longer than the strip bar."

"Too middle-class a neighbourhood?"

"I guess."

"Do you like it as a sports bar?"

"It's all right. I don't pay any attention to the hockey sweaters or the football helmets or the photos of Darryl Sittler somebody bought at a yard sale. And I don't like the trivia games the people at the bar play. Bars are for talking, not for competing. I mean, who cares if you can get the answer to some useless piece of information faster than some guy sitting in a bar in Winnipeg? Who cares if you know more about movies or politics or what the name of some fucking island in the Baltic Sea is." I take a long swallow of my beer. "But if they turn it into a gay bar, then I'll definitely have to find somewhere else to drink."

Jessy says, "It's like you have a philosophy."

I look her straight in the eye. "I do. I have a philosophy about bars. Fucking right I do. I also have a philosophy about goaltending. Hockey goaltending. And I have a philosophy about the sins of pride. Would you care to hear it?"

"No," says Jessy, standing up. "What I'd like to do is go home. It's after one."

"I could tell you about my philosophies at home."

"At *my* home?"

"Terrific idea."

She lays her hand on top of my head. "Down, boy. I'm not that interested in your philosophies. Besides, if I took you home, I'd eat you up."

I raise my eyebrows and look at Trick, but he's disappeared. I scan around, and there he is at the bar talking to Dexter.

"And if I ate you up," Jessy goes on, "Trick would be all by himself. You wouldn't want that, would you? You're his bud."

"After you were done with me," I say, "you could start on him." I stand up suddenly and look down at her. She's tall but I'm huge. I put my hands on her shoulders. "Take me home with you," I say. Everything slows down then, and that's when I catch on to the fact that I'm really and truly gonzo.

Jessy raises her eyes to meet mine. "Let me get this straight," she says. "First, you want me to take you home and bang *your* brains out, then I'm supposed to come back and get Trick, and take him home and bang *his* brains out?"

Over at the bar, Dexter reaches for a switch on the wall. The lights on the Coors sign stop their staggered flashing. Trick wanders towards the men's room, pulling on his overcoat.

I take my hands off her shoulders, and she squirts me hard in the eyes with her spray bottle. "Ow!" I say, or something like that, then she turns me and shoves me towards the door, like a woman pushing a truck.

Outside, the cold hits me like a slap in the face.

Jessy says, "I thought we were friends."

When I can see again, she's standing in front of me with her hands on her hips.

"I'm sorry," I say, "we *are* friends. I was just being stupid –"

"Stupid is right," she says. "Just because you like a girl doesn't mean you have to fuck them."

"It doesn't?"

Next thing I know she's gone, and I'm standing there alone.

I start walking along the sidewalk. Then I stop. What have I done? I respect Jessy. I respect all waitresses. Any woman who wears a pencil behind her ear and chews gum, I respect. Especially if her lower teeth clamp onto her upper lip when she's angry. Makes her look a little like Reg. I laugh and start punching the air. What the fuck was I doing? I just tried to talk someone I actually respect into a one-night stand. Worse, I failed. Failed big time. Been too long since I've had some, I guess. Guess I didn't realize how I feel about her. How *do* I feel about her? Do I just want to get inside her trousers? Is it just sex, or do I have real feelings for her? Well, it's both, of course, so what else is new?

I start walking again. When I get home, I'll have to take Reggie for a walk, but I'm up for it, I'm up for it. And I start punching the air again as I walk along. Punching the air like a boxer.

Fifteen minutes later I realize I'm headed the wrong way. I'm headed east all right – east towards the house me and Tanya used to live in. The house Tanya still lives in.

I spread my arms, bank like an airplane, and turn down Greenwood.

Droning as I go.

When me and Tanya bought the house on Colchester, we both had certain things in mind. Debi was two, and Tanya wanted a safe, quiet neighbourhood. She wanted a backyard and a basement. She wanted a modern kitchen and a modern furnace with a humidifier attached. She wanted a working fireplace and insulation everywhere, a new roof and new asphalt on the drive. All I wanted was a good strong shower with about five different settings on the head: spray, pulse, needles, Swedish massage, and barefoot-Japanese-geisha-girl-walking-on-your-back.

Another thing I wanted was location. I wanted to live east of where I worked. I had been at Homicide for about a year, and I had reason to believe that I would stay there for a while. I was popular. I was hardworking. So I wanted to live *east* of HQ. During my first year there, me and Tanya were in a sixteenth-floor apartment of a high-rise about fifteen minutes *west* of HQ, and every morning that I was on days I would have to drive directly into the sun. Coming home was the same: directly into the sun. Being blinded like that bugged the hell out of me. It made me dread going to work and it made me dread going home. I had this vision of every working day for the next thirty years being the same: my life laid out as plain as a map of the city. As it turned out, the house we bought was twenty-five minutes east of HQ, and I lived there for fourteen years; where I live now is fifteen minutes east, and every morning I snicker at the poor saps driving towards me, their sunglasses on, their visors down. So while it's true that Tanya got everything she wanted in a house, and while it's true that I ended up with fuck-all, it's also true that I have lived almost my whole working life east of HQ. *East* of HQ. First, in the house that Tanya has all to herself, and then in the apartment I currently live in. The door of which I am even now trying to find the key in my pocket for. Behind it, Reg is barking like a maniac.

CHAPTER 6

Sunday, October 11

TRICK HONKS HIS horn at eleven, right on time. We're going to the track this morning. Debi's going to give us the Shedrow tour, then we're going to stay for the afternoon's racing. I give Reggie a Milk-Bone, a vigorous rub behind the ears, grab my jacket, and out the door I go.

"Where the hell did you get to last night?" Trick says as I climb in beside him. He drives a spotless burgundy Cadillac. You practically have to wipe your feet before you get in. "I was standing there with my coat on watching the same damn golf highlights for like the fifth time, waiting for you to come out of the john or whatever. And you never showed."

I clear my throat. "I, uh, I walked home."

Trick's already pulling out into traffic and doesn't look at me. "Well, you could have told me about that little change in plan. I thought we were supposed to split a cab."

"I got a little . . . mixed up. Didn't Jessy say anything? Didn't she tell you I left?"

"Yeah, that's another thing. I don't know if I'll be frequenting McCully's much in the future."

"What are you talking about?"

"Well, it's Jessy. She was rude to me."

"Get out of here."

"No, I'm serious. She didn't seem too pleased with you, either."

"Really? What happened?"

"Well, after I'd been standing there about fifteen minutes waiting for you, I was the only customer left in the place. I knew Dexter wanted to get going, but he was sort of waiting for me to leave. Then finally I saw Jessy stacking chairs – something must have upset her because she was knocking those chairs around like bowling pins – and I asked her if she knew where you got to, and she took this big breath and put her fists on her hips and said you'd gone, and I said that's weird, because you and I were supposed to split a cab, and then she told me to bugger off."

"She said what?"

"She said to bugger off. To be precise, she said – and I quote – 'Trick, I've had a long hard day, so why don't you just bugger off home before you say something stupid like your big stupid friend.'"

The weather's cleared since yesterday, and the sky's as blue Wheeler's left eye. Debi meets us at the Will-Call booth, she gives us both a big hug, we park Trick's Caddy, climb into a beat-up pickup that smells like horseshit, and she drives us around the club-house turn towards the backstretch and through the gates and into Shedrow. Shedrow is like a community of motels, except each room is occupied by a horse. Debi parks the truck beside the cafeteria and we walk a short distance to Barn 3. As we walk down the aisle in front of the stalls, most of the horses swing their heads out to see what's going on. It's dark and cool in the barn, but our eyes adjust, and it smells terrific: hay and liniment and, I think, creosote. As we pass them, Debi names each of the horses under the care of her boss, Shorty Rogers, but then we have to stop and be properly introduced to the four horses she looks after: Cornerbrook, a chestnut gelding with a star the shape of Newfoundland on his forehead; an unraced two-year-old grey filly named Glenora Ferry – "We hope to get her in a couple of races before the meet closes," Debi says – and two old claimers, both bay geldings, Baby Brother and Too Many Men. I know both of them, having lost more than a few bucks on each.

Debi leans her back against the half-door of Baby Brother's stall, and he lowers his massive head over her shoulder. She reaches up and combs his forelock with her fingers. He nickers. His enormous brown eyes study us. He has a blaze that starts between his eyes and runs like the stroke of a paintbrush down the middle of his face, then swerves over his left nostril. "He's got some Northern Dancer in him," I say. "He's got the same blaze."

Debi nods and rubs his forehead with her knuckle. "His daddy's Northern Baby. You're my favourite, aren't you, Babe? Goddamn right you are." From her pocket she produces an apple. She balances it on the palm of her left hand, he takes it in his teeth, chomps it neatly in half, lets one half fall back onto her palm, and noisily devours the part he kept. Then he's back for the other half.

Outside the sun blinds us. Debi leads us past walking rings and straw mountains of manure and horse blankets drying on the fenders of half-tons. I look at Debi – her white-blonde crewcut, her ratty black AC/DC T-shirt, her wrestler's physique – and notice for the first time she's got a tiny silver stud through one nostril.

In the cafeteria I treat Debi and Trick to lunch, and Debi chatters away about the horses and Shorty and some exercise rider named Randy she's seeing – she laughs and says she outweighs him by eighty pounds – and she's so full of life, so *alive*, that I think of the dead girl, Ms. Stevenson, and I think how lucky I am and what Debi means to me, and at one point I lower my fork, still loaded with shepherd's pie, and I say to her, "I can't remember seeing you so happy." She doesn't say anything, but she blushes and then she grins like she used to when she was little, when I would put Bob Seger's 'Betty Lou's Gettin' Out Tonight' on the record player, and Debi would dash out of her bedroom, and I would scoop her up and waltz her around the living room.

"The way I see it," I say, "white trash is a relative term. If there was no middle class or upper class in white society, there wouldn't be anything to compare the scum to. Like all these black basketball players with the bad tattoos. They're black trash."

"Run that by me again," says Trick.

I'm up about forty dollars after three races and feeling good. I've got my daughter with me, my best friend, two or three beers inside me, the sun's shining, and I'm up money. What more could a man want? "Well, now that you have a black middle class and a black upper class – Colin Powell and all that – you can recognize that the Dennis Rodmans of the world are trash – black trash."

Trick shakes his head. "You're saying that before there was a black upper class or a black middle class, all blacks were lower class – therefore, all blacks were trash?"

"That's not what I'm saying at all."

"Oh really, 'cause that's what it *sounds* like you're saying."

"That's not what I meant, and you know it. Who crawled up your ass –?"

"When we were in Africa, we were jungle bunnies, right?"

"For fucksake, Trick."

"And when we came to America, we were slaves. Right?"

"What about House Guest?" Debi says. "He likes a route, and there's no pace in here."

"And then after the Civil War, when we all moved north to Chicago and Detroit and became urban and started carrying boom boxes on our shoulders and rapping on street corners, we became trash. Is that what you're saying?"

"Trick, for fucksake, if you can't have a discussion without going fucking crazy –"

"You know, Camp, sometimes you forget who I am."

"Is that right? How can I forget who you are when everything you do reminds me all the time just exactly –?"

"Everything I do? Like what?"

"Like you wear a fucking tuque all year round! You wore one to the Queen's Plate when it was a hundred fucking degrees. Like you wear more gold than one of them Dominican infielders. Like your *car*!"

"What about my car?"

"It's a burgundy Cadillac, Trick, in case you hadn't noticed. All you need's a pimp hat –"

"You want me to drive a minivan? The parking lot at work's full of minivans, and they *all* belong to white men."

"That's because you're the token black in the shop, and besides –"

"Now wait a minute –"

"And besides, I drive a Volare, of which you are very much aware of!"

"Surely to God you're not suggesting there's something *fine* about that piece of shit you call a car!"

"At least I don't drive a pimp-mobile!"

He stands up and stomps off.

Debi says, "Daddy, sometimes you go too far. Even though he's your best friend in the world, you're still a goddamn racist."

"What do you mean?"

"I can't make it any plainer. You're a goddamn racist."

"I'm not a racist. That's ridiculous."

"I'll prove it."

I laugh. "This should be good. You're going to prove I'm a racist. Well, go ahead."

"Say my baby's name."

This kind of catches me off guard. I open my mouth a couple of times, but nothing comes out.

"Go ahead, say it."

I clear my throat, but again nothing comes out.

"You see! You can't even say my baby's name! It's Jamal, Daddy. Jamal!"

"Why'd you have to give him one of them Afro names? Why couldn't you call him Dave or Bill or Steve. What's wrong with Steve?"

But she's already got up and gone after Trick.

"Or Tyrone?" I say to the two empty chairs across from me. "Or Leroy. What's wrong with Leroy?"

Ten minutes later they're back. Trick won't talk to me, but Debi will. So me and Debi settle on House Guest, and Debi says, "You want in on this, Uncle Artie?" Trick throws in ten and we box House Guest with the favourite, and they finish one-two – House Guest on top at five-to-one – and we high-five each other and order more beers and Trick says, "You can insult me any time you want, man, but don't insult my car," and I say, "Sorry, you know I love your car, I'm proud to ride in it," and then we forget all the nonsense we were talking and start working on the next race, a six-furlong sprint for non-winners of two.

I must have been dozing because the ringing phone startles me so much the half-empty beer can in my hand hops onto my chest and rolls down beside me in the La-Z-Boy. In front of me, Carney Lansford is swinging two bats in the on-deck circle. I can't have been out for long because the lower right-hand corner of the screen tells me there's one out in the bottom of the sixth and the score is still 5–1 Oakland. I pull a fistful of Kleenex out of the box beside me on the snack table and dab at my T-shirt with one hand while reaching for the phone with the other.

"Campbell? Just when I'm getting used to finding you at McCully's, you decide to spend a quiet evening at home."

In fact, I had given serious thought to watching the game at McCully's, but every time I thought about it, I'd get this picture in my mind's eye of Jessy intercepting me just inside the door and steering me back outside.

"You phoned the bar?"

"Yes I did, and Dexter informed me that your whereabouts were unknown."

"Was Trick there?"

"I did not enquire about the whereabouts of Trick. Are you aware that I've never actually *met* Trick? You've mentioned his name to me many thousands of times, but I've never actually *seen* the man. I'm beginning to doubt his existence."

"I'll introduce you. Are you watching the game?"

"Not really. I've been marking papers, but I've been monitoring, so to speak. Looks like a lost cause."

As if in response to Daniel's comment, the fifty thousand fans at Oakland–Alameda County Coliseum in Oakland, California, break into a thunderous cheer, and I look up at the TV in time to watch their sixth run cross the plate.

"They just scored again," I say.

"Yes, I've got it on, too, *sans* sound. Like I said, it looks like a lost cause."

I grunt. I *feel* like a lost cause: my shirt is soaked with beer, my hair needs a wash, my fingernails are orange from the two bags of cheesies I've eaten, the snack table is littered with beer cans, cigarette packs, empty bags, a full ashtray, and a half-eaten bologna, mayo, and coarse-grind black pepper sandwich, there are dustballs the size of tumbleweed under the TV table, the carpet hasn't been vacuumed for a month, and the whole apartment smells like Reg.

"But I've got some news. Those pen names you gave me? One of them stood out, but it wasn't until after I'd eliminated the others that I figured it out."

I sit up straight. "Keep talking."

"The killer's given us another clue. One of the pen names was Lennox Ross, right?"

"Right."

"Well, I don't know why I didn't see it right away. Lennox and Ross were Scottish noblemen in *Macbeth*."

I phone Wheeler, tell her to get dressed and meet me at Ms. Stevenson's apartment building. I'm only there two or three minutes, having a smoke, pacing the curved driveway, when she gets there. We go upstairs and start going through Ms. Stevenson's files. In no time we find what we're looking for: the covering letter the suspect sent along with his submission, complete with his return address – Lennox Ross, 3315 Parliament Street, Apt. 19, Toronto, Ontario.

Me and Wheeler look at each other. "He's right here," I say. "He's right in our own backyard."

"Let's go get him," Wheeler says.

But something makes me hesitate. Daniel could be wrong. Lennox Ross could be some poor sucker of a poet's real name, and the connection with Shakespeare is just a coincidence. But when I start to say as much to Wheeler, I flash back to that business in the Tim Hortons when I let her go in alone after the kid in the Bulls jacket. I feel a prickling sensation spread across my back, and I know the real reason for my hesitation. Fear. I'm scared shitless. Wheeler's about one-third my size, right, but I'm the one with three years left, so all of a sudden I'm the one afraid of breaking down the door of a crazy man, a killer. A loser with nothing to lose.

"Slow down," I say. "Read me the whole letter."

She looks at me, her cheeks flexing like she's about to say something she shouldn't.

In a harder voice I say, "Read the letter."

She clears her voice. "'Dear Editor, Please find enclosed six list poems which I am submitting for your consideration.'" She looks up at me.

"Go on," I say.

"That's it. Except for his signature and his name typed beneath it."

I take the letter from her and stare at it for a moment. "What the hell's a list poem?"

Wheeler lifts her hands in exasperation. "I don't know, but what I do want to know is why we aren't on our way to Parliament Street."

I step over to the telephone and pick up the receiver. "We can't move on this till Bateman gives us the word."

As I'm dialling she's not saying anything. "Homicide," says Gallagher's voice.

"This is Young," I say. "I need to talk to Staff Inspector Bateman."

"He's not in till morning."

"I know that. I want you to find him – at home, wherever – and ask him to phone me at Joanne Stevenson's apartment."

"I'm not supposed to disturb him unless –"

"Charlie," I say quietly, "get him." I give him the phone number and hang up.

Five minutes later, Bateman calls. "This better be good, Camp," he says. "I was on the throne."

"Sorry, boss, but we got a tough call here." I explain the situation to him and, as I expected, he says he'll send a couple of cars to watch the building on Parliament Street, but we won't go in until we're properly mobilized. "We want to make sure it's the right guy, and we don't want to go in till we've got him cold," he says. "I'll get Barkas or whoever's available to check on this Lennox Ross. It's almost midnight, Camp. Get some sleep, and I'll see you bright and early. And Camp?"

"Yes, sir?"

"Good work."

His compliment makes me feel like shit, but at the same time the relief I feel at not having to go to the Parliament Street apartment is like a double shot of Jack. As a rookie, I would have raced there, heart pounding, grinning like an idiot, turned on by the excitement, the danger. Even ten years ago, I wouldn't have thought twice. And I wouldn't have waited for my superior's go-ahead, either. As soon as we found that address I would have been out the door and in the elevator, thinking about which mode of entry to use on apartment 19, 3315 Parliament Street.

I hang up the phone and break the news to Wheeler, but she's already figured it out from listening to my end of the conversation.

"That's such bullshit," she says, and then suddenly she slams her fist down so hard on an end table that a little pot of African violets jumps into the air and nosedives neatly into Ms. Stevenson's big blue plastic recycling box.

As soon as I get home I pour myself a tumbler of Jack. I turn on the television, collapse into the La-Z-Boy, and listen as the sportscaster on CNN tells me the Blue Jays – trailing 6–1 at the end of seven, which was when I left to meet Wheeler – rallied with three runs in the eighth, two in the ninth, and one in the twelfth to win game four.

Cowardice has its own payback. Sometimes it means you sprain your ankle or get a flat tire. But if the coward in question happens to be a 290-pound cop, it means he misses out on one of the great comebacks in the history of professional sports. Furthermore, it will be his favourite team in all the world that will perform this miracle. The team he has followed since it was born, since it was nothing but a bunch of farmboys and has-beens with names like Phil Roof and Alvis Woods who couldn't string together two victories if their lives depended on it. And not to be overlooked is the mixture of guts and more guts the cop's favourite team has summoned up from somewhere to perform this miracle – the very items he's long since left behind in a bar somewhere.

CHAPTER 7

Monday, October 12

BY THE TIME I get to work this morning, we've got a name.

Lawrence Woolley.

Lawrence Woolley is the man renting the furnished room at 3315 Parliament Street. Lennox Ross may be his pen name, but Lawrence Woolley, as a quick search revealed, is his real name. An all-points bulletin went out on him at four a.m. According to the computer, Woolley was released from Poplar Bluff Penitentiary two months ago – Monday, August 10 – after serving six years for sexual assault. Because he has a record, the lab boys were able to send a mug shot along with the APB. At first, looking at the picture, about all you can say is he's pretty harmless looking – thin face, large ears, dark features. He's six feet tall, weighs 178 pounds, no distinguishing scars or tattoos. When I look at the photograph a second time, though, when I look real close, I see the eyes, which like the eyes of all the killers I've ever looked into – and there've been a few – are cold and hard and empty. There's no doubt about it: Lawrence Woolley would just as soon kill you as look at you.

Big Urmson comes in from the all-night stakeout of the Parliament Street address to check in his gun before he heads home. I catch him before he leaves. I ask him what he saw. Nothing, he says. No movement at all.

Me and Wheeler are grabbing our coats for the drive down to Parliament Street ourselves when Staff Inspector Bateman walks up to my desk and says, "Camp, this just arrived." I take the envelope from him. It's addressed to METROPOLITAN TORONTO POLICE, HOMICIDE DIVISION, 40 COLLEGE ST. In the lower left-hand corner, it says, ATTENTION: JOANNE STEVENSON. "I opened it," Bateman says, "and this was inside." He holds up a small rectangle of paper that looks as if it's been scissored from a book. He's holding it by one corner, carefully. He gently lays it on the blotter on Trick's desk and says, "More Shakespeare, from the look of it."

There's rosemary, that's for remembrance;
pray you, love, remember. And there is pansies,
that's for thoughts. . . .
There's fennel for you, and columbines.
There's rue for you; and here's some for me.
We may call it herb of grace a Sundays.
O, you must wear your rue with a difference.
There's a daisy. I would give you some violets,
but they wither'd all when my father died.
They say 'a made a good end.

I hang my coat back up.

Wheeler says, "What are you doing? Let's go," but I ignore her and reach for Trick's phone.

Daniel's not in his office. I leave a message. Urgent, I tell the woman. I scratch my neck. Wheeler and Big Urmson and Bateman are leaning over the quotation, reading it, shaking their heads.

"There's a clue in there," I tell them.

"Maybe," says Wheeler.

"There was last time."

My name is paged over the intercom. I pick up the phone and punch the button for the flashing line. "Young," I say.

"It's me," says Daniel, out of breath. "What's up?"

I read him the quotation.

"*Hamlet*," he says straight off. "It's Ophelia speaking, just after she's gone loopy."

"But what's the clue?" I ask. "There was a clue in the last one."

"Wait. There's something very familiar . . . Wait a minute. Campbell, there's this very strange woman who calls herself Pansy Jones. She runs a small-press operation out of the basement of the Harbour Street Library. It's just a nickel-and-dime operation. She used to churn the stuff out on a mimeograph machine. This is years ago, I don't even know if she's still in operation. She must be sixty –"

"What made you think of her?"

"It's not as if she ever had any credibility. She used to publish anybody – the drugged, the homeless, the addled ramblings of any –"

"Daniel! What made you think of her?"

For a second there's silence. "Well, her name, obviously: 'And there is pansies, that's for thoughts.' And her magazine, just a newsletter, really. It's called *Columbine*. If you ask me, it's a double clue."

Pansy Jones is in the phone book, so while two cars are speeding towards the Parliament Street address, me and Wheeler – siren wailing and lights flashing – race towards a basement apartment near the corner of Gerrard and Broadview. A quick phone call gave us only a taped reply: "Hello, this is Pansy, chief cook and bottle-washer of *Columbine*, a horticultural journal of the arts: floral but never florid. I am not home right now, but please leave a message after the beep."

To reach the apartment we descend a short staircase from the sidewalk. There are several flyers for carpet cleaners and pizza parlours on the black rubber doormat. The mailbox has a dozen letters and magazines jammed into it. Whatever happened here is days old. We knock loudly on the door, then test the knob. It's unlocked.

Inside, lights are on everywhere. "He was here at night," I tell Wheeler. For some reason, I'm whispering; my heart's pounding like a rock drill.

"Could be, or maybe she doesn't get much light down here," Wheeler says.

The apartment is a mess. Magazines and newspapers are every-where – on tables, on chairs, on the floor. Every flat surface is piled and cluttered with books. No television. There are weeks of dirty dishes and empty glasses. There must be two dozen Brio cans scattered around the room. Vases of dying flowers on bookcases and end tables, and the room smells sickly sweet, overripe. As we step forward, I smell cat piss, and when I look at the floor I see litter boxes and feed dishes. As we stand there taking it in, there's a thump in the kitchen. Our fingers jump to our holster flaps. A low shadow crosses the kitchen linoleum, and as we crouch and aim, a grey cat slowly makes its way into our sights. Its yellow eyes widen when it sees us, and it trots towards me. I stand up. My focus is drawn to something on my right. The cat rubs its flank hard against my shin. On a shelf above the sofa, a bookend gives way and several books tumble off the end, like people crowded off a cliff. They crash to the floor, then we hear a high-pitched scream like a baby's. An orange-and-white cat leaps down from the other end of the shelf. In seconds there's a dozen cats emerging from nooks and crannies and meowing towards us.

"Over here," I say, and gesture towards a hallway leading off to our right.

The door to the bedroom is open. The drapes are shut, and even though the lamp on the bedside table is on, the room is gloomy. The sheets on the bed are thrown back, a pair of glasses rests on the bedside table, a photo album lies open on the bedspread. The room is stale: cats and ashtrays and dirty laundry. We sweep our flashlights into the corners of the room, but all we see is books and clothing and shoes.

Back in the hall I see a crack of light under the closed bathroom door. "Open it," I whisper to Wheeler, drawing my gun. She turns the knob sharply and pushes; the door swings away from me and I step in.

Pansy Jones is kneeling in front of the toilet. Her ankles are bound with silver duct tape, as are her wrists behind her back. Her olive-green nightgown is bunched up under her arms, and her buttocks are exposed. There's a sweet, sick-making reek in the air. I breathe slowly through my mouth. There's a heap of dirty laundry and towels under the wash basin and a kicked-over pile of magazines on the floor. A toothbrush and a tube of toothpaste lie on the edge of the bathtub. Tanya did that, too, brush her teeth in the tub. I lean forward and peer into the toilet bowl. The water is rust-coloured, and Ms. Jones's hair has been blackened by the blood and brain matter that have escaped the wounds at the back of her head.

I turn and look at Wheeler, who's staring at the corpse. She points and says, "What's that?"

I lean forward again and look more closely. A piece of paper is balled up in Ms. Jones's right hand. "Looks like a note."

"Read it," she says.

"No. We'll wait for Cronish."

About six of us are standing outside in the fresh air, smoking, when Cronish comes up the stairs from Ms. Jones's apartment. "A serial killer," he says. "How about that? When was the last time we had a serial killer in Toronto?" He seems almost happy. "Most of the bodies I look at belong to stupid people who get killed by people slightly less stupid. The only time things get interesting is when I stumble across the handiwork of someone who has snapped, but has done so," and here Cronish lowers his voice, "with style."

Standing beside me, Wheeler says, "Style?"

Cronish turns and stares at her deadpan over his little half-glasses.

"My dear," he says, "it's the way he killed her. It's the way he killed them both. Premeditated, vicious . . . *stylish*." He turns to me. "I told you he was clever. The tennis ball proved that." Then he smiles and pulls two baggies from a pocket of his overcoat. "Looks like our killer is out for revenge, he's making sport of it, and although he knows he'll lose in the end – as we all will, my dear, as we all will – he's going to have some serious psychopathic fun before he does."

Wheeler says, "Revenge against what?"

"Oh, life and all its grievances. Who knows what they are? But it would appear he has a low opinion of women." Cronish pauses, then holds up the bags, one in each hand. "Which one first?"

When no one says anything, he lowers his left hand and we all stare at the bag in his right. Whatever's in it is dark red and yellow and shiny, and about the size of a baby's fist. "His motto, you might say: 'Killing well is the best revenge.'"

"What is it?" says Wheeler. "Panties?"

Cronish smiles again. "Nothing so mundane."

"It's a flower," I say. "It came out of her mouth."

Cronish looks at me, surprised. "Very good, Sergeant," he says. "As a matter of fact, it's a columbine –"

Before he can say anything more – and I know he wants to – I say, "What's in the note?"

Cronish doesn't like to be rushed. I'm spoiling his fun. He pockets the first bag and opens the second. From it he takes a crumpled sheet of paper, He unfolds it carefully, by the corners. "It reads, 'Oh God, thy arm was here!' It's signed C. Delabreth."

Me and Wheeler grab a sandwich at Subway. My favourite is tuna on white, green olives, green pepper, onion, mayo, extra salt and pepper. The man behind the counter shakes the big tin salt-and-pepper dispenser. It has a handle on the side like a beer stein's.

When we sit down, Wheeler hardly touches her food.

"Wheeler, for fucksake," I say with my mouth full, "eat!"

Behind the counter the phone rings.

"The phone," she says, suddenly looking at me.

"Very good," I say. "Observant."

"*Her* phone. She had an answering machine. We were right there in her apartment and we didn't think to check her messages. Maybe he left a message!"

She's out of her seat and halfway to the car before I can swallow my first bite.

"Terry Robson at PrintCom. Two hundred copies of the chapbook, with two-colour cover, folding and stapling, will run you in the neighbourhood of five hundred. Plus tax, of course. Let me know. Eight-one-eight, four-four-two-five."

"Pansy, it's Audrey. My mother's better, so I'll see you at the awareness meeting, as planned. Seven-thirty, isn't it? Yup, it's right here on the fridge. Bye for now."

"Hello, Pansy. Kemp Stevens here. I'm setting something up for the twenty-seventh at the Ploughshare. Let me know if you want a spot. You could do the bongo thing like last year. Give me a call."

"Um, it's Tom, the super. Listen, I hate to bug you about this, but the people upstairs are complaining about the cats again. It's the smell. They say it comes right up through the floorboards. They say they're going to call the SPCA if you don't do something. Just thought you ought to know. I knocked but you weren't there. Oh, and the howling, too."

"Pansy, it's Kemp again. On second thought, it just struck me that instead of the bongo thing, which might seem a little repetitive since you just did it last year, you could see if that fellow who played the saxophone behind you – what was it, three years ago? – is available. There's no money for him, of course, but it was such a hit he might want to do it just for fun. I would love it if you would read 'Love Is,' which as you know is my favourite among your many fine poems. Let me know what you think."

"Detective Sergeant Young, is that you? How's the investigation going? My guess is she was dead forty-eight hours before you found her. Am I close at least? I must admit I did give myself a head start. I waited a day before sending you the quotation, which the Bard was kind enough to furnish and which I was kind enough to FedEx to your place of employ. Oh, by the way, I killed her Thursday, just before midnight. Yes, Detective Sergeant, my arm was there."

"Pansy, it's Audrey. We missed you at the awareness meeting. Is everything okay? Give me a call. Bernice says hi. She wants to know if you're willing to continue as treasurer."

Back at Homicide Trick comes in with Estabrooks. They were part of the detachment sent to Lawrence Woolley's rooming house. "He's gone," Trick says, slapping down a large envelope on my desk, "but we found some interesting shit, including responses from magazines he sent poems to. This one, for instance, from the new victim." He carefully removes several sheets of eight-and-a-half-by-eleven from the envelope and slides them in front of me.

> *Columbine,*
> *P.O. Box 559,*
> *Station "LK,"*
> *Toronto, Ontario*
> *September 14, 1992*

> *Dear Mr. Delabreth,*

> *Thank you for giving us the opportunity to look at your work. Unfortunately, it doesn't meet our needs at this time. Do try us again.*

> *Regards,*
> *Pansy Jones, editor*

"Delabreth," I say. "The same name was on the note we found at the scene." I scratch my head. "But he used Lennox Ross when he submitted poems to Ms. Stevenson."

"So he's using more than one pen name," says Trick. "That's all that means. Keep reading. Three of his poems are there."

DR MANNING'S GARDEN

White Feather
Pincushion

Red Hot Poker
Love Lies Bleeding

Bee Balm
Blazing Star

Canterbury Bell
Cloth of Gold

Moss Rose
Monarda

Viola
Veronica

Hosta
Hollyhock

Hibiscus
Coneflower

Wallflower
Windflower

Lythrum
Pyrethrum

Portulaca
Potentilla

Shasta Daisy
Painted Daisy

Pacific Giant Guinevere
Pacific Giant Summer Skies

MIXED DRINKS

Allies
Atom Bomb
Depth Charge

Hell
Dawn
Commodore

Cowboy
Horse's Neck
Blood and Sand

Monkey Gland
Serpent's Tooth
Corpse Revival

Cupid
Between the Sheets
Bosom Caresser

Bikini
Slippery Nipple
Sex on the Beach

Starboard Light
Honeymoon
Round the World

White Lady
Green Room
Blue Star

Deauville
Brazil
Bombay

Mind Eraser
Gloom Chaser
Glad Eye

BLUE MONK

Bemsha Swing
Brilliant Corners
Bright Mississippi

Bye-Ya
Rhythm-a-ning
Ba-lue Bolivar Ba-lues Are

Trinkle Tinkle
Hackensack
Nutty

Epistrophy
Pannonica
Misterioso

Crepuscule with Nellie
Ruby, My Dear
Just a Gigolo

Straight, No Chaser
'Round Midnight
Ugly Beauty

I Mean You
Don't Blame Me
Well, You Needn't

Evidence
Off Minor
Introspection

After I've finished reading, I look across at Trick. "At least now we know what a list poem is," I say. "Well, maybe we don't know what it is, but we know what it looks like. Who's this Dr. Manning?"

"I did some sniffing around," he tells me. "Turns out Dr. Manning's the head shrink up at Poplar Bluff."

I'm sitting at my desk an hour later when the phone rings.

"Young, this is Andy Bartle of *The Standard*. A little voice just told me another woman's been killed. Another poetry type. Is this true?"

Andy Bartle is an asshole. He's a worm. In fact, I would rather have worms in my gut than talk to the son of a bitch. He's an ambulance-chasing bastard. A couple of years ago, I was standing outside a high-rise in Scarborough trying to talk down a jumper on the twentieth floor. I had a bullhorn, and I had people inside the guy's apartment, but they were scared to go out on the balcony because the guy said he'd jump if they came near him. He'd been up there an hour when Andy Bartle and his photographer showed up. The first thing Bartle said was, "Good, he's still up there." Then he told his photographer, who looked like a trainee – he didn't look any older than about seventeen – to get ready, to try to get "before," "during," and "after" shots. A minute later, as if on cue, the guy jumped. The only sound I could hear as he fell was the clicking and whirring of the camera. He fell for about a minute and a half, it seemed like, and landed on a big air-conditioning unit about ten feet tall, and stayed there, one arm dangling over the side. "Awesome!" Bartle said, beside me. "Fucking awesome!" He turned to the photographer. "Did you get it?" The photographer nodded. "Good work, good work," Bartle said. "If you want to make a name for yourself in journalism, you can't miss opportunities like that."

So I'm not too fond of the asshole. He's only about thirty, a little weasel in two-tone shoes and a homburg. Not that I can see them now, over the phone, but I bet he's got them on.

"No comment," I say. "You know I'm not going to tell you any-thing about an on-going investigation."

"Come on, Young, if I don't get it from you, I'll get it somewhere else. If I get it from you, there's a much better chance you'll look good than if I don't."

"Is that some kind of threat, you little weasel?"

"Fine, be that way. But this news is big, and if it's not handled right, the public's going to be all over you. A *serial* killer, Young. Imagine the hysteria."

"Look, Bartle, we're on the case. We've got leads, and we're moving."

"Do you think he'll strike again?"

"You said it yourself, he's a serial killer. If you want to know anything else, you'll have to talk to my staff inspector. Now that's it."

"Did he use a hammer on this one, too? What else did he –"

I hang up on him.

It's the bottom of the sixth by the time we get to the bar. I was getting cold feet at the last minute, but Trick told me not to be a dickhead. Seems he was here last night, and Jessy asked where I was.

"Blue?" Dexter calls from behind the bar as we make our way to the only empty table in the place.

"Four of them," Trick responds, and we take off our coats and get settled. The score is 6–1 Oakland, Cone is already out of the game, and unless a miracle like last night's takes place, I will shortly have to fork over twenty dollars to Daniel.

Trick sees Jessy coming with the beers and heads for the john before I can say a word.

She doesn't look at me or speak. She just puts the beers down.

"Jessy," I say, "can I talk to you?"

"You gonna pay for those or start a tab?"

"We'll start a tab. Listen –"

But she turns on her heel and disappears into the crowd, and when Trick comes back and asks me how the little reconciliation went, I tell him to stop smirking, he looks like Eddie Murphy. That shuts him up for a whole inning until Daniel arrives. Before I left the station, I phoned Daniel at his office and told him what had happened to Ms. Jones. "My God," he said at one point during our conversation, "she rejected his poems? I didn't think she rejected *anybody's* poems." I told him about the three list poems, and he asked me to fax him copies, which I did. He asked if I'd be at McCully's this evening, and when I said yes, he said he'd see me here.

I introduce him to Trick. "After all these years," he says. "I thought Campbell just made you up. I thought you were the stuff of legend. What a pleasure it is to meet you." So while I'm still smouldering away about Jessy and stealing glances all over the joint to see if I can see her, Trick and Daniel are getting along like a house on fire, wondering out loud why I've never introduced them before, complaining to each other about what a slob I am, and talking about people named Joshua Redman and Jamaica Kincaid – whoever the fuck *they* are – and generally rubbing it in that they'd probably be better off as friends to each other than friends to me.

After a while, a different waitress comes over. I've never seen her before. We order a round, but I keep quiet. I don't say to her, Isn't this Jessy's section? Or, Where the hell's Jessy?

When the game ends (Oakland: six runs on eight hits, no errors; Toronto: two runs on seven hits, three errors), I pull a twenty out of my wallet. "Daniel, you piece of shit, here you go, but remember it's *forty* bucks on Cone's next start."

Daniel smiles and reaches for the money. "By my calculations, the Jays will have to make it to the World Series for Cone to get another start."

I pull the money back. "I can't believe my ears. You don't think the Jays are going to make it to the Series. Trick, don't tell me you like this man."

Trick's expression is grim. "I *thought* I liked him. I *wanted* to like him."

"Tell you what," I say to Daniel. "I'll surrender this twenty if you'll wager it back on Wednesday night's game. Guzman against Moore."

"Nope. Only bet on Cone. Or, rather, *against* Cone. Secret of my success. Now give me my money and order some beer. And wings. *Hot* ones."

The new girl takes our order and returns a minute later with a pitcher of beer.

When she's gone, I say, "Okay, two questions, one for each of you."

"What's the topic?" Trick asks. "Baseball?"

"No, this is business."

He leans forward.

"Trick," I say, "how did the killer know I was on the case? The message on Pansy Jones's answering machine was addressed to me. And Daniel, these list poems. What kind of a person makes list poems? What would his personality be like?"

From the inside pocket of his blazer Daniel takes the copies of the poems I faxed him. He unfolds them on the table and says, "I've been thinking about it. It's hard to judge from just three poems, but my guess is he's probably obsessively neat. Orderly. The idea of reducing language to its barest bones appeals to him. Maybe he's trying to see things in their purest, simplest form. There's something he's trying to understand. Himself probably, but there's nothing special in that. All serious writers do it."

"Hold it a minute," I say. "You think he's a serious writer?"

"Well, like I say, it's difficult to evaluate someone's work on the basis of just a few samples, but yes I do. And I'm fairly certain he does, too. And I'll tell you something else. Even though his poems are just lists, I – and I say this with some reluctance – I like them. They're like abstract art. They don't *mean* anything. They're nothing more than what they appear to be — the names of flowers or cocktails or jazz tunes — but there's an integrity to them that baffles me, considering that his other principal interest in life seems to be murder."

"Well, he's sick, right? The other day you said he's a psychopath."

"Yes, I think he's sick. Don't you?"

"I'll let you know. I'm driving out to Poplar Bluff tomorrow to visit Dr. Manning, the institution guru. He's the guy who treated Lawrence Woolley for six years, and I want to know what he's got to say."

Daniel points at one of the list poems in front of him. "He's the man with the flowers."

"The same." I turn to Trick. "So, how about your question?"

Trick shrugs his shoulders. "Pretty simple, if you ask me. We've had a good fifty, sixty phone tips by now, right? Some come with names, but most are anonymous. Crackpots, most of them. We trace them and most wind up at pay phones. But we have all sorts of people fielding the calls, right? The crackpot asks the right question, he gets the answer he wants. Especially Gallagher, you know how he likes to talk."

Daniel says, "Who's Gallagher?"

Trick says, "Desk sergeant. Good guy, but he talks too much. If he took the call, and the caller said, 'This is a pretty scary case, but I guess you've got some of your best people on it,' Gallagher would probably say, 'That's right, sir, Detective Sergeant Young is definitely one of our best.'"

Daniel says, "Remember, Campbell, he's making a game out of it."

"Yeah, right, but it gets kind of personal when he does that. The thing is, the manhunt's on, and he knows it. He can't go back to Parliament Street. We're looking for any relatives right now, but there's no guarantee he'd go to them. We think we understand his motive: he's showing these women who've rejected his poems who's boss. He's saying, 'You think you can reject me? Watch this.' And then he tortures them. He's not just getting even. He's making a point.

"We know his method. We're in the process of contacting all the editors of literary magazines across North America. The problem is he uses a different alias with each submission, so all we can tell them is to key on submissions of list poems. And anything sort of vaguely Shakespearean. The note he left today, for instance."

"What note?" Daniel says.

"I told you, didn't I? Pansy Jones had a columbine stuffed in her mouth and a note crunched up in her hand."

"A columbine? You didn't say anything about it."

I rub my face. "Sorry, my man, I can't remember who I've said what to."

"What did the note say?"

"Something about the arm of God. And it was signed. Not Lennox Ross. Some other name. Delahanty or something." I search my pockets for the scrap of paper I wrote it on. "I can't remember what it was. It's at home. I'll get it for you tomorrow. It's the name he used with the poems he submitted to Ms. Jones. The letter of rejection she sent him had the same name on it."

Daniel looks worried. "The name could be important."

I look at Trick. "Do you remember?"

He shakes his head. "I wasn't there, man. Wheeler was with you. Ask her."

I peer through the haze of cigarette smoke at the Blue Light clock above the bar. "It's midnight. She'll be asleep. I don't want to wake her."

"This is important," says Daniel.

I reach for my cigarettes. "I know, but I'm not going to wake her. She's wound tighter than a spring as it is."

Daniel says, "But if this Lawrence Woolley really is a serial killer –"

"I know, I know, if he's going to strike again, it'll be soon. He's going to do as much damage as he can before we take him down. I'll find the name for you tomorrow. It wasn't Delahanty. Dela-something."

"'The arm of God . . . ,'" Daniel says. "Doesn't ring a bell, I'm afraid."

The wings arrive in their wicker basket. Celery and carrots and blue-cheese dip on the side. Little plastic bowls for the bones. The new girl brings them. By now I'm so exhausted I don't even look around for Jessy.

CHAPTER 8

Tuesday, October 13

I DON'T THINK I'VE been out of the city in two years. Since me and Tanya split up and sold the cottage, I never have reason to. I'm not much for camping – sleeping on the ground's too hard on my back, and I'm not too fond of bugs, either. Clouds of mosquitoes buzzing around your ears. Earwigs in the tentpoles.

But it's nice driving down an empty highway, the yellow line twisting and turning in front of you. Half of me says, the hell with Poplar Bluff, let's just keep going, mapless, see what's around the next bend.

But I can't. I've got a job of work, as my old man used to say, pulling on his boots. Six-foot-ten. Bigger than me. Died at the Legion, forty-four years old, face-first into his mashed potatoes. Never got to see me play college ball. Not that he would have showed up anyway.

Poplar Bluff Correctional Facility is up near Penetanguishene, a small town two hours from Toronto. The only time I've ever been to Penetang, as everyone calls it, was in 1973, when Secretariat won the Belmont Stakes. I was in college then, and a bunch of us were up at somebody's cottage for the weekend, but I wasn't about to miss the Belmont, not with the greatest racehorse since Man O'War running in it, so I drove into town by myself – nobody wanted to go with me – to watch it on TV at the bar of a hotel. Only three or four horses went in against him: Sham, My Gallant, Twice a Prince. There was one other, I think. Before the race I got talking to this old guy on the next stool, and he wanted to bet. Native guy. Said his name was Ezekiel Hand. I remember it like yesterday. I said no, it would be a crime to take his money, nothing in the race could touch Secretariat. But he insisted, started getting all upset, so I said okay, I'll give you the rest of the field. He agreed. He thought I was crazy. So we bet a dollar. Secretariat won by thirty-one lengths. The old guy paid up, grumbling. Not only did he not know anything about horseracing, he didn't know much about television either, because when the replay came on, he thought it was another race with the same horses. Insisted on betting again. I tried to make him understand, but he started getting all indignant, so I took another dollar off him. He didn't even twig when they showed the replay in slow motion. It didn't bother him that Secretariat won again by exactly thirty-one lengths. Ezekiel Hand. He told me he worked up at the Douglas Point power station. Wanted me to send some books up from the city for his son. School books. Like I say, I was still in college then. I forget the rest. We were drinking.

Penetanguishene. More letters in the name than people in the town. The man behind the desk at the Humpty Dumpty Motel gives me the key to number 17, and as I walk across the parking lot towards it, I pass the pool. It's too late in the season to swim, but I take a gander anyway. Bottom's about two feet deep in mud and leaves and fast-food garbage. In my room, I put six cans of Blue in the bathroom sink. I make a couple of trips to the ice machine with a wastepaper basket till I have a mountain of cubes on top of the beer. You can't even see the beer. Then I want to wash my face before I head off to Poplar Bluff, but I can't because of the ice in the basin, so I lean my face into the shower and wash it that way, and then I leave.

Dr. Burns Manning is medium height and slim, about fifty or fifty-five. He has wavy grey hair, and there's a glint to his eyes, like in photos of Charles Manson. We're in his office on the main floor of Poplar Bluff. I had to pass through four or five sets of sliding barred gates just to get into the place – like the opening to "Get Smart." There's a dead tree in a pot in one corner of his office and a yellow retriever asleep on the floor. Dr Manning's desk is piled high with papers, and there's a big black ashtray and a pipe rack with about six pipes in front of him.

The first thing he says to me after I sit down is, "So you're here about Larry." When I say yes, he leans back in his chair. "Describe the crime scenes, please."

Not what I had in mind. I was planning on asking the questions. I've interviewed enough "professionals" to know they mostly think cops are stupid, and I know they like to control situations like this one, but I do as he asks because I want him to know exactly what "Larry" has done. It takes about fifteen minutes to properly describe the crime scenes, and the whole time I'm talking he seems like he's only half listening. He seems more interested in the photocopies of the Shakespearean quotations and the list poems I placed on his desk when I sat down. By the time I'm finished I'm in a sweat.

"You know, what is very interesting, Detective Sergeant," he says, looking up when I finally stop talking, "is that Larry's obsession with lists does not stop with his own poems: the quotations from Shakespeare he uses are, in and of themselves, lists. A list of dogs and a list of flowers. Very interesting indeed. I'm sure you'd already noted that yourself."

I hadn't. Neither had Daniel. A list of dogs and a list of flowers. "He's a killer, Dr. Manning, that's all I know. He's killed twice, and because of the evidence I've just described, we think he'll kill again. My partner, who trained at Quantico with the FBI, thinks he may be a serial killer."

"With all due respect to your partner, killers aren't generally regarded as serial until they've killed three times." He holds up three fingers like I'm a moron. "However, I agree with you. I wouldn't be surprised if he did kill again."

This makes me angry. He treated Lawrence Woolley in prison, and Woolley came out worse than when he went in. "We need your help, Doctor," I say, controlling myself.

Manning smiles. He looks at the pipe rack. "I'm afraid I have to respect the rules of patient confidentiality."

Fine, hardball. "We can subpoena your files if we need to. You know that. Or you can be the Boy Scout, because of how dangerous he is, and give us what you got."

Manning takes one of the pipes from the rack. He's still smiling. "My relationship with Larry was amiable – we went duck hunting together – but perhaps I can help you."

"You went *duck hunting* together?"

Manning puts a finger to his lips. "Therapy. Unorthodox, I admit. But then I'm an unorthodox therapist. I must say that Larry seemed to enjoy himself, although he wasn't very comfortable around guns."

Fuck you, I think. Fuck you. "How can you help us?"

"Well, as it happens, Larry fancied himself a writer, so I asked him to write a series of creative pieces for me. Not fiction, mind you. I asked him to write about the most traumatic events of his life. My request was motivated strictly by a desire to gain greater insight into his background, but he clearly thought I was interested in his literary abilities, and I did nothing to disabuse him of that."

"You have these pieces of writing?"

Again the smile. "He made me promise that what he wrote would be private, like diary entries." The smile broadens. "But in my business, Detective Sergeant, it's publish or perish, so before I returned them to him I made copies. Research. I haven't used them yet, and if I do, I won't name him. I have the highest regard for the privacy of my patients."

Privacy. When Manning says "privacy," the first four letters rhyme with "shiv."

"When can I see them, Doctor?"

"I didn't say you could see them. It contravenes my professional –"

"You said yourself, he's going to kill again."

He's loading his pipe from a clear plastic pouch. "You can have them this afternoon, if you wish. There are about two dozen of them all told, if I remember correctly. And, if you like, I'll include a copy of a little character sketch I put together on him just before his release. I do it for all departing patients. Standard procedure. Just part of our approach to demobilization, I guess you could say. I'll call it up on my computer and update it for you. I can have that for you this afternoon as well."

"Thank you. Whatever you've got that might help us. We don't want him to kill again."

Some of the bluster seems to go out of him. "Nor, I assure you, do I, Detective Sergeant. Don't mistake my attitude as cavalier. It's not. And don't think I wasn't listening as you described the crime scenes. I was. I heard every word. We . . . shrinks . . . get a little defensive at times like this. The public usually blames us, you see," he points to his chest with the stem of his pipe, "when offenders reoffend. You, too. The police, I mean. I know what you're thinking. Larry Woolley came to us a rapist, and when he left he became a murderer." Manning looks down at his dog whimpering in her sleep, legs moving in a dream chase. "It's wearying."

I stand up to leave.

"Where shall I send the, um, material?" Manning asks.

"The Humpty Dumpty," I say, feeling stupid, "room seventeen."

"Ah, so you're staying overnight in our fair burg. And at the lyrically named Humpty Dumpty, no less. I've never had the pleasure, but I've often wondered why the owners chose that name. Do you suppose it was because they conceded that it was a dump they were running, or do you think it had something to do with the amount of *humping* going on in their, oh, what would you call them, love chambers?"

It's a reasonable question, I suppose, and so I answer it. "I thought it had more to do with the big wall behind it that separates it from the highway. Maybe they had little kids at the time, and it just sort of occurred to them."

Manning is still smiling at me. "Oh, by the way, you may want to talk to a young man named Mark Thorogood." He strikes a wooden match against the underside of his desk. "He was a volunteer here who had a lot to do with Larry's poetic aspirations. He works in the Collingwood Library, about forty miles from here."

He waits until the flame settles, then lights his pipe.

In winter, Collingwood is the centre for downhill skiing in southern Ontario, but in mid-October the people you see on Main Street are locals in lumberjack shirts and feed caps; it's still two months until the rich city folk with their condos and their pink and purple ski gear begin to crowd the sidewalk in front of the Gift 'n' Gab and Rutherford's Hardware. An hour after leaving Dr. Manning, I'm standing beside the book-return receptacle at the Collingwood Public Library, introducing myself and showing my badge to Mark Thorogood, who looks up at me without interest. Once I've made the purpose of my visit clear to him, however, he agrees to answer a few questions and leads me downstairs to the staff lunchroom in the basement. I could use a coffee, and I even see a pot stewing on a hot plate in the corner of the room, but he doesn't offer.

"You're the Mark Thorogood who worked as a volunteer at Poplar Bluff?" I ask him when we're seated.

"Still do." Thorogood is maybe twenty-five years old. He's slim and handsome with blond hair to his shoulders and black-framed glasses. He looks more like a card shark than a librarian.

"Did you work with a man named Lawrence Woolley?"

"Until his release, yes."

"He was released in August."

"That's right."

"You and Mr. Woolley shared an interest in poetry."

"That's right. What's this about?"

His tone is wiseass, but I can tell he's nervous by the way he plays with his hair. "You'll understand soon enough. Did you encourage Mr. Woolley to send his poems to magazines?"

"You could say so, yes."

"Can you tell me what magazines these poems were sent to?"

"Not really. He asked me to suggest some places where he might submit them, so I did. I gave him the names of about twenty places. I can tell you which magazines I recommended, but I don't know which ones he actually sent stuff to."

"Were some of them in Toronto?"

He thinks for a few seconds. "Probably ten or so in Toronto. The rest across the country."

"Were two of the magazines called *Good Return* and *Columbine*?"

Suddenly the young man doesn't look so sure of himself. "I can't remember, but it's possible. I've sent stuff to those magazines myself."

"I want you to give me the names of all the magazines located in Toronto which are edited by women which you gave to Mr. Woolley. Toronto and vicinity. Do you know which magazines are edited by women?"

Mr. Thorogood has turned white. "What's happened?"

"Do you know which magazines are edited by women?"

"Yes, but all that information is at home."

"I'll phone you tonight. Will you be home?"

"I'll be home by seven."

"Write down your phone number for me. Do you live here in town?"

"Yes."

"I'll phone you at eight and you can give me the information. I'll need telephone numbers and mailing addresses, too."

The young man's trembling. "Tell me what's happened."

"Mr. Thorogood, do you know if any of Mr. Woolley's poems were accepted for publication?"

"No, I don't. He sent them out in June or July and I've never heard from him since he was released. It usually takes three or four months before you hear anything."

"I don't follow."

"Before you get a reply from a magazine about the stuff you sent in to them, it usually takes three or four months. Please tell me what happened."

I don't know why I'm twisting the knife. None of this is his fault, really. He was just doing the volunteer thing, making himself feel good. But I twist it anyway. "Don't you watch the news, Mr. Thorogood? Or read the papers? Other than the *Collingwood Beaver*, or whatever the local rag's called?" He's looking at me with his mouth open, like I've sucker-punched him. "Mr. Thorogood, I regret to inform you that Joanne Stevenson, editor of *Good Return*, and Pansy Jones, editor of *Columbine*, are dead."

His eyes widen.

"They were murdered, Mr. Thorogood."

The young man's as pale as a blanched almond. "Larry killed them?"

I stand up. "Looks that way. I'll phone you at eight."

I get back in my car and leave Collingwood. For about two hours I drive around the countryside. I pass through tiny towns with names like Angus, Guthrie, Fesserton, New Lowell, Sunnidale Corners – towns that have probably never experienced a single murder in their entire histories, let alone serial killings. Of course, Larry's not really a serial killer yet. He's still a minor-leaguer. He needs to kill again. Once more. Then he's made it to the bigs.

By the time I get back to the motel, it's a quarter past seven. There's a large manila envelope for me at the desk. I hurry to my room, fish a beer from the lukewarm lake that's all that's left of my mountain of ice, and tear open the envelope. Inside are two stapled sheaves of paper. The first consists of typed pages, the second is photocopies of handwritten sheets of foolscap. I make myself comfortable on the bed – both pillows and an extra blanket moulded into a backrest, cigarettes and can of warm beer handy on the bedside table – and begin to read.

LAWRENCE WOOLLEY: AN OVERVIEW
BY DR. BURNS W. MANNING

[NOTE: *Detective Sergeant Young, this afternoon I was able, to the best of my knowledge and ability, to update these notes for you. I hope they prove useful.*]

Lawrence Clifford Woolley was born August 28, 1957, in Toronto. His father, Norman, worked as an orderly in the same hospital in which his son was born; his mother, Alfreda, was a housewife and fervent Catholic; his older sister, Mary, was born in 1954.

Larry attended Briar Park Public School, Gordon McLean Junior High School, and West Scarborough Collegiate. For the first 18 years of his life, he lived with his family at 28 Miranda Court, a quiet residential street of inexpensive bungalows in Scarborough, a Toronto suburb.

Throughout his elementary and high-school career, the grades on Larry's report cards indicate that he achieved very well academically. In fact, at age eight his I.Q. was measured at 144, and he was recommended for an experimental "gifted" class at another school, but his parents declined the offer.

Larry's father, an unrecovered alcoholic, died of a heart attack when Larry was 12. Spousal abuse had been common in the house, and Larry had been traumatized by his father's violence – on more than one occasion he had seen his father punch his mother in the face; once, when he was five or six, he heard his father throw his mother down the cellar stairs, and he heard her screams. As was revealed later in interviews, he felt helpless in the face of his father's violence. His father, interestingly, never physically abused Larry; when he misbehaved as a youngster, however, up until the age of eight or nine, his mother used to pull his pants down to his knees and make him lie on his stomach on her bed, and she would spank him with a hairbrush. It was extremely humiliating for him. The only punishment Larry received from his father consisted of periods of enforced isolation in his room. Nor did his sister ever suffer corporal punishment. And despite the mother's suspicions, there is no evidence of father/daughter sexual abuse.

Following her husband's death, Alfreda Woolley turned on her son. Larry told me later that in hindsight it seemed to him that his mother was exacting a revenge on him that she was never able to exact on her husband. For example, when he was 13, Larry's voice broke, a moustache sprouted on his upper lip, and he grew three or four inches almost overnight. His mother's reaction was to make him sleep in the basement recreation room instead of in his own room. His mother was afraid that because of the proximity of the bedrooms on the main floor, Larry might interfere with his sister.

Larry was made to feel ashamed of his sexuality. He never dated in high school. Nor did his sister, who was expressly forbidden to do so. [NOTE: *According to my information, Mary still lives with her mother – in a high-rise apartment on Birchmount Avenue in Scarborough. Alfreda Woolley sold the house on Miranda Court shortly after Larry was sent here to Poplar Bluff.*] Larry's only success came at school. Although he was a loner, he was not disliked or ostracized. In fact, he was respected for his intelligence, and at one point acted as a peer tutor in English Lit. for less capable students. But despite the high marks he earned, his mother belittled him. She told him he would never amount to anything, he would never go to college, and respectable girls would never have anything to do with him because his carnal appetites would always show through.

Like most boys entering puberty, Larry began to masturbate. At first he used magazines, but his psychopathy eventually led him to use photos of his sister and mother from the family album. [NOTE: *This information, as well as much of the other information in this character profile, was revealed in Larry's journal entries, not in interviews.*]

At 18, Larry won a full scholarship to Queen's University in Kingston, Ontario. He left home and spent the next four years earning a Bachelor of Arts Degree (Honours) in Literature. Then he completed his Master's Degree in Shakespearean studies. Throughout these years he lived in a basement apartment off campus. He had two friends, a chess friend and a literary friend. Because all three were intellectuals, they never attended football games or residence parties. They did, however, travel to New York City one weekend when Larry was nineteen. The literary friend was sexually experienced and masterminded the expedition. Larry and the chess friend lost their virginity to prostitutes. When Larry told me about this, the memory disgusted him.

After graduation, Larry secured a teaching position at a small liberal-arts college in Peterborough, about an hour's drive north of Toronto. He was there for five years – until his arrest for rape in 1985. At the time of his arrest he was single, unattached, and friendless. His two friends from university were no longer part of his life, and his new colleagues regarded him as brilliant, eccentric and unapproachable. [NOTE: *His colleagues and mother and sister all referred to him as Lawrence; at Poplar Bluff we called him Larry to make him feel more like "one of the boys."*] One colleague testified at the trial that Larry seemed meek on the outside, but very angry underneath. At the time of his arrest, he was living off campus – in a basement apartment.

In my capacity as Chief Psychiatrist at the Poplar Bluff Correctional Facility, I came to know Larry Woolley quite well during the next six years of his life. He struck me as a man of tremendous intellect – he is a Shakespearean scholar and an American-history buff – whose self-confidence and self-esteem had been undermined by the circumstances of his childhood – an abusive, alcoholic father, an abusive, castrating mother. It is no surprise to me, therefore, that he became a rapist or, more recently, a rapist/murderer – possibly a serial killer. In one of his journal entries, in fact, he spoke briefly about a growing interest in watching someone die, that he could and would orchestrate the death of a human being if he felt there was sufficient reason for that person to die. [NOTE: *The rejection of his "list" poems by female editors may have provided Larry with "sufficient reason" and certainly provided a classic scenario in which his mother's predictions of failure came true. So he did what his mother further predicted: he cast aside his intellect and chose carnality. He made a conscious conversion to evil. He embraced evil. He punished these women with sex. That he killed them first only emphasizes his fear of sexual intimacy. Leaving them in demeaning sexual postures was their real punishment.*]

In conclusion, it became evident to me through my association with Larry Woolley (through my interviews with him, through his journal entries, and through input from other staff here at Poplar Bluff) that he is unlikely ever to be rehabilitated; in light of what he has done since, I am sure of it. He felt no remorse for any of the rapes he performed – not even the rape of his student – and I am certain he feels none for the murders he has committed. On the contrary, because he is white, male, and intellectually superior, and because he feels cruelly cheated out of the conventional successes – romantic, sexual, and intellectual – that he thinks should have been his, he no doubt feels entitled to some payback, to indulge in evil, to rape and murder those women. He used them as revenge against the unfairness of life just as surely as his mother used him for the same purpose. Just as she was entitled, so is he. Larry's anti-social behaviour was made worse by his time in prison; before being incarcerated, he raped and released his victims, indicating that he may have hoped that some sort of relationship would ensue; since his release from prison, he murders, then rapes, indicating that he no longer entertains any illusions about women – or his chances with them. At one point in his life he may have wanted to fall in love and experience a normal relationship, but now he sees women only as enemies, as debilitators, and, in my opinion, he will continue to kill them until he is apprehended, or until he commits suicide.

[NOTE: *Finally, and I address this comment specifically to you, Detective Sergeant Young, it should be pointed out that we at Poplar Bluff successfully opposed early parole for Larry, but once he had served his full sentence he became, under the letter of the law, a free man.*]

I get up off the bed and go into the bathroom for another beer. I should've gotten more ice. I could get some now, but fuck it. Back in the bedroom I sit down in front of the TV. The channel that lists all the shows tells me it's almost eight.

I go through all my pockets looking for Mark Thorogood's phone number. I can't find it. I can't even remember if he gave it to me.

I sit on the side of the bed and leaf through the telephone directory. There are only two Thorogoods in Collingwood, Mark Sr. and Mark Jr. I dial Junior's number. He answers immediately. His voice sounds broken, empty, and I go easy with him. After two or three minutes I hang up. I have the information I need – addresses, phone numbers, titles of magazines, names of female editors.

1. *The Barnes College Quarterly* (editor, Elizabeth Arthur)
2. *Blue Cohosh* (Karen English)
3. *Bugle* (Megan Wong-Rutherford)
4. *Columbine* (Pansy Jones)
5. *A Feminist View* (Trudy Lemelin)
6. *Good Return* (Joanne Stevenson)
7. *No Frigate* (Miriam Qureshi)
8. *Nun's Habit* (Ellen Frank)
9. *T'Ain't* (Monique Mbale Farmer)
10. *Yarn* (Caley Kellogg)

No ballgame tonight. I'm so hungry my stomach's making the same whimpering sounds Dr. Manning's dog did. Hope Trick remembers to feed Reg, take her for a walk. I reach inside the manila envelope for Lawrence Woolley's "creative" pieces. Wonder what an expert would make of his tiny precise handwriting. I try to read the first one, "In the Bahamas," but my eyes are tired and if I read any more I'll have a headache so bad I won't be able to read anything tomorrow. I'll read them in the morning, before I head back to the city. Get back in time for tomorrow night's game. Jays are up three games to two. One more win over Oakland and we go to the World Series. The World Series, boys. But right now, I'm going to get me something to eat. Find me a bar, some locals to talk to. Eat a party-size pizza, drink about twelve cold ones. *Cold* ones.

PART TWO

CHAPTER 9

Wednesday, October 14

IN THE BAHAMAS

The first one was from Florence, Kentucky. I don't know what her name was, but while we were still in the casino of the Queen Lucaya, before I raped her, she told me where she was from. I was sitting at the horserace table. I wasn't gambling. I was just watching and trying to calculate which numbers would come up. The next thing I knew she was sitting on the stool beside mine. She was at least forty, she was dressed impeccably, and she was drunk. It was after midnight, and I suppose she was looking to get lucky. She leaned towards me and asked me how the game was played. I explained how you wagered on these little mechanical horses that move around the track by dropping a dollar coin down the slot and punching the numbers of the horses you like. She took a coin from the little plastic bucket she had with her and dropped it in the slot. What number should I choose? she asked me.

Try number two, I said. When the race started, she began to jiggle up and down and she grabbed my arm. Come on, number two! Come on, number two! After the race ended, she leaned her head on my shoulder. Did I win? she asked, looking up at me. For a woman her age, she was very well preserved. She had long dyed blonde hair, ruby lips, a golden tan, and spectacular green eyes, empty of anything except animal cunning.

Yes, I said, you won. And she had. Sixteen dollars.

The reason I was in the Bahamas was because *I* was a winner, too. I had won a week's vacation when I purchased a lucky-draw ticket from a student raising money for charity. I remember the student, too, because she played Titania in our department's ill-fated, ill-attended production of *A Midsummer Night's Dream*. I don't remember *her* name either, which in itself is not surprising. I do, however, remember that it was a ticket for two that I won, but I preferred to go alone. This was in late May or early June, about five months before the woman under the bridge, and about seven months before Andrea, so I guess I was already getting ideas. I hardly talked to anyone down there. To occupy my mind, I began making lists of things: local species of fish (Puddingwife, Pygmy Filefish, Stoplight Parrotfish, Jolthead Porgy, Neon Goby); mixed drinks available at Skipper's BeachBar (Bikini, Slippery Nipple, Desperate Virgin, Sex on the Beach); given names of black croupiers in the casino (Deniro, Dellareese, Jevan, Altermease); unclaimed stolen items being auctioned off by the Royal Bahamas Police, as published in *The Freeport News* ("black frame of Ray-Ban shades," "one window with two louvres," "one teapot," "one fishing line on a bottle," "one bag containing a power stick deodorant"). If I wasn't people-watching in the casino, I was in my room going through the phone book or the newspapers looking for lists.

At some point, as I say, the woman told me she was from Florence, Kentucky. She asked me where I was from with my funny accent. Moose Jaw, Saskatchewan, I told her. That made her laugh.

I asked her if she wanted a drink. She mentioned something exotic, an Alabama Slammer or a Mind Eraser. She played the horserace game a few more times, choosing her own numbers. She lost every time. When her drink came, she sucked it down in seconds. Then she said, Let's go for a walk. I thought she meant outside in the moonlight, so I said okay, but all she did was guide me around the casino. I watched the sunburned tourists in their brightly coloured clothing pulling the arms of slot machines as if there were no tomorrow. Automatons, barely aware of what they were doing, or whether they were up money or down, or how ridiculous they looked. They just needed an activity, like mice on a treadmill. Then we were out in the lobby, and she asked me if I wanted to come up to her room.

As we entered the elevator I started to freeze. I became very angry. At the time I didn't understand my anger, but I do now. I was angry because she was a slut. I was angry because I knew exactly what kind of a woman she was the instant I laid eyes on her. And I was right. Just like I knew the number-two horse would win the race.

We were alone in the elevator. When we got off at the tenth floor she took her room key out of her purse and handed it to me. She gave me what I suppose was her idea of a wicked smile and said, This way you can't ever accuse me of dragging you into my web.

I looked at the number on the key. We didn't see anybody else as we made our way along the hall. She linked her arm through mine and tried to unbuckle my belt as we walked. She was singing something, or humming.

I unlocked the door and shut it behind us. I turned towards her. She was facing me, leaning forward, eyes closed, lips pursed, waiting to be kissed. I clocked her in the jaw instead, as hard as I could with my fist. Right on the point of the chin, like a boxer would do it. She went down like a bag of hammers.

I got her onto the bed and undressed her. It was difficult. I'd never undressed anyone before. But I got the job done, my heart beating like a piston the whole time. When I had her naked I rolled her so that she was face down, and I was just about ready to start when she groaned and rolled over.

What —? she said, but that's all she said, because I hit her across the side of the head with a big blue jar of Noxzema from the bedside table. You never know what will come to hand. I rolled her over onto her stomach again, and tried to do her like that, but she kept sliding, so I pushed her forward until her head was up against the headboard. I had to put two pillows under her hips. Then I was able to finish.

I left the room and walked to the emergency stairwell and ran down the ten flights. Fixed my tie as I walked across the lobby. Nodded to the doorman.

My hotel was about a half-mile along the beach. I sprinted the whole way. Pumped, focused, in control. I'm the man, I'm the man. You should have seen me, Burns. You wouldn't have recognized me. I was out there. That particular tropical evening, I was something very special.

For the rest of the week I went to the casino at the Bahama Reef Hotel. It didn't have a horserace table, but that was all right because I didn't bet much anyway. I just watched the assholes in their floral shirts. I did think about flying home early, but I didn't want to appear suspicious in case the feds were watching the airport.

I never saw the woman from Florence, Kentucky, again. On the beach, in the bars. I don't imagine she even reported what had happened to her. Maybe *she* flew home early. Or maybe this sort of thing was routine for her. She was so drunk, maybe in the morning she couldn't remember anything. Too bad, if that's the case. I wanted her to remember. She must have wondered, though, why she had a whanging headache, and where she got the bruise on her temple, and why there was dried blood in her ear.

RED-TAILED HAWK

Like me, the Turkey Vulture is a coward. It waits until its prey is already dead before feeding on it. It is a carrion-eater, as I am. A scavenger. If I could change my nature, I would be a bird of prey: a Red-tailed Hawk. I'd soar around the sky, searching the fields below until I saw something of interest – a field mouse, a snake, a vole – then I'd swoop down and scoop it up and take it back to my nest where I'd kill it and eat it. Other species of hawk common to southern Ontario include the Red-shouldered Hawk, Cooper's Hawk, the Marsh Hawk, the Duck Hawk (Peregrine Falcon), and the Fish Hawk (Osprey).

From my window I can see a meadow and a far line of trees. Sometimes I watch a Turkey Vulture circling. Sometimes more than one. They're looking for dead animals to tear apart. I've seen them on nature shows, the way they group around the carcass, sitting there with their wings spread to conceal the shameful thing they're doing.

From my window I can also watch my hawk. When he cruises the friendly skies, he is rock-steady; his wings don't waver at all. Vultures are unsteady. Because they are cowards their wingtips tremble. But the hawk is cool and deadly, and once when it was late in the day and the sun was sinking behind the far line of trees, the light caught the hawk's tail just as he flew past my window, and I could see its true colour, and I understood how it got its name. It was a rusty red. I only saw it for an instant, which is the way it should be with all things beautiful. It was the colour blood turns when it dries, before it turns black.

SUNGLASSES

The second time it was a woman in her fifties. I was teaching in Peterborough at the time, and I had come to Toronto for the weekend. The purpose of my visit was entirely specific: I was going to find a woman to rape.

She was walking towards Bloor Street across the viaduct. It was late October or early November. It was almost dark, sixish, drizzly and overcast; the sun hadn't shone in a week. Despite the gloom of the day, she was wearing sunglasses. A dark blue raincoat, a head kerchief, and sunglasses. I think it was the sunglasses that did it. She seemed to think she was safe behind them, that they somehow protected her from the world.

As she reached the west end of the viaduct, I ran up behind her and said, Have you seen a white poodle? Before she could answer I had my hand high under her chin and her right wrist twisted up between her shoulder blades. I dragged her down the embankment. Her shoes came off. I was all business.

Under the bridge, in the light from the streetlamps, I was on top of her, my black raincoat spread like wings. I made her get on all fours. I flipped up the skirts of her raincoat the way an early photographer would flip up the black cloth that covered his camera. I made her crawl forward until her head was against the dripping stone buttress of the bridge.

After I was finished, she stayed on her stomach. Look at me, I said, but she wouldn't. I grabbed her hair and yanked until she rolled over. Take a good look, I said. Her sunglasses were still on. I ripped them off and tossed them away. Her head kerchief had come off. There were dead leaves in her hair.

She said, Why would I want to look at you? Her voice was dead. I had killed something in her.

I stood up. It smelled like piss under the bridge. She lay there in the leaves and the cigarette butts and the beer bottles and the condoms.

I climbed back up the embankment and sprinted the three blocks back to the car. I was wired. I'm the man, I said. I drove to a bar and had three shots, one after the other, and about six cigarettes. Some floozy on the next stool started telling me about the

white Siberian tigers you can rent if you're getting married in Vegas.
I said, That's very interesting, that's *really* interesting, and she said,
What's *your* problem? and then — Burns, you would have loved this
— I gave her Hamlet's suicide speech, the whole thing, right down
to "Nymph, in thy orisons, be all my sins remembered."

HARD TIMES

I took a pair of the sweat socks that Gloria sent me for Christmas
out of the drawer. Clean, unused. Virgin. Grey with white at the
top and a red ring. I laid them on the rad. Then the guard came
and took me for my shower. When he returned me to my cell I
dried my feet thoroughly, clipped and cleaned my toenails, and
put the socks on. It was like stepping into warm oatmeal.

Gloria has been sending me gifts for almost four years. In her
first letter she said that she had read about my case in the *Vancouver
Sun*, that she thought I was "very unique," that she admired my
being a Shakespearean scholar and for doing what I wanted, for
satisfying my needs. She said that very few women could handle a
man like me, that I was misunderstood. She wished that she could
come and stay with me in my cell. I wrote back, and she smuggled
me some photographs of herself inside a hardcover copy of
Dickens' *Hard Times*. In her letter she told me that it was a play on
words. Some of the photographs are unusual. I keep them inside
my *New Webster's Dictionary and Thesaurus and Medical Dictionary* and use
them whenever I need a little relief. For your information, Burns,
I keep them on page 950, in case you want to take a peek, where
there is an entry for "pygal — pertaining to the buttocks."

Gloria lives in a suburb of Vancouver. Thousands of miles
away. She says she's single but I have no reason to believe her. She
looks like she's had about six kids. She's a big girl. She writes
every month though, without fail. I've come to expect her letters
and gifts. She says she has needs, too, but unlike me she's never

satisfied them. I suspect that she's all bark and no bite: if I were to send for her, she wouldn't come. If I were somehow to get out of here and go out to B.C. and show up one evening at her house in Surrey, just about dinnertime, she'd bar the door and scream for Hubby. For her, writing letters to rapists is just an exotic act, an *erotic* act. The only excitement in her humdrum life. A fantasy. A good work. I wonder if she tells the girls at bingo about me. I wonder if she tells her buddies in the bowling league that she writes to a rapist.

Anyway, I have needs, too, and if I ever get out of this place — sorry, *when* I get out of this place — I'll be sure to satisfy them.

FAMILY CIRCUS

A few months after my father died, my mother made me move out of my bedroom and down to the rec room in the basement. The pull-out sofa I had to sleep on was a bed of nails. I don't want you anywhere near your sister, she told me. She said men only care about one thing. She made me move all my belongings downstairs. No one helped me. The crystal radio, the chemistry set, the chess game made of marble, my clothes, my bedding, and all my books (the complete Arden Shakespeares; the thirty-volume *Encyclopedia Americana*; over three hundred books in total, all catalogued — even at thirteen, I was making lists!). I wanted to move my bed, too, but she wouldn't allow it. Your old room is the guest room now, she told me. We need the bed upstairs. In the eighteen years I lived in that house I can't remember a single guest.

I had to eat down there, too. It's not like I was locked in, but my meals were laid out on a tray, and when she rattled the clapper of the little dinner bell at the top of the stairs, I would come up and get my food and take it back down.

I was allowed upstairs for one bath a week, Wednesday nights (while Mary was at piano class), and the rest of the time I was expected to stay in the basement. I had a portable TV and I ate off one of those cheap folding TV tables. Pretty soon I was addicted to television, and I had no interest in seeing my sister (not that I ever had) or anyone else for that matter. I liked my isolation. Now I was being treated at home as I was at school — everyone was indifferent to me. I didn't mind it at all.

But a few months into this new situation, things changed. It dawned on me that my mother was treating me as she wished she had treated my father — whose death had made her crazy with joy, savage with joy. She would scream at me, You may be getting 90's, and you may have your teachers convinced that you're some kind of whiz kid, but I know the truth! You're an animal — like your father was — and when it comes right down to it, you'd choose filthy fornication over good grades every time!

How perceptive she was! I had just discovered jerking off — I was thirteen, I could have done it every twenty minutes, twenty-four hours a day — but eventually the nudist magazines and *Playboys* I had smuggled into my room lost their appeal. I was bored with them. I needed something new and different to arouse me. That's when I remembered the family album under the coffee table in the rec room, which featured several photos of my mother and sister in bathing suits. They were taken two summers earlier, a year before my father died, when he and my mother made one last stab at family life and took us to a lodge in Haliburton for a week. We had our own cabin, "Edgewater," and I can still remember awaking to the aroma of the special cake they made for breakfast as it wafted from the dining room down through the pine trees. At some point during the week, my father was sober enough to take several photos of my mother — who spent most of the week chatting on the big screened-in verandah of the lodge with a pair of spinsters from Michigan — and my sister in their bathing suits: my mother frowning, rigid, pretty; my sister posing like a pin-up girl, sitting with her knees drawn up, her head thrown back, her arms straight down behind her to the planks of the dock. She was fourteen. My mother was thirty-five.

I have to tell you, Burns, when I found these pictures in the basement two years later, something clicked in my brain. As I reached for myself, I remember thinking that I'd made an important discovery. It had something to do with making a conscious decision to cross the border between two countries. I was leaving behind me the country known as Social Convention, and I was stepping boldly forward – chin high, full of purpose and a new and wonderful sense of belonging – into the country known as Evil.

HOW I LOST MY CHERRY

You'll like this chapter, Burns. *Es muy piquante.* I dedicate it to you.

The whole idea was Jamie's. He was the only one of us who had had sex with someone other than himself, and whenever he was in one of his vindictive moods, which was most of the time, he would rub it in. Nineteen years old, he would say, looking at me and shaking his head, and still uninitiated? We would be in his room in residence or one of the coffee shops along Princess Street. We might have been talking only moments earlier about Nicaragua or aliens or "Let me not to the marriage of true minds admit impediments" when suddenly he would get it into his head to torment us. Carlyle or me. He could be quite rough on Carlyle, who was small and red-headed and was always pushing his glasses to the bridge of his nose. What's your favourite pull subject, Carlyle? Magazines? Videos? The remote in one hand, your sad little red-faced pecker in the other, kneeling before the great god Panasonic. A perfect feel for where the pause button is. Or what about the Barbie Doll you keep in the drawer of your bedside table? Your sister's, wasn't it? Dear girl no doubt sniffled around for weeks wondering where poor Barbie had disappeared to. Little did she know big brother had pulled Barbie's head off and was sucking on her little plastic titties as he whacked. And you, Lawrence, that was a huge mistake telling me about those photos of Mummy and Sis. But tell me – I can't stand not knowing – which one did you prefer? Which one *did* it for you? I'm certain one of them had more *influence* than the other, hmmm? My guess is . . . Mummy! Am I right? I am, I am, I can tell by the way the colour rushes to your cheeks!

Jamie thought he was superior – maybe because his family had money – but even though he lorded it over us, he was no Casanova himself: he had bad dandruff, worse acne, and an Adam's apple the size of a lemon. And sometimes we would give it back to him. So you got lucky once, I would say. The maid got horny, right? Hadn't had any since Bubba got deported. Big deal. She never came back for seconds, did she?

Despite his limited experience, Jamie insisted that black women were the best, and that's why one Reading Week we drove down to New York in his Volkswagen Beetle. How better to get you two initiated, Jamie said, than with a couple of Manhattan's finest? We stayed at a hotel on 43rd Street. The TV in our room didn't work, the window was opaque with filth and wouldn't open, and the water that came out of the faucets was brown. When I went down to the desk to complain, the girl said, So you don't want to stay here? It had taken us three hours to find a hotel we could afford that actually had a vacancy – and she knew it. We just want a TV that works, I said, and clean water. So you don't want to stay here? she repeated, real "New York," and that was the end of that. The first two nights we were there we just soaked up the atmosphere. We discovered Jimmy's Corner, a narrow bar frequented by some of the strangest people I have ever met in my life. At one point, I had Peewee Marquet – a black midget in a green uniform who told me he was the doorman at Birdland – on my left, and a six-and-a-half-foot-tall black transvestite in a midnight-blue sequined gown on my right. They thought we were cute — three fresh-faced college kids from Canada.

The second night we went to a sex show on 42nd Street. A black woman wearing nothing but a pair of suede riding boots forced her slave — a balding, pot-bellied, middle-aged white man, naked except for his glasses — to lie on his back and spread his legs. Then she used a claw hammer to drive what looked from my vantage point in the third row like a two-and-a-half-inch common spiral nail through the edge of his sac and into the floorboards. He screamed with pain — and delight, it seemed to me — and I was still trying to decide if I liked watching this sort of thing when Carlyle bolted up the aisle. Jamie and I ran after him. He was outside at the curb, retching, while a black man not ten feet away with a shell game set up on a card table laughed his guts out.

The third night — our last in the Big Apple — Jamie took Carlyle and me to a "massage parlour" about five minutes' walk from Times Square. He said he had scouted it out, that various people he had talked to had assured him it was safe: we wouldn't get ripped off and we wouldn't get a disease. We walked up a long flight of red-carpeted stairs and passed through a curtain into a kind of large waiting room with a very high ceiling. Sitting in chairs and on sofas around the edges of the room were seven or eight women in negligees. They were reading or smoking or watching television, and paid almost no attention to us. We stood there stupidly for a moment — even Jamie looked unsure of himself. One of the women — there were five or six black women and a couple of white women — leaned her head back and called through an open doorway, Mother, we gots company! And a moment later out came a tall black man in a canary-yellow double-breasted suit, a black fedora, and sunglasses. Rings glittered on his black fingers. I don't remember much of what was said, but I do know that we had to pay him forty dollars each, not twenty-five as Jamie had promised. I remember Mother saying,

You wants some black pussy? Don'tchall gets no black pussy at de univoisity? Heh heh heh. Then I was being led by the hand down a darkened hallway by a heavy, very black woman who smelled of Old Spice. I was so nervous she must have known it was my first time. Don't worry bout nuttin', baby. Rita do all de woik. We went into a small bedroom illuminated dimly by bedside lamps. She knelt in front of me and unbuckled my belt. I squeezed my eyes closed. I felt my pants fall to my ankles. Then I felt a warm liquid on my genitals, and I opened my eyes and looked down. She had a cloth and a bowl of water and she was washing me. It felt so good that I gasped. It felt so good to be handled that way. Then she towelled me dry and told me to finish getting undressed. I kicked my pants and underpants off and left them on the floor. I unbuttoned my shirt and took it off and hung it on the back of a chair. When I turned around she was sitting naked in the middle of the bed, her legs spread. Her breasts were enormous, and as she lay back they settled on either side of her chest like big sacks of mercury. Come here, she said, but before I could make it to the bed I knew it was all over. I reached the foot of the bed, grabbed my dick, aimed it at Rita, and came like a firehose. Ooh, Rita squealed, it rainin' in heah. She sat up, massive and jiggling, and pulled me down on the bed beside her. She wiped herself off with paper towel. Then she wiped me off. I felt ridiculous there beside her, naked except for my socks. I felt like an infant. Now, jus' you relax, honey, she said. She got on all fours over me and slowly dragged her breasts up and down the length of my torso, her nipples like electrical contacts with my body, then gradually lowered her head to my groin and took both of my balls in her mouth. It was so excruciating I almost screamed. She began to knead my dick with her hand, and in a minute I was hard again. From somewhere she produced a condom, already unwrapped, and expertly sheathed me, then she rolled onto her back, pulled me on top of her, and guided me in. She began to move under me, and I began to drive. I moved her hands up above her head like I'd seen in Jamie's movies and as I worked I watched her face contort. Fuck me, she said. Fuck me! And I did, and when I came for the second time, it was agony, it was like dying, it was utter release, and I loved it and knew that there was nothing in the world I would ever love more, and as I collapsed on top of her, my head slipped from her breast to her armpit, which was still exposed, her hands still extended above her head, her fingers still clamped around the vertical rods of the headboard, and I lapped like an animal at the black stubble.

ANDREA

She liked me. She sat in the first row and never took her eyes off me, except when she dipped her head to write something in her notes. After the first two months of the semester we became friendly. I had marked a couple of her assignments and I knew she was bright. Sometime in November she began hanging around at the end of my lectures (two a week, one tutorial), offering opinions about *Hamlet*: The real tragedy, as I see it, sir, is what happens to Ophelia. Here he is, like, supposed to love her, and he just totally uses her to trap the king, and it makes her crazy. And Mr. Woolley, the business about the pirate ship is just ludicrous. I mean totally. As if something like that could actually happen. At which point I would suggest to her that the ghost was equally improbable, but critics praise it in the same breath that they pan the pirate ship. As you can see, we conducted our conversations on a high plane. At first they took place as I was packing up my papers at the end of class; a few weeks later we were adjourning to the cafeteria for a coffee; finally, we were visiting a roadhouse called Misty's, some distance off campus, up Highway 28, where we drank beer.

Andrea Sunstrum was tall, broad-shouldered and small-breasted, the volleyball type. She had long reddish blonde hair and pale blue eyes that tracked you closely, like a bird's.

One night in December, a few days before the holidays began, she got very drunk at Misty's, and asked me to take her to a motel. We'll just lie down together, she said. We don't have to do anything. Our Christmas present to each other. I won't *see* you for three weeks! By this point she was drinking Southern Comfort, and when we got to our room, she smoked half a cigarette and passed out on the bed.

I leaned over her to take the cigarette from between her fingers, and suddenly, as if someone – the devil, more than likely – had reached into my stomach and twisted my guts, the old thoughts I used to have about my mother and sister came back. The thoughts about someone untouchable. Because of what had happened in Freeport and then under the viaduct about a month earlier, I thought I had it under control. I thought I would be able to target only certain types of women: party girls, working girls on vacation, women walking alone at night. Strangers, in other words. Not people I knew. And especially not students.

But as I looked at Andrea, her cigarette in my hand, I became excited. The next thing I knew I was pulling her shoes off, and her jeans, and her panties. She was on her back, and I spread her legs and began working the back of my thumb against her, and to my amazement she got wet. I was in and done in seconds. It wasn't until I got up that I saw the blood. It was all over the bedspread. It was on my stomach and shirt. It was all over her thighs.

I went into the bathroom and washed myself. When I came out, she was sitting up on the bed. She was looking down at the mess between her legs, and she was shaking her head and her hands were in her hair. She must have heard me then, because she looked over to where I was standing at the bathroom door. At first she looked confused. But then her expression changed, and it took my breath away. Disbelief, betrayal, and horror, in quick succession, like a transmogrifying face in a nightmare.

I began to tremble. Andrea stood up unsteadily. She made her way towards me. I thought she was going to hit me, but she walked right past me into the bathroom. Over the running taps, I could hear her vomiting.

After about ten minutes, she came back out. I was sitting on the edge of the bed. She hadn't showered. I stood up and moved away from her, around to the far side of the bed. Slowly, deliberately, she got dressed. She didn't say a word. She wouldn't look at me. When she started towards the door, I said, Andrea, listen, wait, but she just walked out of the room with a bloody towel in one hand and her cigarettes in the other.

THERAPY

I was getting the thoughts again tonight, so I took down one of my Civil War books and made a list of some of the names of the Rebel officers who fought at Gettysburg. I think these names evoke the spirit and romance of the antebellum South. What do you think, Burns? I'd be interested in your opinion.

CONFEDERATE OFFICERS AT GETTYSBURG

Jubal Early
Kirkwood Otey
Birkett Fry

Isham Page
Page Willet
Willet Parham

Peyton Manning*
Pichegru Woolfolk
Collett Leventhorpe

Mahlon Miller
Lunsford Lomax
Lafayette McLaws

Risden Bennett
Bolter Grantham
Talcott Eliason

Chiswell Dabney
Selfridge Gilbert
Jefferson Bulger

Marmaduke Johnson
Hamilton Jones
Zebulon York

Arley Gibson**
Eppa Hunton
Elzey Mays

Goode Bryan***
Speight West
Cullen Battle

* Any relation?
** Curiously effeminate, the three names in this stanza, don't you agree?
*** Aren't these three names wonderful? If I was a soldier, I'd want my name to be Cullen Battle.

VOLUNTEER (1)

You asked me if I would be interested in having a volunteer assigned to me. We all know that volunteers, as well-meaning as they may appear, have their own agenda. Usually they see themselves as heroes, white knights, Shane riding into the valley, but they don't usually hang around too long after they've seen the sickness up close, and after they've come to realize that our only interest in them is the cigarettes they bring or the change we cadge or the games we trick them into playing. It must be humbling for them when they finally realize that while we have a tremendous impact on them, they have virtually none on us. They're just wood we burn to keep warm.

Anyway, I said yes. Can it be a girl?

You almost smiled. You know better than that, Larry.

What it turned out to be was a pimple-faced young man from a nearby town who claimed to be a sociology student at the University of Toronto. His name was Roger, and he wasted no time in revealing his real purpose in visiting me. He began by asking me questions. How many women had I raped? How did it make me feel? Would I do it again if I was released? We were facing each other through the Plexiglas window, each of us holding a phone receiver to his ear. His "gifts" — a deck of cards, two packs of cigarettes, issues of *Time* and *Maclean's* — were in a shopping bag beside me on the floor. The guard had brought them in to me.

I narrowed my eyes. Twenty-seven, I said, lying ninefold. Powerful, in control, dominant. Roger looked left and right, but we were the only people in the cubicle. Yes, I whispered. The first chance I get. Roger was trembling by this point; either he was terrified or he was pulling like a madman. I couldn't see below the level of his pocket protector and the seventeen pens bouncing off each other like rush-hour on the subway.

Hey, I said. Hey, Roger.

His eyes were half-closed.

Pilot to bombardier, I said. Pilot to bombardier.

Finally he focused on me, perspiration beading his forehead.

Aren't *you* supposed to be helping *me*? I said. Aren't *you* supposed to be telling *me* about God? Aren't *you* supposed to be singing "This Land is Your Land" on your fucking ukulele?

He had stopped jiggling. He said, I've got to go.

And he ran out.

He returned once more, but I had no further use for him. I could have said, Sorry, I'm not here to jerk you off, but instead I said, They're giving me a four-day pass over Christmas, as long as someone will sponsor me, so I thought I could come and stay at your place –

What! But my mother and father – he stammered.

Oh, you live with your parents? I said. That's wonderful. It's been years since I've enjoyed a real family Christmas. Will your mom be cooking a turkey? Will there be mistletoe? Will there be cousins? Do you have any little girl cousins?

Roger dropped the phone and stood up. He looked like he had just swallowed a bad oyster. I never saw him again.

ARREST

I was on my way to class the next morning. Walking down the hall from my office. Dean Ferris walking towards me with two men in business suits. Plainclothes cops, as I would very shortly learn.

Mr. Woolley, he said as he approached, these gentlemen would like a word with you.

I'll be with you in just a moment, I said, and turned back in the direction of my office. I've forgotten my lecture notes!

Somehow I thought she would forgive me. I was almost at my office door when I felt a firm hand grip my left arm above the elbow, then another grab my right. I hadn't heard their footsteps. My ears were full of a sound like surf crashing.

The officers identified themselves, explained the charges against me, and read me my rights. I was handcuffed and led down the hall past staring students. Mr. Woolley? someone said. I don't know who. A bright young voice full of concern.

What really *burns* me about the whole business, Burns, is that I never got to make my lecture. I had been looking forward to it. I was going to talk about the massacre of Macduff's family. What, you egg? Young fry of treachery!

And later, All my pretty ones? Did you say all?

WHAT REALLY TURNS ME ON

I remember renting a video called *Images of Death*. It contained real footage of people dying – on battlefields, under fallen buildings, from high-rise balconies, and off bridges. Suicides, accidental deaths, deaths by misadventure (skydiving, bungee-jumping, wherever someone might be pointing a camera at the about-to-be-deceased). Some of the scenes were filmed by witnesses to car accidents. Zooming into the back seat before the ambulances arrive. America's funniest videos.

I became obsessed with death. It was the new pornography, far more interesting than sexual pornography or the pornography of violence. (I managed to squeeze in a "snuff" film once, during an off-Broadway theatre trip I was supervising – this couldn't have been more than three or four weeks before Andrea took me to the Friendship Inn; at first the film disgusted me – an overweight young black woman, naked and spreadeagled on a bed, thinks she's starring in a skin flick, but discovers to her horror that she's about to die, by knifewound. By the time the film ended, however, I felt quite differently. I realized there were people just like me out there, with the same tastes, and they were *committed to* and *creative about* their passions.)

It's true that I've never had a "normal" relationship with a woman – boyfriend/girlfriend, that sort of thing. The women I've fucked I've either raped or paid. But even so, at some point during the sex, their faces (those that I've been able to see!) have taken on a beatific expression, a kind of calm resignation, like a face settling into death. Even the face of the girl being killed in the snuff movie becomes calm towards the end. Maybe it's just shock, but I prefer to think of it as acceptance of the inevitable.

In one of the scenes from *Images of Death*, a British cameraman caught the death throes of a Serb soldier. The dying man was on his back, turning his head from side to side – slowly, rhythmically. He had a thin beard that followed the line of his jaw from ear to ear. His eyebrows met. He had one hand behind his head like a man on a hammock. These details humanized him. But it was his eyes that fascinated me. They were half-closed, and each time his head turned towards the camera, the surer you were that he would die the next second. And then he did; his head stopped midway through a turn, and he was dead – the lips slightly parted, the eyes still at half-mast.

It was a beautiful thing to watch, and I admired the dispassion with which the cameraman recorded the event. He was not interested in comforting the man (who was past comforting anyway). He was only interested in recording this most exquisite of moments: the instant of human death.

In the snuff film it was difficult to tell the precise moment at which the black girl died. There was too much blood, and the camera wasn't very steady.

I would like to do this, too. I would like to witness someone's death.

But I don't know that I could ever set it up. Certainly I couldn't do it gratuitously, like in the snuff film. And I'm not likely to begin a career as a photojournalist. It would have to be someone I know. Someone who deserves to die. Someone who made me incredibly angry. Then I could do it.

VOLUNTEER (2)

This one's an English major, you told me. Then you added, mean-ingfully, And a poet. Your lists, as I've told you, Larry, are poems. At least to me they are. I thought the two of you would have something in common, that with encouragement you might come to feel good about your poems, that you might produce more of them, even get some of them published.

So again I said yes. More out of boredom than anything. And a few days later this kid named Mark showed up. Ponytail. Black leather jacket. He began talking and he reminded me of any number of students I'd had: bright, curious, talented, self-centred. Anyway, for his second visit he brought a few of his poems, and he asked to see some of my lists. Dr. Manning told me about you, he said. I'm really interested. I gave him a few and he said he wanted to take them away with him — he wanted to read them in total seclusion — and I told him if that's what he wanted all he needed to do was rape somebody. He looked at me strangely for a few seconds, then off he went. I read his poems — they were good all right: free verse, incidental rhyming like Robert Lowell's, exper-imentation with various narrative voices — and the next time he visited me we formed this mutual admiration society, and he encouraged me to submit my lists to literary journals. Around southern Ontario at first, he said. Then, with luck, a few will be accepted, and then we'll try some of the American quarterlies. He praised the spareness of the poems — like you, Burns, he, too, called them poems — how I'd reduced language to its simplest form of expression; just the thing itself.

His enthusiasm was infectious, I must admit. Truth be told, I think the idea of being literary agent to a convict appealed to his vanity. Norman Mailer and Jack Henry Abbott, that sort of thing. And, truth be told, I've always wanted to publish — the few schol-arly papers I submitted here and there over the years I was teaching were always rejected. Maybe I've found my métier. I'm a poet. I'm going to publish my list poems. But make no mistake: I'm not simply a compiler of lists. I can make real poems, too.

Watch, I'll prove it:

LAMENT

The devil in me.
Poison in me.
Satan in me.

The killer in me.
The coward in me.
Satan in me.

PART THREE

CHAPTER 10

Thursday, October 15

THE THIRD CLUE IS in my hand. It came by mail – to Homicide, addressed to me. Why did he send it to me? I found it on my desk when I got to work just now. It looks like a regular letter, except it has no return address on it. Sometimes I think I should be more careful with my mail, but I usually figure I'm just being paranoid. Anyway, I opened it. It's a single sheet of paper, a photocopy of more Shakespeare, from the look of it.

> The names of those their nobles that lie dead;
> Charles Delabreth, high constable of France;
> Jaques of Chatillon, admiral of France;
> The master of the cross-bows, Lord Rambures;
> Great master of France, the brave Sir Guichard Dolphin;
> John Duke of Alencon; Antony Duke of Brabant,
> The brother to the Duke of Burgundy;

And Edward Duke of Bar: of lusty earls,
Grandpre and Roussi, Fauconberg and Foix,
Beaumont and Marle, Vaudemont and Lestrale.
Here was a royal fellowship of death!

I glance at my watch. Seven-fifteen. I phone Daniel at home. The sound of his voice tells me he was sleeping.

"Jesus, Campbell," he says, his voice hoarse. "My aching head!"

"Listen," I tell him, "I have to read you something."

"Good God, what a game!"

"Daniel, listen."

"American League Champions!" Daniel shouts. "Oh baby!"

"Daniel!"

"What? What's the problem?"

"Listen."

He shuts up finally, and I read the quotation to him.

He grunts. "Henry the Something. It's the dead soldiers at Agincourt."

"Charles Delabreth," I say to him. "The first name."

"What about it?"

"The name on the note in Pansy Jones's hand. It was signed C. Delabreth."

"You said Delahanty."

"I said it was something *like* Delahanty."

"You were supposed to get back to me."

"I know. I forgot."

"Jesus, Campbell, it's a clue."

"I know that. But how? *How* is it a clue?"

"Wait. Did you read me the whole quotation?"

"Yes."

"Because that's curious." He's silent for a moment. "It's another list all right, but he stops halfway through."

"What do you mean?"

"Well, what you read to me is the list of the French dead. He goes on to list the names of the English casualties as well."

"The English casualties," I repeat, something flipping around inside my skull. "The English casualties." I reach inside my suit jacket and pull out the list that Mark Thorogood dictated to me over the phone yesterday. I unfold the piece of paper and find the name I'm looking for. "Karen English."

"It's *Henry V*," Daniel says. "I remember now. Who's Karen English?"

"She must have rejected his poems." I hang up and dial the station.

Last night I got to McCully's just in time for the first pitch. I had come straight from Penetanguishene, and after reading Woolley's diaries – or whatever you want to call them – I was in serious need of a drink.

Joe Carter homered in the bottom of the first, and the bar was jumping. This is it, I thought, we're going to the World Series. What a night. How could a man not have a good time on a night like this? Especially a diehard Jays fan, a man who's been rooting for them since the beginning (1977: 54 wins, 107 losses), a man whose favourite trivia question is "Name the Blue Jay pitcher who won their very first regular season game (clue: he only won one more game in the Majors)," a man who's waited fifteen years for this, a man who's watched his team blow three league championships (to Kansas City in 1985; to Oakland in 1989; to Minnesota in 1991). Hell, in the midst of the celebration, I even found Jessy beside me, her hand on my shoulder while she's yelling over the noise at Trick. Then a big smile on her face when she looks at me. The place was blue with smoke, electric with excitement. Daniel was there. I introduced him to Wheeler, who was looking gorgeous in a suede jacket with a Blue Jays cap backwards over her blonde hair. "Daniel Curry,"

I said, "this is Wheeler." She shook Daniel's hand and said, "Lynn." "What?" I said. "Lynn," she repeated, and turned to me. "It's my first name. I happen to have a first name, and the first name I happen to have happens to be Lynn."

Anyway, like I say, I'd come straight from Penetanguishene. Well, not quite straight. I stopped for ten minutes at home, had a good short wrestle with Reg, took her for a trot around the block, read Trick's note – "Fed your dog, walked your dog, watered your dog. She's fine, she told me she prefers me over you as a caregiver, and she told me to tell you to haul ass down to McCully's, we've got a serious ballgame to win tonight!!!" – then hauled ass down to McCully's, downed a double shot of Jack, high-fived everybody in the bar, had another double, watched the first thee innings, watched the Blue Jays pad their lead to 6–0 – and then it hit me.

It hit me.

I had no interest in the game. I couldn't concentrate. I couldn't think about baseball. I was distracted. I couldn't think about Trick yelling "Joltin' Joe, Smokin' Joe Carter!" in my ear twice an inning. I couldn't think about the fact that *my team* was actually going to the World Series, against the mighty Atlanta Braves, no less. I couldn't even think about the fact that Jessy and Wheeler, the two women who hate me most in the world – excluding my ex, of course – were being nice to me. I couldn't think about Jessy's smile or her hand on my shoulder, or Wheeler's squeal when Candy Maldonado hit the three-run dinger in the third, or the fact I was surrounded by my best friends in the world, having a once-in-a-lifetime, knock-down-drag-'em-out, no-holds-barred blast.

All I could think about was Lawrence Woolley.

We break the lock on the door to Karen English's tenth-floor apartment in Toronto's old Parkdale district, a neighbourhood of quiet, tree-lined streets and Victorian houses. Inside, it's like déjà vu: lots of artwork on the walls, hundreds of books neatly arranged on the shelves – just like Joanne Stevenson's. And it doesn't stop there. I feel like I'm walking underwater as I follow Wheeler towards the bathroom, the door closed on purpose just to add a little suspense, like wrapping paper on a parcel no one should have to open.

This time she's facing us. She's seated on the toilet, naked, her ankles duct-taped, and her wrists, too, behind her. With more silver tape across the forehead and stretching back to the wall behind her, he's positioned her so that the first thing we see after we swing the door inward are her protruding green eyes. He's taped them open, narrow strips from eyelid to eyebrow. The whites have gone yellow, and one of them is bloodshot. Long strips of tape across her collarbones and shoulders attach her to the toilet tank. Her short blonde hair is muddy brown on the side where she took the hammer blows. More tape covers her mouth. The piece across her chest holds the note in place. I step forward and kneel in front of Karen English's body, and I read: 'This happy breed of men, this little world, This precious stone set in the silver sea . . .'"

I stop at Homicide just long enough to do the preliminary paperwork and drop off my gun. And take a phone call.

"Andy Bartle here, Young. Correct me if I'm wrong, but my usually reliable sources tell me you've found another girl."

I don't say anything. I feel like a wasp is buzzing around my head, and all I can do is stay still.

Bartle clears his throat. "Unless I'm mistaken, in our last conversation you said – and I quote – 'We've got leads and we're moving.' That's an accurate quote, isn't it?"

I don't say anything.

"I thought so. Also, when I asked you if you thought he'd strike again, you as much as said yes. 'He's a *serial* killer,' you said. My italics. So my point is, Young, it doesn't look so good for you. What am I supposed to say? The lead investigator fucked up? The lead investigator can't keep up with the killer? The killer's too bright for him? Tell me what to say, Young. Give me a quote."

Then there's silence. I don't know how long it lasts, but finally I speak. "We're doing the best we can," I say. "We deeply regret this latest tragedy. We have new evidence, and we're confident we'll ground him soon."

Bartle says, "Ooh, '*ground* him,' that's colourful. Anything else?"

Quietly, I put down the phone.

I hold on until I get downstairs and I'm alone in the locker room. Then I let go. And when it's over, eight or ten minutes later, five or six of my colleagues are sitting on my chest, and the lockers – once as orderly as soldiers standing at attention – are everywhere, like pick-up sticks, like a log-jam. Like soldiers suddenly sent flying by an explosion.

Like in a weird movie with lockers for soldiers.

Playing the parts of soldiers.

Lockers instead of soldiers.

I'm at home.

Trick's in the kitchen making coffee. He asks if I want any.

I tell him no.

He asks if I want him to phone Debi.

No.

Tanya?

I don't even answer.

They handcuffed me – for my own good, they said – and put me in the wagon and drove me to Emergency. The doctor gave me some Valium. No booze tonight, he said. Go home. Get some sleep.

Bateman told me to take a day or two off. Cool down. You'll be fine. We'll get him. Patted me on the shoulder. We're bugging your phone, Camp. You've gotten under his skin. He's sending you stuff through the mail, so he may phone you. Okay?

One moment was all it took. She's dead because I let up for one moment. All I had to do was think a little harder. All I had to do was go home, get the name out of my other pants, go back to the bar, and give it to Daniel. Or even just phone him there. Delabreth. It's Delabreth, Daniel, not Delahanty. But I was too tired to think. Or move. And now another girl's dead. I even forgot to phone him Tuesday morning. How could I forget? I went to Penetanguishene. Did some work there, found out some information. Then said to myself, Good work, Camp, take a breather. And I did. And while I was napping, Lawrence Woolley was awake.

And busy.

And when I read Daniel the quote this morning, he recognized it immediately. "It's *Henry V*," he said.

There's no doubt about it. If I'd worked a little harder, Karen English would still be alive.

Trick comes in with two steaming mugs of coffee and sets one down near me.

"I don't want it," I tell him. "I told you I didn't want any."

"Suit yourself," he says. Then he sits down on the sofa, picks up the remote, and turns on the television.

CHAPTER 11

Friday, October 16

WHEN I OPEN MY eyes this morning, Trick's still on the sofa. Snoring like a bear. I'm still in the La-Z-Boy. I get up to use the bathroom. I'm standing there shaving when he sticks his head in.

"I thought Bateman told you to take some time off."

"That's right," I answer. "He did."

As soon as I get to Homicide I send Barkas and Estabrooks back to the Parliament Street rooming house to have another look. As well, I tell Wheeler to write me up short bios of the female editors whose names are on the list Mark Thorogood gave me.

Sure enough, about eleven, Estabrooks comes into my cubicle waving a sheaf of papers.

"What are those?" I ask him.

"These," he says, making a big production of it, "are more of Woolley's poems. More lists. They were inside an old suitcase."

"A suitcase? Where was this suitcase the first time you searched his room?"

"In a dumpster behind the building."

I speak slowly and clearly, like I'm talking to a moron. Maybe I am. "Wasn't the dumpster searched the first time?"

Estabrooks shrugs his shoulders.

"Anything else in the dumpster?"

"Not so far. Barkas is still inside it, rooting around." Estabrooks smiles.

"What's so funny?"

The smile disappears. "Nothing, Sarge, I was just, like . . . picturing Barkas."

"Well, you just hustle back there and climb back inside with Barkas and picture away until you find something else."

"Sorry, Sarge, I just thought you'd want these pronto, so I –"

"That's good, Estabrooks. You did the right thing. Now get back over there and help Barkas. Examine every square inch of that dumpster. I don't care if you're up to your neck in garbage. Every square inch, understand?" I stop and take a deep breath. "He's killed three women. There's nothing funny about it."

"Sorry, Sarge." Estabrooks looks like he's never seen me before.

A moment later Wheeler rolls in. She's got date of birth, place of birth, race, colour, religion, social insurance number, education and occupation, and whatever else she could dig up for the other seven female editors. Caley Kellogg was born in Lincoln, Montana. ("Where all those weird militia groups are based," Wheeler whispers over my shoulder as I'm reading.) Megan Wong-Rutherford is Chinese, second-generation Canadian, married to a sculptor. Monique Mbale Farmer, a nurse, came to Canada from Africa when she was fifteen. ("A nurse?" Wheeler whispers again. "Odd line of work for someone who runs a literary mag.") Elizabeth Arthur and Trudy Lemelin are professors. Miriam Qureshi is an "out" lesbian. Ellen Frank is a homemaker married to a rich stockbroker.

After Wheeler leaves, I pick up Woolley's poems, tell Gallagher I'll be back in an hour, walk outside and down the street to the Burger King. I buy a coffee and two bacon double cheeseburgers and find a booth in the corner. I eat the burgers and drink the coffee. I walk back to the counter and order another coffee, a large one this time. When I get back to my booth, I'm ready, and I open the folder and start reading. The first thing I notice is he's typed out each list on a separate sheet of paper and he's included notes for each one.

—⚬—

During my last semester of teaching at Trent, I took my drama class (the class Andrea was in, as a matter of fact) to see a production of *The Merchant of Venice* at the Stratford Festival, in Stratford, Ontario. There is a special public garden in the town which contains all of the flowers and plants and herbs that Shakespeare mentions in his plays. Each one has a little plaque beside it with the quotation from the play in which it appears. For example:

"Where the bee sucks, there suck I,
In a cowslip's bell lie I."
— *The Tempest*

P.S. I consider "Shakespearean Garden" my first legitimate list poem.

SHAKESPEAREAN GARDEN

Rue
Sage

Anise
Angelica

Purple Basil
Yellow Bedstraw

Lemon Balm
Lemon Thyme

Garden Thyme
Wild Thyme

Wild Marjoram
Wood Betony

Sweet Woodruff
Salad Burnet

Summer Savory
Winter Savory

English Lavender
Fringed Lavender

French Lavender
Finochio

Tarragon
Bergamot

Lady's Mantle
Coriander

Costmary
Catnip

—⁓—

Walter, Cleveland, myself, and a couple of others used to play cards in the lunchroom. Listed below are some of the games we played.

POKER

Straight
Seven Card

Four Fourteen
Seven Twenty-seven

Woolworth's
Indian

Fiery Cross
In Between

High Chicago
Blackjack

Bung
Blind Baseball

Screw Your Neighbour
Lewd Lucy

Follow the Queens
Kings and Little Ones

One-eyed Jacks,
  Man with the Axe,
  Bitch with the Brooch,
  and a Pair of Natural Sevens
  Takes All

I haven't been plagued at all lately by the thoughts. All I think about are the lists. Below are the names of some of the Arikara, Cheyenne, and Sioux warriors who fought at Custer's Last Stand, June 25, 1876, at Little Big Horn Creek in Montana. Also included are the names of several of Custer's Crow Indian scouts. NOTE: The names with asterisks beside them denote men who were killed in battle.

LITTLE BIG HORN

Belt
Bush
Pine

Gall
Rectum*
Coffee

Whirlwind*
Stabbed
Soldier

Bear Soldier
Bear's Eyes
Bear Comes Out

Bearded Man*
Blind Man
Cloud Man*

Lame White Man*
Black White Man*
Half Yellow Face

Rain-in-the-Face
Scabby Face
Red Face*

Good Face
Goose
Hawk Man*

Owl
Chased-by-Owls*
Strange Owl

Turkey Legs
Fools Crow
Crow King

Ghost Dog
Sitting Bull
Blue Horse

High Horse*
Crazy Horse
Owns-Red-Horse*

Long Dog*
Long Robe*
Long Road*

Kills Him*
Kills Alive
Kills Pretty Enemy

Kills-a-Hundred
Afraid-of-Him
Did-Not-Go-Home

Moves Camp
Goes Ahead
Comes Again

Drags-the-Rope
White-Man-Runs-Him
Walks-Under-the-Ground

I showed this one to Burns. He read it closely, and commented that each name was a poem unto itself. He actually said unto itself.

I said, Even Rectum and Scabby Face?

He smiled his smile and said, Yes, even Rectum and Scabby Face.

I said, Do you want to know which name is my favourite?

Yes, he said eagerly.

Take a guess, I said.

He looked at the list. After a while he said, I don't know.

Take your time, I said.

He hesitated. He shook his head.

I said, Come on, you wimpy little fuck, take a guess.

No, he said, just tell me.

That's too easy, I said. Tell you what, though. I'll give you a clue. A very big clue.

What's the clue? he said.

My favourite, I said slowly, is the forty-second name on the list.

—⚹—

I don't know what it is about American history that fascinates me, but it does. The frontier spirit, I suppose. The names alone thrill me. Here are the names of all the followers of the emancipator John Brown who assembled for the attack on the armouries at Harpers Ferry in October 1859.

JOHN BROWN'S RAIDERS*

Oliver Brown 1
Owen Brown 3
Watson Brown 1

Jeremiah Anderson 1
Osborn Anderson 3
Aaron Stevens 2

Barclay Coppoc 3
Edwin Coppoc 2
F.S. Meriam 3

William Thompson 1
Dauphin Thompson 1
William Leeman 1

John Kagi 1
John Cook 2
John Copeland 2

Charles Tidd 3
Albert Hazlett 2
Stewart Taylor 1

Lewis Leary 1
Shields Green 2
Dangerfield Newby 1

* five blacks, sixteen whites (one Canadian)
1 – killed at Harpers Ferry, October 1859
2 – executed at Charles Town, December 1859
3 – escaped

The names of battles are sometimes as interesting as the names of the men who fought them. I got this list out of the encyclopaedia in the library and present them to you, dear reader, in chronological order.

BATTLES OF THE CIVIL WAR

Fort Sumter
Philippi

Pea Ridge
Prairie Grove

Corinth
Shiloh

Front Royal
Mechanicsville

Gaines's Mill
Frayser's Farm

Seven Pines
Bull Run

Harpers Ferry
Bloody Lane

Marye's Heights
Stones River

Vicksburg
Chancellorsville

Seminary Ridge
Cemetery Hill

Little Round Top
Devil's Den

Chickamauga
Chattanooga

Orchard Knob
Missionary Ridge

The Wilderness
Spotsylvania Court House

Yellow Tavern
New Hope Church

Bermuda Hundred
Brice's Crossroads

Cold Harbor
Hatcher's Run

Peachtree Creek
Kennesaw Mountain

Five Forks
Appomattox

—⁓—

Two weeks ago, Burns mentioned my interest in lists at Session, and ever since then people have been coming up to me with suggestions. Most of them don't qualify, however; they are merely lists of mundane articles — clothing or food or the parts of a motor. To be poetic lists, each item must have poetic integrity. Like the names of the Indians in "Little Big Horn." Still, some of the suggestions haven't been bad. The names of butterflies, for example (Mourning Cloak, Saga Fritillary, European Cabbage), or British pubs (Green Man, The Fox, Crossed Foxes), or obsolete models of cars (Biscayne, Bel Air, Strato-Chief), or famous Canadian racehorses (Fearnaught, Heresy, Slaughter, Inferno, Uttermost).

Cleveland, whose claim to fame is the murders by shotgun of three of his fellow postal workers, is a baseball enthusiast. He gave me this one. It is a list for Whitey Ford, a Hall of Fame pitcher for the New York Yankees.

WHITEY FORD

9—1
18—6
16—8
18—7
19—6
11—5
14—7
16—10
12—9
25—4
17—8
24—7
17—6
16—13

2—5

2—4

—m—

Burns himself suggested this one. His wife has a book at home called *A Handweaver's Pattern Book,* and the names of the patterns are rich in folklore. Because he was aware of my interest in American history, he brought it in for me. Wasn't that nice of him? He must have hoped his gesture would rid me of my desire to rape and pillage.

ROSE IN THE WILDERNESS

American Frontier
Conestoga

For the Mountains
Mountain Homespun

In Old Narragansett
Home Life in Colonial Days

Indian March
Scottish Chiefs

Martha Washington
Molly Pitcher

Lee's Surrender
Swedes on the Delaware

China at Work
Overseer

Seed
Pique

Consider the Lilies
Rose in the Wilderness

—ᴍ—

Here's one for Walter, who told us in Session about how, as a boy, he enjoyed stuffing cannon-crackers down the throats of toads and tree frogs, then lighting them and watching them explode. This was some years before he took an axe to his parents in the century farmhouse he grew up in and then set it on fire.

As well, I must thank Burns for acquiring a crate of fireworks for our Victoria Day festivities. And for assigning me guardian of the crate; it was thus that I was able to copy down their names.

FIREWORKS

Twelve Ball Candle
A Baker's Dozen

The Dirty Dozen
The Outlaw

Rebel
Fiesta

Shimmering Cascade
Oriental Splendour

Giant Hi-Flyer
Jack-in-the-Box

Chain Reaction
Galactic Storm

Magic Tree
Burning Schoolhouse

—m—

About two months ago we were at lunch and the topic of conver-
sation was pussy. Various opinions were being expressed around
the table about massage parlours and escort services and whore-
houses and where in the world the best pussy could be had.
Somebody said New York City. Somebody else said Miami.
Cleveland said Chicago. When it was my turn I agreed with New
York City (ah, Rita!), but I also added Berlin (just to impress,
never having been to Berlin). Then this new guy Kevin said Las
Vegas, and he talked at length about the Yellow Pages in Las
Vegas and how there are over a hundred pages of escort services.
He said they're listed under the heading "Entertainers" and some
of them have really kinky names like Rampage and Centerfolds
and Burn Baby Burn and Fantasy Room Service.

So the next time my young friend Mark Thorogood came
calling, I asked him to do me a favour. Since you work at the
Collingwood Library, I said, I want you to contact a library in Las
Vegas, any library, there can't be too many, and ask the librarian
there to ship us a copy of the Las Vegas Yellow Pages. What do
you want the Las Vegas Yellow Pages for? my young friend asked
me. It's for a poem, I told him, and he was only too willing to help.

"ENTERTAINERS"

Adult Singing Strippers
Ancient Chinese Secrets

Asian Deviations
Asian Party Girls

Babes Who Flunked College
Bored Secretaries

Call Me Up I'll Come Down
Daddy's Little Girl

Dirty Dancing
Dirty Deeds Done Dirt Cheap

French Maid Strippers
Full Service Off-Duty Stewardesses

Girls on the Menu
Girls of Glitter Gulch

Good Luck Charm for the Gambler
Heidi's Hardbodies

I Leave My Husband at Home
I Try Harder

Large Ladies
Lipstick Girl

Nasty College Girls Direct to Your Room
Oriental Girls Know Secret Ways of Pure Pleasure

Pretty Feet Polished Nails
Red Shoe Ladies

Silk Stockings
Sizzle

Student Nurses Working Their Way through School
This Trooper's Looking for a Few Good Men

U-Pick-Em
Voluptuous Female Body Builder

Watch Us Play
What Do You Want

When the Cat's Away the Mice Will Play
You Want Me Don't You

—⁓—

I look up from my reading. An East Indian man in a Burger King hat wants to mop under my table. I lift my feet.

The last piece of paper in the sheaf is not a list poem, but a list of a different kind. And even though I didn't know it before I started reading, it's what I've been looking for all along.

SUBMISSIONS UPDATE

Good Return – Battles of the Civil War
                    Confederate Officers at Gettysburg
                    Little Big Horn
                    John Brown's Raiders
– *All rejected* 14/9/92

Desperate Angel – Poker
　　　　　　　Whitey Ford
　　　　　　　"Entertainers"
　　　　　　　Fireworks
– *All rejected* 16/9/92

Columbine – Dr. Manning's Garden
　　　　　　Mixed Drinks
　　　　　　Monk
– *All rejected* 26/9/92

Horn of Plenty – Battles of the Civil War
　　　　　　　Confederate Officers at Gettysburg
　　　　　　　Little Big Horn
　　　　　　　John Brown's Raiders
– *All rejected* 27/9/92

Blue Cohosh – Shakespearean Garden
　　　　　　Rose in the Wilderness
　　　　　　Dr. Manning's Garden
　　　　　　Monk
　　　　　　Mixed Drinks
– *All rejected* 30/9/92

No Frigate – Poker
　　　　　Fireworks
　　　　　Whitey Ford
– *No response yet*

I haven't touched my coffee. On my way out of the Burger King, I leave it on top of the garbage disposal, where you're supposed to leave your trays. Outside, the East Indian man is taking a smoke break.

Back at Homicide I put in a long-distance call to Mark Thorogood at the Collingwood Public Library. I have to wait for him to come back from lunch. When he phones back fifteen minutes later, his information is exactly what I expect. The reason *Desperate Angel* and *Horn of Plenty* were not included on the list he gave me was because I only asked for the names of magazines whose editors were female, and the editors of *Desperate Angel* and *Horn of Plenty* are men. That might also explain why "Entertainers" was submitted to *Desperate Angel*, but not to *No Frigate*; Woolley figured what with its "chauvinist pig" subject matter it was more likely to be accepted by a male editor. As well, it would appear that he never did submit poems to the other six magazines on Mr. Thorogood's list: *The Barnes College Quarterly*, *Bugle*, *A Feminist View*, *Nun's Habit*, *T'Ain't*, and *Yarn*.

Then I tell Mark Thorogood about Karen English, and I have to listen to him sob for about two minutes before he more or less pulls himself together. I'm starting to feel sorry for the kid.

When I hang up I ask Wheeler to locate Miriam Qureshi, the editor of *No Frigate*. She's the only female editor still at risk.

At noon Trick and I go out for a sub.

When we get back I try to get in touch with Daniel to tell him about the poems Barkas and Estabrooks found in the dumpster, but I can't reach him at school and nobody answers at his house. I leave messages at both places, then I sit around and wait for the next piece of the puzzle to appear.

About half past four Wheeler comes in and tells me they can't find Miriam Qureshi. She also tells me a missing-persons report was filed yesterday morning by Ms. Qureshi's roommate.

CHAPTER 12

Saturday, October 17

IT'S SATURDAY, MY day off. I get up early, and me and Reg walk down to the Busy Bee where I buy a program for this afternoon's harness races at Mohawk, but none of the horses I like to lose money on are entered, so we go home again. I try to watch some TV, but ever since Pee-wee Herman went off the air, Saturday mornings just haven't been the same. I make a feeble attempt at housework, but at ten o'clock or thereabouts I drop the vacuum in mid-stride, abandon the garbage bag in the middle of the living-room floor, take a shower, get dressed, walk outside where my trusty rusty Volare waits at the curb, and drive down to the station.

Staff Inspector Bateman isn't thrilled to see me. He tells me to go home. I tell him no. He looks at me. He takes me into his office and asks me if I'm all right now, or am I feeling any after-effects of that business the other day in the locker room. I tell him I'm fine, what's new with Ms. Qureshi?

According to Bateman, Miriam Qureshi received a phone call about nine o'clock Thursday evening, told her roommate she was going out for an hour to have coffee with the sales rep of a printing company, and would be back by ten. The roommate, a slim woman with a shaved head, L-O-V-E tattooed across the knuckles of one hand, H-A-T-E tattooed across the knuckles of the other hand, and silver rings all the way around the rims of both ears – Bateman shakes his head as he describes her – finally went to bed around midnight, but woke up alone and phoned the police.

On Friday, Ms. Qureshi did not show up for work at Cirillo's Vegetable Market on the Danforth. Her parents, twenty miles away in Mississauga, haven't heard from her. Neither has anyone else.

Staff Inspector Bateman shows me a copy of the APB that's been issued and the accompanying photograph of an unsmiling dark-skinned woman with a short, mannish haircut. Unlike her roommate, Ms. Qureshi looks more or less normal.

Because Daniel didn't get back to me last night I call him now.

"You're lucky you caught me," he says. "Alice and I are just about to leave for Niagara-on-the-Lake to see a couple of plays and do the B&B thing."

Me and Tanya did that once. Somewhere in Prince Edward County. A little town called Cherryville or Cherry Valley. I hated it. Not the town, the B&B thing. I felt awkward, like a fake relative in someone's house. The people who owned the house were retired. Lawyer and his wife. The room we slept in had mints on the pillow and a bowl of fruit on the dresser. But it'd belonged to one of the sons in the family who'd gone off to university, and his high-school textbooks and model airplanes were still on the shelves. I figured if I looked under the bed I'd find a dusty old *Hustler*.

"I left a message on your machine yesterday afternoon," I tell him.

"Really? Julie's home from McGill for the weekend and she erased them by mistake. She told me, but I had no idea who, if anyone, had called. I should have shown her which buttons *not* to push."

"We've found more of Woolley's poems. They were in a dumpster behind the building he was living in. Would you take a look at them?"

"Sure. Fax them to my office. I'll read them Monday morning, first thing."

"Another thing. What do you know about a magazine called *No Frigate*?"

"*No Frigate*? It's women's writing, with a feminist or lesbian orientation. Was Woolley sending poems to them?"

"Yes."

"I don't get it. As far as I know, they only publish women writers."

"I guess he didn't know that," I say. "Or he thought the brilliance of his stuff would change their minds."

"Listen, Campbell, I've got to get a move on here, but I was going to call you on the car phone once we were on our way."

"Why?"

"I've got news for you, too. It just came to me in the shower this morning. Remember the note Woolley left at the Pansy Jones murder site?"

"Right. Something about arms."

"'Oh God, thy arm was here!'"

"That's it."

"Well, I found the source. It's another line from the *Henry V* speech."

"It is?"

"Yes, it's a clue, just like you figured it would be. Woolley was telling us which speech he would use with his next victim. The quotation killed two birds with one stone: he was saying that he has God's power to take life away, and he was also telling us that the clue – 'English' – was in the King's speech."

"So what you're saying is, the note he taped to Ms. English might give us a clue about the *next* victim."

"Exactly. 'This happy breed of men, this little world, This precious stone set in the silver sea.'"

"What do you make of it?"

"Well, each item is symbolic. Woolley's the happy man because he's killing women. The world may be small, but he can do what he wants in it, get away with whatever he likes."

"You sure you're not just being a professor here, coming up with all sorts of shit the author never intended? I hated when teachers did that."

"Campbell, just because *you* didn't see the symbolism doesn't mean it isn't there."

"Fine. Keep going. What about the last part of the quotation?"

"I think he's being ironic. The precious stone is his next victim. It's ironic because she – whoever she might be – is precious to someone, but not to him. He fully intends to kill her."

"The fucker."

"Campbell, listen, Alice is making faces at me. I've got to get going. We're running late as it is."

"World Series starts tonight, you aware of that, buddy?"

"Oh yes. We're catching a matinee, *Lady Windermere's Fan*, in case you've ever heard of it, and I'll be happily ensconced in front of a TV by seven-thirty."

"Cone pitches tomorrow," I say.

"Of that I am aware as well. Forty dollars aware, *n'est-ce pas?*"

"Right. You're coming home tomorrow night?"

"That's right, sailor."

"Well, drop by McCully's. You can pay me there."

I make a second phone call – to Elliot Cronish.

"Young! Have you been avoiding me, Young? I'm dying to know how the case is going. When the third body came in the other day I said to myself, 'Well, how 'bout them apples, our boy has graduated to serial status after all.'"

"Save it. Just give me the news. How did he kill Ms. Jones and Ms. English?"

"You really aren't much fun, you know. You used to be. I think you're too much in the company of that ill-humoured young woman."

"Cronish –"

"All right, all right. In both cases there was trauma to the head – a hammer, likely – and that's what Karen English died of. Pansy Jones, like Joanne Stevenson, drowned. Or, more correctly, *was* drowned. And again like Joanne Stevenson, Pansy Jones was raped after death. The good news is the DNA from the semen confirms Lawrence Woolley. The bad news is that Karen English wasn't raped."

"How is that bad news?"

"No DNA for one thing, but it's also bad because he's broken his pattern. Something happened – he couldn't get it up, he heard a noise, a distraction – whatever it was, he didn't rape her."

"If he'd heard a noise," I put in, "he wouldn't have had time to tape her to the wall."

"Well, there you are: I guess he couldn't get it up. Anyway, it's bad news because now that his routine's been disturbed, he may change his modus operandi entirely."

"Why do you think so?"

"I've been doing some reading. I just find the whole business fascinating, and our boy, you have to admit, is really quite creative. Mind you, serial killers are usually clever, and because they're playing a game – a game of elusion – they have to make changes. They can't allow themselves to become predictable. Ask your little partner of the multicoloured eyes if I'm wrong."

"I'll be sure to do that."

"Oh, and Young, Forensics got in touch with me about the car. Joanne Stevenson's car?"

"What about it?"

"It's clean. Fibre samples, hair samples, et cetera, suggest that Woolley was never in it, as driver or passenger."

"Well," I say, "now that we know who the killer is and what he's like, it figures. He wasn't her boyfriend, or any other kind of friend, and he wasn't planning to leave town in any kind of hurry. That simplifies things."

"But if he wasn't a friend, why would the silly girl let him into her apartment in the first place? That's what I can't grasp about any of these murders. Why did all three of these women let him in?"

"He probably phoned them up and said he was Lennox Ross or Charles Delabreth – whichever name he used with each of them – and asked could he talk to them. Or maybe he said he wanted to drop off another submission of poems. Something like that."

"And they fell for it. All three of them."

"So it seems."

"One more thing."

"What's that?"

"Well, I thought you'd want to know what was in Karen English's mouth."

I shake my head. "I hadn't given it any thought."

"I'm surprised at you, Detective Sergeant. His patterns, such as they are, are still your strong suit. Am I right, or am I right?"

"What was it?"

"After all, the surprise in mouth number one was a tennis ball, and in mouth number two it was a hothouse flower, a columbine. I'm shocked that you aren't more curious to find out what little treasure he left in mouth number three."

"I'll ask you again, what was it?"

"Guess."

"Cronish, you're making me mad, so just cut the crap and tell me."

"You really are no fun. Karen English had a tea bag in her mouth. With the tag attached. Twinings English Breakfast."

I make a third phone call – to Miriam Qureshi's shave-headed room-mate, whose name is Sandra Mulligan. I ask a long string of questions and get some interesting answers. *No Frigate* is running on a shoe-string, has a small but growing reputation, and is badly in need of financial backing. Yes, it seemed strange that this "sales rep" should call in the evening and ask to meet Ms. Qureshi immediately, but they live a pretty bohemian lifestyle, Ms. Mulligan tells me, and stranger things have happened. The caller asked Ms. Qureshi to meet him at the Second Cup on Yonge Street, just a short walk from the high-rise on Dundonald where the two women live. No, Ms. Mulligan was not told the man's name. She did not tag along, because Ms. Qureshi did not invite her to do so. Although Ms. Mulligan's name appears on the masthead as an associate editor, it's really Ms. Qureshi who runs the magazine. Ms. Mulligan helps out from time to time, but she doesn't enjoy "dealing with all those egos," as she puts it, and besides, the whole operation is a money pit. Yes, a Staff Inspector Bateman visited her last night and asked her to check whether or not a letter of rejection had been sent out recently to a writer named Lennox Ross or Charles Delabreth, and she did con-firm that such a letter, in response to a submission of three list poems, was sent out ten days ago, on Wednesday, October 7, to Lennox Ross. Ms. Mulligan then asks me if there's a female cop on the case, and I say yes, why? and she says she would rather deal with a woman than with a man just now, which kind of shocks me, and I say, Why is that? And she says, I can't deal with men right now, okay? I mean look what's happened to Miriam, so I say okay and give her Wheeler's badge number and telephone extension.

The Second Cup isn't even a full block from the apartment building. It's just around the corner. In plainclothes, me and Wheeler pay the owner a visit and show him two photographs: Ms. Qureshi, solemn, looking like a handsome young man; and Lawrence Woolley, whose update photos, having finally arrived from Criminal Records, reveal a thin pale face with small eyes, a straight nose, a long jaw, large ears, and medium-length dark hair. When Wheeler first saw the photo she said, "He's scary. He's got a weak mouth. He looks like Nicolas Cage in *Wild at Heart*. The owner studies the photos carefully then shakes his head. "I worked Thursday night," he tells us, "and Miriam didn't come in. I know her well. She comes in two, sometimes three times a week. But this man I've never seen before. I would remember him if he was here. He has a face you don't forget."

As we drive the short distance around the corner towards the high-rise, I say to Wheeler, "He intercepted her between her apartment and the coffee shop. How did he get her to go with him? When she realized he wasn't taking her to the Second Cup, she must have wondered."

"She would have put up a fight."

"He must have had a car."

"Stolen, maybe. Or rented."

"He must have forced her into the car. Held a knife to her throat or a gun to her head."

I wait in the cruiser outside the high-rise while Wheeler goes in. Wheeler had the day off, too, but when I phoned her at home and told her about Ms. Mulligan's strange request for a female cop, she said she'd be right in. "Look," I said, "I don't want you to give up your day off," and she said, "Then why did you call me?" I didn't know what to say to that. "Anyway," she said, "I want to come in, so don't sweat it."

We've phoned ahead, and Ms. Mulligan's agreed to speak to Wheeler – alone.

"Careful in there," I say as Wheeler gets out of the car. "She's one of them bull-dykes, eh? If you're not back in twenty minutes, I'm coming in."

Wheeler tugs down the brim of her HOYAS ballcap, sets her mouth grimly, turns and *winks* at me – maybe she doesn't hate me, after all – then marches off towards the entrance of the apartment building.

While I'm waiting, my mind begins to wander, and between fielding staticky checkup calls from Dispatch and gazing around at the revamping of what was once a rundown white-trash neighbour-hood into a trendy community of actors and lawyers and boutique owners, I flash back – for reasons I can't even guess at – to an epic eleven-minute arm-wrestling match at a bar full of shouting friends between me (290 pounds) and Daniel Curry (185 pounds) when we were still in our twenties and he wasn't a professor yet and I wasn't a detective yet, and to everyone's surprise except mine he won; and then for some reason my thoughts drift to my ex-wife, who I haven't seen in about two years, but who, in our last telephone conversation, proudly informed me she has a personal trainer ("I thought those went out of style," Daniel laughed when I told him about the phone call, "sort of like eunuchs"); and then I think about Debi, who I'll see tomorrow, and her almost total lack of concern for her future (all she can think about is Wayne or Randy or whatever the exercise rider's name is, and the baby, of course, half-black and fatherless, whose name I still have trouble getting my mouth around; she's a good mother, but she doesn't seem at all concerned about her prospects – career-wise, financial-wise, marriage-wise); I think about Wheeler being more or less nice to me the last couple of days; I think about Jessy being nice to me last Wednesday when the Jays clinched (I'll see her tonight at McCully's – and tomorrow, if she's working); I ponder the sad fact that I haven't *had any* in over a year, not since my friendship with a woman who made the trophies for our slo-pitch league (divorced, two teenagers both angry at every-thing and everybody; a big attractive chest when holstered; unhol-stered, they dropped like hanged men) went belly up; I think about Wheeler on Woolley's sense of entitlement ("He figures it's his right to kill these women. Like Dr. Manning said, because he's white and educated and sees himself as a failure, he thinks the world owes him, and that makes him very dangerous, a very brutal kind of criminal. Everyone is capable of evil, but in our society no one is more capable of it than white men. Like that guy in Pickering a couple of years ago who raped and murdered his daughter's best friend. She was only fourteen years old. He'd even been friends with the girl's parents. Cribbage on the porch, and so forth. But after he was convicted, and the dead girl's father begged him to tell where the body was, he refused. He wouldn't do it. He had his appeal to consider. Like Woolley, this guy thought of *himself* as the victim. He had no compassion or sympathy or regret. He wasn't sorry for what he'd done. I don't know what he did to rationalize it to himself, but he must have succeeded. After all, not only did he not kill himself, but he remained *defiant* about what he'd done – as if in some twisted way, what he'd done, raping and strangling this child, was justified").

Then I look up and Wheeler's walking towards me with a comic look of exhaustion on her face – tongue hanging out like a panting dog's – and I wish I was fifteen years younger, and not so huge, and not so ugly, and not so stupid.

"So what did she say? Why was it so important she talk to you?"

"It wasn't me, per se. It just had to be a woman."

"Right, but why? Just because she's a lesbo she's allergic to men?"

"Well, actually, she did open up. When she was seventeen, she was hitchhiking, and she was in some small town up near the Lakehead. She was in a bar or a pool hall or something, and she had nowhere to sleep, and this guy offered to take her to a youth hostel in the next town, so she agreed. But the guy and his buddy drove her into the woods and took turns with her and then tied her to the trunk of a tree. They gagged and blindfolded her. They left her there to die. She struggled for hours and finally freed herself and made her way back to the highway. So yeah, she is kind of allergic to men."

It's almost four by now, and I'm fighting traffic to get back to HQ. In my mind's eye I see Karen English again, the horror in her taped-open eyes. The evil she suffered. Ms. Mulligan *survived* something just as bad. Stress prickles spread across my back and down my spine like a rash. At a red light I take a couple of deep breaths, and when it changes to green, I say, "Yeah, so go on."

"So she thinks maybe Miriam made up the story about the sales rep and eloped with an old boyfriend."

"What?"

"It seems Miriam's only been out of the closet a year or so – actually Sandra thinks Miriam's bisexual – and Sandra admits she gets insanely jealous whenever Miriam pays attention to a man. Plus, things have been kind of rough between them lately."

"Why?"

"She figures it's the magazine. Apparently, Miriam eats, sleeps, and breathes the magazine, and Sandra feels rejected. She feels the magazine is more important to Miriam than she is."

"Wheeler, I'm sorry, but will you please stop calling them by their first names? This isn't 'Days of Our Lives,' for fucksake."

"I know it's not 'Days of Our Lives.'"

"What about the ex-boyfriend?"

"I have his name. He lives in California."

"California? What's he doing in Toronto?"

"Um, she doesn't actually know that he's *in* Toronto. It's just a hunch on her part."

"What the fuck? Doesn't she understand that this has nothing to do with her? Did you explain about Lawrence Woolley?"

"Yes, she knows all about him. Staff Inspector Bateman filled her in last night. But she's obsessed with this other idea."

As HQ comes into view, I take another deep breath. "All right. So what do you think?"

She's quiet for a moment, then shakes her head. "Three things bother me," she says. "First, what Cronish told you: for some reason Woolley didn't rape Karen English. That's a break in his usual routine. Second, there's been no clue whatsoever about Miriam. No Shakespearean quotation. No clue of any kind. Up to this point, he's always given us a clue. Which leads to the third thing, which is my conclusion: he's playing the game differently this time. More extreme. More dangerous." She pauses and closes her eyes and rubs her fingertips into her temples. "For one thing, the first three attacks were in the women's homes. This time he's abducted his victim."

"Or so we think," I say.

She looks at me. "Oh, he's got her. Of that I am positive. They're in a motel somewhere, and he's taking his time with her. He knows we're going to catch up with him sooner or later. So he's having his fun while he can. He's got her in a motel somewhere, and he's torturing her to death."

We hang around Homicide till seven, mostly on the phone to tipsters, but nothing materializes. That both Miriam Qureshi and Karen English might be safe at home right now if I hadn't suffered that little spell of laziness is front and centre in my mind, like a bulletin in huge letters projected onto my frontal lobe. And if it's not the message I see (COP FUCKS UP; ONE WOMAN DEAD, SECOND MISSING), then it's Ms. English's enormous green eyes I see, and then without any urging at all, my imagination goes to work, and there's Ms. Qureshi in various situations, each one worse than the one before, each one enough to break your heart, or make you think about tucking your service revolver up under your chin, each one enough to make you wonder whether there's any limit to the evil men can think up, each one enough to convince you there is no God, there can't be a God, because God would never allow it, He would never permit innocent people to suffer like they've just suffered in your imagination – which is probably nothing compared to how they *really* suffered, or how Ms. Qureshi is suffering right now, at this very instant, while you're dicking around the office, talking to all these fools on the telephone.

I invite Wheeler to watch the game with me at McCully's but she says no. She doesn't offer any excuse or tell me what she plans to do instead. She just says no. And here I was thinking we were making progress.

Trick's already there when I arrive. I tell him I'm going to meet Debi in the Clubhouse tomorrow. Does he want to come?

No, he's got a date, he says, and points at this amazingly beautiful woman in a bright yellow dress making her way towards us from the ladies' room.

"You old smoothie," I say. "Who is she?"

He smiles sadly and tells me she's his cousin Eartha from Lockport, New York, and she's up here for an educational conference – she teaches physics to high-school students. She's made Trick promise to take her to the museum and the Science Centre tomorrow afternoon. The track's out.

When Eartha reaches our table, Trick introduces us, and just as I'm about to fall in love, Jessy shows up to take our order. Trick says, "Eartha, this is Jessy, the feistiest barmaid in the city."

Eartha smiles and says, "Pleased to meet you."

"She's so feisty," Trick continues, "that even though Camp and I don't like this bar, we can't drink anywhere else. Jessy won't let us."

"She won't hear of it," I say.

"She's too feisty," Trick says.

Jessy shakes Eartha's hand and then she says, "Watch out for the big guy, Eartha, he's a convicted sex offender."

In game one of the World Series, a Jack Morris forkball fails to fork in the bottom of the sixth inning, and Damon Berryhill clouts it out over the right-field wall for three runs, all Atlanta will need for a 3–1 victory.

With the final out, McCully's empties like somebody pulled the plug. Eartha kept glancing at me all evening like I was on a day pass from a halfway house, and Jessy, admiring her work, laughed a whole lot, made unkind faces at me, and reminded me of Carla from "Cheers."

I walk home alone, but I'm not unhappy. Comfortably numb, as they say. I had a lot to drink tonight – what with the tension of the ballgame, and Eartha thinking I was a pervert, I *had* to have four or five shots, as well as my usual boatload of beer – and I know I'm weaving noticeably. As I try to fit the key in the hole, I can hear Reg tearing the furniture apart. I get the door open, roughhouse with Reg for about thirty seconds, find the leash, and then we head out for a walk. And gradually I calm down. Baby Brother's running in the eighth tomorrow afternoon, so Debi'll be all excited about that. That'll be good. And tomorrow night, it's Cone against John Smoltz in game two. Daniel will be there, back from the B&B thing. I'll win forty smackers, and like the man says, all will be right with the world. I keep thinking this, even mouthing the words, then saying them out loud – "All will be right with the world" – as the numbness brought on by the booze begins to fade, and the faces of dead women start showing up at the edges of my mind.

CHAPTER 13

Sunday, October 18

BY THE TIME THE fifth race rolls around I'm down a few bucks, but I'm having a good time because of the father-daughter thing. Debi calls me Daddy, I call her Sweetie. Because I'm treating her to the roast beef buffet in the Clubhouse, we're both looking our best. She's wearing a knee-length dress that's fire-engine red with these sort of little white lighthouses or cannons or something all over it, and a pair of white eight-hole Doc Martens. She's also wearing little round granny glasses with purple frames, and when I tell her I didn't know she wore glasses, she looks up from the *Form* and says, "I just got them. Now I can read all about the horses I'm about to lose my money on."

I smile and shake my head. "You sound just like me," I say.

I'm wearing a beige polo shirt under a navy blazer, grey flannels, and my favourite shoes – a pair of size-16 brogues Trick calls the Pacific Feet. They're scuffed and warped and broken at the heels. I never tie the laces because they slip on just fine – besides, it's too far to reach.

Soon, Debi will have to make her way back to the barn to get Baby Brother ready. Already she's very excited, and when she's excited she gets talkative, so maybe that's why she's talking about her mother, a topic she usually avoids like the plague. The conversation began normally enough, then switched saddles in midstream. We were talking about Christmas:

"Do you know what I remember, Daddy? I remember putting out the plate of cookies and the glass of milk and the note."

"On the hearth."

"That's right. And in the morning, the cookies would be gone –"

"If I remember right, Santa always left a few crumbs."

"– and the milk, and there would always be an answer."

"'Dear Debi, hope you enjoy your gifts. Be good to your mommy and daddy. Love, Santa.'"

"Yes, just like that." Debi claps her hands and laughs, and behind the bruise-coloured lipstick and the heavy mascara, and despite the crewcut and the nose stud, I can see her little-girl face, full of curiosity. "I used to love lying in front of the tree, trying to figure out what my presents were. I remember one of them especially – a square box, about a foot square – and for the life of me I couldn't figure out what was inside."

"What was it?"

"A plastic cash register! With plastic coins – red and yellow and blue!"

"I remember. You played with it non-stop. Brought it to the dinner table. Had to play restaurant. Had to play store."

"Christmas is only two months away, Daddy. Maybe I'll see if I can find a plastic cash register for Jamal."

"He might be a little young for it."

"That's okay. He'll play with it soon enough. I'm going to make sure his Christmases are just like mine were."

"Just make sure he doesn't swallow the coins," I say, and stand up to get some more roast beef. When I come back to the table, Debi's got mascara all over her face, and she's making it worse by swiping at it with her napkin.

"What's wrong?"

She looks up at me, her eyes brimming. "The bitch," she says. "Why'd she have to ruin our family? We had a perfectly good, normal family."

"Oh, Sweetie, that's all in the past."

"No, it's *not* in the past! It's with me all the goddamn time! How could she screw around on you? You're the most wonderful goddamn man in the world."

"Sweetie, it's not that simple. I –"

But she's really bawling now, and people are turning to look.

"And with a fucking *Nissan* dealer!"

Eventually, she collects herself and, still sniffling, exits the Clubhouse to go get Baby Brother ready for the eighth. I move to the bar to escape the stares of those diners who think I'm some old sugar daddy who's just told his beefy young mistress the party's over.

I bet fifty across on Baby Brother, and although he puts in a strong bid down the stretch he can't get to the first two and ends up third, a good six lengths off the winner. At 8–1 he pays five and change to show, so I get back most of my investment.

I head outside and hurry down to the rail where the grooms wait for the horses. Most of the grooms are tiny men. The young ones hope to be jockeys some day. Some of the old ones *were* jockeys at one time, before they lost their nerve, or couldn't make the weight any more. Anyway, they're all small – five feet, a hundred pounds – so Debi looks like a giant among them, this huge girl in a red dress and blonde crewcut, shank in hand, carefully watching the action of her horse as he canters towards her, then slows to a trot, and then to a walk.

"Hey, Baby," she says, as he exhales heavily and leans his forehead into her chest. "How was he, Ron?"

The jockey tosses his whip to his valet and prepares to dismount. "Run good once he got going," he says breathlessly. "Got into some traffic on the far turn, took him a while to get untracked."

"Any bad steps?"

"No, he's made of iron, this old dude." He slaps Baby Brother's wet neck and hops off, landing as light as a feather beside Debi.

"He come back okay?" I call from the rail, and Debi turns and smiles at me.

"Just fine, Daddy. Hope you didn't lose too much."

"Not much. I had him across."

She pulls the blinkers off and is ready to lead him back to Shedrow to cool him out.

"How about next Sunday?" I shout.

"All right." She smiles again. The tears are all gone. "I'll be here."

I radio in on the off chance there might be a new lead. I'm in my car heading from the track to McCully's – with a short stopover at home to let Reg out. I get through to Barkas, and he says there's nothing much, but one interesting call did come in. Lawrence Woolley's mother phoned. About the time we discovered the Parliament Street address, her and her daughter had been questioned, and although they hadn't been willing or able to offer any useful information, they did agree to have their phone bugged and surveillance established outside their apartment building. Now, Barkas says, she wants to talk.

"Why now?" I say.

"She says it's because of the three dead women. She wants to help."

"That's good, that's good," I say. "Phone her back and see if nine o'clock tomorrow morning's okay. Then phone Wheeler and tell her I want her to go with me."

I shut down the radio and punch in a cassette. Bob Seger's singing "Shinin' Brightly."

"How was the Science Centre?" I ask Trick when I get to McCully's.

"Great," he says. "We rode a mine cart through an active volcano, I saw what I would look like if I was a Klingon, and I was embraced by a robotic dinosaur. Eartha was embraced by a flying pteranadon."

"I wish I was a flying pteranadon," I say.

"I'm sure. How was the track?"

"Debi's horse finished third. We had fun. So . . . where *is* Eartha?"

"On the bus back to Lockport. I offered to buy her a beer and then put her on a later bus, and she considered it." He pauses. "Then she asked me where we would go for our beer, and I said McCully's, and she said is that where we were last night, and I said yes, and she said will your friend who likes little boys be there, so that sort of iced it."

"You could have lied. You could have told her I was out of town, and then I could have just showed up. Change of plans or something."

"Yeah, and then what?"

"And then, let's see, and then your beeper would go off, and you'd have to go in to HQ, and *I'd* have to escort Eartha to the bus –"

"Yeah, and *then* what?"

"Um, and then . . ."

"This is my cousin you're talking about."

"Yeah, right. So then we'd go . . . dancing!"

"Dancing? You don't know diddly about dancing."

"Oh yeah? Watch this." Then I'm on my feet and doing the Jerk. Then I do the Swim. I do the Mashed Potatoes. There's no music, but it doesn't matter.

Trick says, "Camp, sit down, that isn't dancing. You're embarrassing me."

By then I'm doing the Twist. Jessy's walking by with an empty tray and starts doing the Twist with me. "I didn't know you could dance, big guy," she says. She twists a full circle around me and then she disappears among the tables and the people and the smoke.

At the beginning of the sixth inning of game two, Daniel arrives, home from the B&B trip to Niagara-on-the-Lake. I quickly bring him up to date on the case. Then Daniel hears the score: Atlanta 4, Toronto 2. Cone has been pulled. Daniel cackles and starts counting the money he thinks he's already won.

"Sixty bucks we bet, right, Campbell? Or was it eighty?"

In the eighth, Alomar doubles and scores. Atlanta 4, Toronto 3.

"No problem," says Daniel, but there's tiny beads of sweat on his brow.

In the ninth, Borders singles and Eddie Sprague cranks a Jeff Reardon fastball deep into the left-field bleachers: Toronto 5, Atlanta 4.

"I think you're right," I say to Daniel. "It *was* eighty bucks."

In the bottom of the ninth, Henke come in and shuts the door. Series tied at one.

"I'm a broken man," Daniel says, and hands me forty dollars. "I'm disconsolate and I'm going home." Then he looks at me. "Did you bring those poems you wanted me to read?"

"You told me to fax them to you tomorrow," I say.

"Okay," he says, "but don't forget," and he looks at me, suddenly serious.

"I won't."

Then he leaves.

Five minutes later, Trick stands up. "Me, too. Gotta work in the morning. You coming?"

"No, you go on," I say. "I'm having one more, then I'm on my way."

"I'll wait for you."

"No, you better go. I might make it two."

Two hours and three beers later, I'm still sitting at the bar. And feeling fine. After all, it's been a great day – I spent some quality time with my daughter, the Jays put together a very gutsy comeback victory, I won forty dollars off Daniel, and I'm looking forward to this interview with Mrs. Woolley tomorrow.

Jessy suddenly appears at my shoulder. "Big guy, give a girl a ride home?"

She's been eyeing me all night long like I was something in a store window, but I'm still surprised.

Jessy, as I discover, lives eight or ten blocks from McCully's. "If I'm working days I ride my bike," she says, sitting beside me in the Volare. "But if I have to go home late, like tonight, it makes me nervous, so I leave the bike at home and take a cab instead." I can feel her smiling in the dark beside me. "Usually that's what I do."

When I pull up in front of her place, she says, "I've got a nice joint upstairs. Want to come in?"

"Joint" used to mean "place," as in "Boy, you live in a really cool joint," and I'm so square that's what I thought she meant. I'm about to say something stupid, but I twig just in time.

"Sure," I say, debonair as all get-out.

Jessy's got the entire second floor of a brick semi. Very cozy. Very nice. She tells me to sit down in the living room. She disappears for a minute and comes back with a Bart Simpson pencil case. From it she takes one of those really thin joints you know's probably going to hurt you.

Sitting side by side on the sofa, we smoke it.

After a few minutes she says, "Do you like the hip?"

"The what?" I say.

"The *hip*," she repeats, like I'm foreign or something. I don't think about it much, but I'm really more of a leg man. Luckily, I don't say anything, because then Jessy pushes a plastic CD case along the coffee table towards me, gets up, and hits a couple of buttons on her hi-fi, or whatever you call it – CD player – and leaves the room.

I look at the case. Oh, I say to myself. Out loud, maybe.

Then she's back, dancing. She says, "This one's called 'New Orleans Is Sinking.'" She hands me a tallboy of Foster's – frosty – and watches as I crack it and take my first sip.

"Oh, that's beautiful," I say, wiping my mouth with the back of my hand. "I was thirsty. And when you're real thirsty, that first sip of cold beer, it's like . . . I don't know, it's like –"

"It's like paradise," she says. "It's like an angel's pissing on your tongue."

Then she's gone again.

The music's amazing. I get up and go over to the stereo and find the volume knob and crank it. Jessy rushes in and turns it back down. "The U*krai*nians," she says and points to the floor. Then she disappears again.

There's a bookshelf nearby, and I turn my head sideways to read the titles. Daniel says you can tell a lot about a person by the books they read. *Magister Ludi. Eyeless in Gaza. Anthem. The Prophet. Choose Your Own Adventure.* Well, that last one sounds good. Anybody visiting my place wouldn't learn a thing. I don't own any books. Magazines, yeah. *The Blood-Horse. Canadian Horse. Sport of Kings.* And copies of *Racing Form* by the thousands. I never throw them away.

When Jessy comes back she's taken off her maroon McCully's T-shirt and she's wearing an oversize Dallas Cowboys jersey. Number 33. It falls to mid-thigh, below which, it would seem, there aren't any more clothes. By which I mean she's bare-legged.

"Tony Dorsett," I say, as she settles on the couch beside me.

"Eh?" she says.

"Running back," I say. I'm starting to feel the dope and I can't seem to speak in full sentences.

"Oh, this old thing?" she says, looking down at her chest. "My brother gave it to me for Christmas a few years ago. I don't know much about baseball myself. You should know that from all those dumb questions I ask. Nine-seven-one double play? Makes no sense to me." She looks down at her chest again. "No, I just like to sleep in it."

I'm just looking at her.

Then she says it again. "I just like to *sleep* in it."

"Oh," I say. Then there's this kind of awkward silence, so I glance over towards the bookshelf. "Boy oh boy, lots of books."

"Oh, those," she says, sort of pissed-off sounding. "Those are my other brother's. He went to university. For six weeks."

"That one book, *Choose Your Own Adventure?*"

"What about it?" she says.

I nod at her stupidly. "Interesting?"

She bites her upper lip with her lower teeth. Reg'll need a walk. "Oh, that one," she says. "I don't know how *it* got up there. It belongs to my nephew. Jason. He's eleven. Want to see my room? I've got a waterbed."

I gulp and try to speak, but nothing comes out.

"Come on," she says. She takes my hand and stands up.

"I thought you didn't like me," I manage, as she leads me down the hall.

"I do like you, big guy. When you're being a gentleman and just having a good time. Like tonight."

She stops midway down the hall and squints up at me in the dark. There's candlelight flickering from somewhere, and for an instant I catch the green of her eyes. Her hair's not so red in this light. It's more bronze. I remember Daniel using the word "burnished" to describe someone's hair.

"Your hair's sort of burnished," I say.

"Come on," she says, "before I change my mind."

The dope's kicking in nicely. I haven't done any since me and Trick took some off a kid a couple of summers ago down at the Beaches. Hash. Through a plastic soda straw, off the coal of a cigarette. It was beautiful. The stars, man. And laugh? Trick doing impersonations of Big Urmson and Estabrooks and Bateman. I was on my back, helpless on the boardwalk. Lucky we weren't in uniform.

Jessy leads me into the bedroom. Candles on the bedside tables throw a romantic glow. The bed itself is covered with a white bedspread, and it's so big it reminds me of the time me and Daniel played football against Vaughan Road Collegiate in four inches of snow.

Jessy sits down on the edge of the bed, facing me. She reaches towards my belt. Maybe I flinch or something because she says, "That's okay, big guy. I only want to see if it's true what they say about big men."

"What's that?"

"That they've got these really tiny dicks? Small little stubby things?"

CHAPTER 14

Monday, October 19

I SHOULD BE THINKING about Alfreda Woolley and what questions we're going to ask her, but I can't seem to think about anything except what happened last night. When Wheeler said something about Karen English a few minutes ago, I flashed to the murder scene and Ms. English's green eyes. Then I remembered Jessy's green eyes last night, how they caught the candlelight, how I didn't connect them to Ms. English's, how I was able to sort of mindlessly relax in Jessy's bed and Jessy's arms without getting distracted by the faces of dead girls.

"Will the daughter be there?" Wheeler asks.

And I don't even feel guilty. I mean, I could *love* Wheeler, I know that. I could marry her, except it's impossible because she's way too young, and besides she doesn't love me. Fact is, she thinks I'm a racist coward bastard.

Jessy's more of a pal. The kind of pal you sleep with. It's like she knew I needed sleeping with and so she slept with me.

"Are you listening to me?"

I didn't stay the night. It didn't feel right, and when I got ready to go, about four in the morning, Jessy didn't argue. She sat at the top of the stairs with the hem of her Tony Dorsett jersey pulled forward over her knees as I tiptoed down. At the bottom I turned and looked up at her. I think I was still stoned and I was about to say something stupid, like, Listen, I'll call you, I'll call you, but she just put a finger to her lips and pointed downwards from her perch and whispered, "*The Ukrainians*," and waved at me till I was out the door and in the car and singing along with good old Bob. "Against the Wind."

"Answer me!"

"What?"

"Will the daughter be there?"

"Beats me, girl."

Wheeler looks at me in silence. Then she says, "What's the matter with you?"

"Nothing. There's nothing the matter with me. Don't you think we should be talking about what we're going to say to Mrs. Woolley?"

"No kidding."

"Yeah, and I wonder what she wants to say to us."

Wheeler nods, still studying me. I turn left onto Birchmount and head north towards the apartment complex where Mrs. Woolley and her daughter live.

I feel like I've been in about a dozen apartments lately, but this one's different: for one thing, it doesn't have a dead girl in the bathroom. For another, it doesn't have artwork on the walls, unless you consider pictures of Jesus artwork – especially the one I remember from my own Sunday school days, a copy of which overlooks Alfreda Woolley's dining-room table. The one where Jesus is looking straight at you. The one where he looks like a rock star with long reddish brown hair down to his shoulders.

Mrs. Woolley is a thin woman with a narrow face and salt-and-pepper hair pulled back in a bun. Schoolmarmish. In my opinion a far cry from pull-subject material, but hey, I'm not her little boy. She shows me and Wheeler into the living room, and Wheeler sits on the sofa and I sit in an easy chair across from her. This forces Mrs. Woolley, who sits in a hardback chair at one end of the coffee table, to look from one of us to the other, which allows whichever of us isn't being looked at to observe her mannerisms and scan the room.

"Thank you for calling us," I say, once we're settled. "We understand you want to talk to us about Lawrence, that you have some information that might help us along with our investigation."

There's not the slightest trace of softness in Mrs. Woolley's expression as she turns to face me. "He's an animal!" she spits. "He's a predator and he should be kept in a cage. He's just like his father was, whose soul is even now writhing in hellfire."

"Um, your daughter, Mrs. Woolley, will she be joining us?"

"Certainly not." Mrs. Woolley's eyes remain fixed on mine.

"Is she here?"

Her eyes narrow. "What interest is it of yours where she is?"

"She may have useful information as well."

"Mary's just a girl. She knows nothing." She gives one hand a little backward flip. "Besides, she's at a piano-teachers' conference. In Quebec City."

I glance at Wheeler, and, like a tag-team wrestler, she jumps into the ring. "Mrs. Woolley," she says, "what in particular do you want to discuss?"

She turns to face Wheeler, and I notice her left fist bunching the material of her skirt, one knee pumping like a piston. "Several months ago, before he was released from prison, he sent his sister some papers and told her to keep them for him. I found them in her room."

Wheeler looks at me quickly and then back to Mrs. Woolley. "What are they?"

Mrs. Woolley leans forward and takes a manila envelope from a shelf underneath the coffee table. "I don't know much about

Shakespeare, but they seem to be quotations." She hands the envelope to me.

I unwind the string fastener and pull out a sheaf of papers – forty or fifty sheets in all. I riffle through them and recognize many of the list poems I first read last Friday when Estabrooks and Barkas found them in the suitcase in the dumpster on Parliament Street. But the first few sheets, as Mrs. Woolley guessed, are quotes from Shakespeare.

"Look at these," I say to Wheeler as I spread them out on the coffee table.

Wheeler kneels beside the table and scans the sheets. "They're all here," she says. "Ophelia's speech. The list of the French dead at Agincourt. The dog speech from *Macbeth*."

"And one more," I say, pointing at a fourth piece of paper.

Wheeler leans forward and reads out loud:

"This royal throne of kings, this sceptr'd isle,
This earth of majesty, this seat of Mars,
This other Eden, demi-paradise,
This fortress built by Nature for herself
Against infection and the hand of war,
This happy breed of men, this little world,
This precious stone set in the silver sea,
Which serves it in the office of a wall,
Or as a moat defensive to a house,
Against the envy of less happier lands,
This blessed plot, this earth, this realm, this England,
This nurse, this teeming womb of royal kings."

"I'm not sure what it means," I say, "but it sounds like another list, and it's got the lines he used with Ms. English."

Wheeler says, "It's about England."

"But it's not about Ms. English," I say. "It's about whoever he's going after next. I'd better get a hold of Daniel." I turn to Mrs. Woolley. "Can I use your phone?"

She nods. "There's one right beside you."

Daniel's wife, Alice, answers and says Daniel's at the college. I phone the college, and the receptionist for the English department tells me Daniel's in class. Get him out of class, I tell her, this is police business.

Five minutes later Daniel's on the line. "What is it?"

"Another clue. Another quote. You remember the note we found at the Karen English murder scene? The one about the happy breed of men?"

"It's from *Richard II*," Daniel says. "I looked it up. 'This happy breed of men, this little world. . . .' I forget the rest."

I finish it for him. "This precious stone set in the silver sea."

"Campbell, sometimes you amaze me."

"The point is," I tell him, "he used those two lines on Ms. English but he hasn't used the whole quote yet. Altogether, he sent four quotes – the three he's already used and this one – and a bunch of list poems to his sister. His mother intercepted them. I'm at her place now."

"But haven't we accounted for all the women editors he sent submissions to? Why would he go after women he hasn't even sent poems to? Women who haven't even rejected him yet."

"I don't know. Maybe the fact they're women's enough."

"Has any clue shown up for the Qureshi woman?"

"No, nothing. I don't know if it will. He seems to be breaking his pattern with this one."

"If, in fact, he did abduct her. Maybe she *did* run off with a boyfriend."

"Oh, he took her," I say. Then I use the same words Wheeler used as we were leaving Ms. Mulligan's apartment building. "Of that I am positive."

"Well, what do *you* think? I read through the whole speech and I couldn't come up with anything. All I know is John of Gaunt is worried about England's fate and he's listing her virtues. I figured it applied only to Karen English."

I shake my head. "I don't know what to think."

"What are the titles of the other magazines?"

I pull a folded piece of paper from my shirt pocket. I catch Mrs. Woolley watching me. I look across at Wheeler but she's not there; the sofa's empty. "*Barnes College Quarterly*," I read. "*Bugle. A Feminist View. Nun's Habit. T'Ain't. Yarn.*"

"Hmm. I'm going to look at the speech again. I'll get back to you post-haste. How much time do you think we've got?"

"We should be all right. I'll contact the six women right away. We may be ahead of the game this time. Phone me at the shop."

"Hey, weren't you supposed to fax me the new list poems?"

"Shit! I'll do it as soon as I get back." Then I stop, and there are ten seconds of silence on the line.

"Campbell?"

"Just thinking. This may be a little radical, but if we can figure out which of the women he's got his eye on, maybe we can ambush him."

"You mean like bait him and trap him?"

"That's exactly what I mean."

I hang up and dial Homicide. Gallagher puts me through to Bateman. I give him the six addresses and ask him to make sure each of the women is accounted for. "One of them is Woolley's next victim," I tell him. "Don't alarm them. Just make sure they're okay."

As I hang up the phone I see Wheeler's back from wherever she went. The john, probably. She sits back down on the sofa.

"Where's the bio file I asked you to put together on the female editors?" I ask her. "The one with the dates and places of birth and so on."

"It's right here," she says, and reaches for her attaché case.

"Let's have a look," I say. "Let's compare your information to the stuff in the Shakespearean quotation."

She spreads the seven sheets – one for each woman – across the coffee table.

"You can put that one away," I say, tapping Miriam Qureshi's, and Wheeler removes it.

Then as she slowly reads the speech again, I scan up and down the six remaining sheets. As she finishes, I shake my head. "I don't see anything."

"There it is," Mrs. Woolley says quietly, her right arm extended, the trembling forefinger pointing at one of the sheets. "'This nurse,'" she recites, "'this teeming womb of royal kings.'"

Wheeler picks up the sheet. "'Monique Mbale Farmer,'" she reads. "'Born in Ghana, eight, four, fifty-seven. Came to Canada at fifteen. Educated at the University of Toronto. Editor of *T'Ain't*. Currently employed at Mount Sinai Hospital in Toronto . . . ,'" Wheeler looks up from the paper to me, "'. . . as a registered nurse.'"

"In the maternity ward, I shouldn't be surprised," Mrs. Woolley says. Her arm is still stretched out in front of her.

"Thank you, Mrs. Woolley," I say, but she doesn't answer. She looks like she's just watched someone die.

In the car I say, "Wasn't she an outfit?"

Wheeler turns the key in the ignition and says, "Maybe so, but she's on our side."

"Soon's we get back, ask Bateman what he's found out. I'm going to call Daniel."

Then Wheeler says, "The daughter was there, you know."

"What?"

"While you were on the phone to Daniel, I excused myself to use the washroom. Mrs. Woolley was so engrossed in your phone call that I took the opportunity to snoop around a bit. I poked my head into both bedrooms. The first one was Mrs. Woolley's. The second was Mary's."

"She was in there?"

"She was sitting at her vanity, brushing her hair. She looked up at me in her mirror. 'Sorry,' I said. 'I'm looking for the bathroom.'

She just stared at me. Then she said, 'I know why you're here.' 'You do?' I said, and she said, 'He didn't do it, any of those awful things *she* says he did,' and she jerked her hairbrush in the general direction of the living room. Then I asked her if she'd seen her brother lately, but she just looked away and started brushing her hair again. You should have seen her. She looks like she hasn't been outside in years. Her skin's so pale it's almost blue. Her hair's long and black. She's beautiful. You'd never guess she's thirty-eight years old. She looks about nineteen. She looks like Rapunzel."

Back at Homicide, Staff Inspector Bateman tells us about the six remaining female editors: Ellen Frank has been spirited away by her rich hubby – their lawyer would only say she's out of the country; Elizabeth Arthur has moved on-campus at York University; Trudy Lemelin has taken temporary shelter with relatives in Oakville; the other three – Caley Kellogg, Megan Wong-Rutherford and Monique Mbale Farmer – have chosen to stay at home, and all three were successfully contacted by phone. Unmarked cruisers have been dispatched to all three locations pending the next move.

"Which is what?" Wheeler asks.

"Which is we pay Ms. Farmer a visit."

Half an hour later, Ms. Farmer is showing us around her studio loft on Queen Street West, Toronto's new "bohemian" district, according to Wheeler. The ceilings are twenty feet high and the living space itself – which is really only one huge room – seems as big as a hockey rink.

Ms. Farmer is small and businesslike. Her skin is very black, and the whites of her enormous brown eyes are yellow. She's wearing a gold floor-length dress made out of what looks like upholstery. On her head she has a little flat, brimless cap made out of the same gold material. She leads us into a sort of living-room area of the loft and asks us to sit down. Four black sofas create a square around a large oval carpet of red and black stripes. An old wooden chest serves as a coffee table in the middle. On it are a clean ashtray, copies of *Ebony* magazine, a sky-blue pack of Gauloise cigarettes, and CDs by King Sunny Ade, Ladysmith Black Mambazo, and somebody called Dudu Pukwana.

Once we're seated, I get straight to the point. "Ms. Farmer," I begin, "we have reason to believe the serial killer Lawrence Woolley, who is still at large, has you in mind for his next attack."

Ms. Farmer has her hands folded on her knees where she sits across from me. She looks down for a moment, then back up. "Continue."

"With your co-operation, Ms. Farmer, we're confident we can apprehend him . . . here."

"Here?" she says, her eyebrows lifting. "I don't think so." Her voice is high, sort of singsong. East Indian almost.

"We have to get him, Ms. Farmer. To do so, we have to go where we know he'll be. And he's going to be here. Very soon."

She stares off at the walls of her living room, at the posters of black men with their fists raised, at the carved masks. "What about me? Where will I go?"

Wheeler clears her throat. "A hotel, with police protection. Or," and she clears her throat again, "or here."

"Here? Why would I be here?"

"To help us catch him," Wheeler says. "Let me ask you a question. Is it possible Lawrence Woolley knows what you look like or sound like?"

"It's more than possible. My photo appears beside the editorial I write for each issue of *T'Ain't*. As well," and here she pauses, "I have spoken to this man."

"What?" I ask. "When?"

"He phoned me in September. He wanted to send me some of his poems."

"What did you tell him?"

"I said no. I told him I only publish the work of women of African origin."

"How did he take that piece of news?"

"He called me names."

"Do you remember what he called you?"

"Oh yes," and she smiles as if at a private joke. "I never forget what people call me. He said I was a castrating bitch. He added that I would never castrate him."

"Anything else?" I ask. Wheeler is scribbling like crazy on her notepad.

She pauses. "Yes. He asked me if I enjoy fucking white men, because he certainly enjoys fucking black women. Then I hung up."

"Did you report this call?" I ask her.

Ms. Farmer stiffens. "No. And don't try to suggest that if I had, those other women would still be alive, because I couldn't have identified him even if I'd wanted to. He never told me his name. It was only when one of your colleagues phoned and asked if I'd received any submissions of list poems that I remembered the phone call. The caller had mentioned list poems. I remember thinking – after the phone call in September – not only is this man an obscene crackpot, but he thinks you can make poems out of lists. How could a list be poetical?"

"But why," I ask, "didn't you mention this phone call to our colleague?"

She narrows her eyes at me. "I didn't think about it till afterwards."

"Well, why didn't you phone back afterwards when you *did* think about it?"

She sighs heavily. "Because I didn't want to get involved, that's why. I'm easy prey, Detective. I'm a woman. I'm five feet tall. I weigh ninety pounds. You have no idea what it's like. Look at you. How big are you? Three hundred pounds? You've probably never been physically afraid in your life."

She takes a breath and probably has more to say, but Wheeler jumps in. "Ms. Farmer, please. If Lawrence Woolley knows what you look like and what you sound like, and since we have no small black female officers who could stand in for you or duplicate your voice or speech, would you consider acting as . . . well, as the bait? We need you in case he phones or knocks at the door. You'll be fully protected – in here," she waves her arm to indicate the loft, "and outside."

"This is not my problem," Ms. Farmer says angrily. "Why should I do your job –?"

"He's killed three women."

"I have no control over –"

"And I might as well tell you, he's abducted a fourth. There's a good chance he's torturing her. We can't find her. We don't even –"

"Who? I haven't heard anything about an abduction!"

"Miriam Qureshi. She's the editor –"

Ms. Farmer stands up. "Miriam?"

Wheeler stops. She waits a moment and then says quietly, "We need your help, Ms. Farmer, to catch this monster."

Ms. Farmer sits down again. Suddenly, all the resistance is gone. She has the grim look of a soldier about to go over the top. "Tell me what you want me to do," she says.

CHAPTER 15

Tuesday, October 20

AS IF ON CUE, the fourth quotation appears on my desk this morning. Because it's addressed to me, and because it's in a small package about the size of a deck of cards, Staff Inspector Bateman insists the bomb boys take a look before I do. While we're waiting, I get Big Urmson to fax the sheaf of list poems to Daniel at Seneca College, which I was supposed to do yesterday. As well, the receipt that came with the package tells us it was sent from Hamilton, Ontario, forty miles west of Toronto, via courier. Which makes me think about all the other clues we've received so far and the way they were delivered. So, while we're waiting, me and Wheeler make a list of our own:

CLUE #	VICTIM & TYPE OF CLUE	MEANS OF DELIVERY
1.	Joanne Stevenson; dog list (*Macbeth*)	inside tennis ball taken from victim's mouth (Oct. 6)

2.	Pansy Jones; flower list (*Hamlet*)	Federal Express to Homicide (Oct. 12)
3.	Pansy Jones; note from C. Delabreth	crumpled up inside victim's hand (Oct. 12)
4.	Pansy Jones; personal phone message to CY	left on victim's phone-message recorder (Oct. 12)
5.	Karen English; dead soldier list (*Henry V*)	regular postal service to CY at Homicide (Oct. 15)
6.	Karen English; "This happy breed of men . . ." (*Richard II*)	taped to victim's body (Oct. 15)
7.	Karen English; Twinings English Breakfast tea bag	in victim's mouth (Oct. 15)

An hour later, an explosives expert named Hutchison arrives. He X-rays the package, and although there's a small amount of metal in it – in the shape of a finger ring, Hutchison says – there's no explosive device. We gather round my desk – by now the whole team has assembled: me, Wheeler, Bateman, Trick, Barkas, Estabrooks, Big Urmson – and watch as Hutchison opens the package with an X-Acto knife. What he finds inside is a tube of paper with printing on it and, it would seem, something inside the tube. Something cigar-shaped, only smaller. As he slowly unrolls it, Wheeler leans in and turns her head sideways. I watch her squinting and her lips moving. Without lifting up her head, she says, "It's the 'teeming womb of royal kings' speech." Hutchison keeps slowly unrolling the paper. Nobody's saying anything. All I can hear is Big Urmson's breathing behind me. He sounds like one of those things you squeeze air into a fire in your fireplace with. Hutchison gets to the last roll and all of a sudden there's a human finger, complete with signet ring, lying on my desk.

"Christ," Estabrooks says, stepping back.

Bateman shouts, "Gallagher, get Forensics up here!"

Trick says, "Brown-skinned."

Wheeler, still leaning close, studies the ring. "An onyx cameo," she says, "of a woman's face."

"Phone Ms. Mulligan," I tell her. "Describe the ring. Let me know what she says."

I tell Big Urmson to get me an evidence bag. While he's off doing that, I finish the list:

8.	Miriam Qureshi; severed finger	United Parcel Service (UPS) to CY at Homicide (Oct. 20)
9.	Monique Mbale Farmer – potential victim; England list; "teeming womb" (*Richard II*)	United Parcel Service (UPS) to CY at Homicide (Oct. 20)

Then she's back. Her face looks grey. "It's definitely Miriam's finger. Sandra gave her the ring."

"What else did she say?"

"She still thinks it's the California boyfriend. She thinks the finger is a message to her because Sappho's face is on the cameo."

"Who the hell's Sappho?"

"An ancient Greek poetess. She symbolizes lesbianism. Sandra told me."

I look at Wheeler. "Great. Something new every day. Now help me out here: did we or did we not establish the boyfriend actually *is* in California?"

"Yes. Urmson located him yesterday, in Fresno. But Sandra thinks he's hired somebody, a 'hitperson,' she called him, to abduct Miriam."

I scratch behind my ear. "And why would a hitperson hired by Miriam's boyfriend cut Miriam's finger off?"

"I mentioned that to Sandra."

"And what did Sandra say?"

"She said there must be a reason. She said she'd think about it and get back to me."

"Well, that's good to know," I say. "That's a comfort, as my old man used to say when the barman delivered his next pint. Is surveillance in place at Ms. Farmer's?"

"Yes. We're as ready as we'll ever be."

"Good," I say. "What do you say we bring this bastard down?"

The phone call comes about noon. Lawrence Woolley must think it'll take us forever to figure out the nurse clue, but we're ahead of him for once. Me and Wheeler are with Ms. Farmer when the phone rings. Estabrooks, equipped with a bucket of paint, a roller and tray, and dressed in stained painter pants and one of those paper Colour Your World hats, is redecorating the hall outside the loft. Barkas, done up as a wino in an old ski jacket, sweatpants, and laceless oxfords, is picking through garbage outside on the street. Trick is in an unmarked cruiser thirty yards down the block in a shady spot under a tree. He's got a radio receiver in his hand. Another hundred yards away Big Urmson and Silliphant and the black guy with the red hair from 52 are sitting in a cube van that says *FLOWERS BY ERWIN* on the side. Around the corner is a tracer truck.

When the phone rings, me and Wheeler and Ms. Farmer, who's wearing the gold upholstery dress again, all jump.

"Be calm," I say to Ms. Farmer as she reaches for the phone. "Be very, very calm."

She looks at me, terrified. Then she takes a deep breath, and at the end of the third ring she picks it up. "Hello," she says. "Yes, this is she. Mr. Langley? Montano Press? No, I'm not familiar with it, but go ahead." She listens for a moment. "A cost-reduction scheme. Well, naturally, I'm interested in ways to reduce costs. Certainly. Yes, I would. How about later this afternoon? I work out of my home, so you could drop by here. No? Tomorrow?" She looks at me. I nod. "About two? At the Greek Garden on Danforth. Yes, I know it. That's fine. Right, thank you for calling. I'll see you then. Tomorrow, about two, yes. Thank you. Goodbye."

She hangs up the phone and falls back into the sofa. "I remember the voice," she says to no one in particular.

"Good work," I say. "Great work."

"I'm holding," Wheeler says to someone on her radio.

"Tracer truck?" I ask.

She nods. "They need a minute or two."

Ms. Farmer sits up and looks at me. "But why tomorrow?"

"I don't know. But we'll be there to meet him." I look at Wheeler, who's watching me as she waits, radio to her ear. I hear a pop outside, like a car backfiring, then a horn start up.

Wheeler says carefully, "A booth on Queen West near Soho." She looks at me. "That's nearby."

Something's wrong. I can feel it in my arms, like a weakness. I pull my radio out of my jacket pocket. "Estabrooks, you there?"

"You bet, Sarge. I've got most of this wall done. You want me to start on –?"

I hit Barkas's channel. "Barkas?" I can hear garbage pails being moved around and bottles clinking and the scuffle of newspapers on the ground.

"I'm here," Barkas says. "Just neatening up. What's going on?"

"Stay where you are." I hit Trick's channel. "Trick, something's not right. What do you see from where you are?"

But he doesn't answer. All I can hear is the solid blare of a car horn.

"Wheeler, stay here! And get an ambulance!" Then I'm across the floor of the loft and out the door and down the hall past Estabrooks, down two flights of stairs, Estabrooks's running footsteps behind me, out the door onto Queen, Estabrooks shouting "Barkas!" and the three of us racing down the middle of the street through trucks and streetcars, people turning to look from the sidewalks as we charge, guns drawn, towards the sound of the car horn and into the crowd that's gathered around Trick's cruiser, Estabrooks and Barkas shouting, "Police! Back off! Move back!" and pushing people away – an old man in an alpine hat, a skinny kid in a muscle shirt, a half-black kid in a Pistons jacket – until I'm up to his window and there's a hole the size of a dime through the glass and another one in the side of his neck, red blood on his black skin like a splash of paint, his forehead resting on the steering wheel, the one eye I can see open and staring, his jaw working.

I pull at the door handle.

"It's locked!" a voice shouts over the sound of the horn. "All the doors are locked. We tried to get him out."

Another voice, speedy, shivering – the kid in the muscle shirt: "He only got the one shot off. He fuckin' flew. Tall fucker. We was standin' right over there, wasn't we, Stevie?"

I smash the window with the butt of my Glock. The glass crystallizes and turns white, and I punch it in. I reach in and unlock the door and open it. "Trick!" I shout. But he doesn't react. I lean in and see a long spatter of blood across the passenger seat and up the far door. I lift him off the horn and the noise suddenly stops and little chunks of glass fall off him. I lean him back against the headrest. His left eye swivels and looks at me. His lips move. "What is it?" I say. I put my ear close to his mouth, but I can't make out what he's saying.

Behind me I can hear people talking excitedly. I can hear Barkas and Estabrooks telling them to back off. I can hear someone laughing. I wonder if it's him, if he's right behind me in the crowd, but I don't take my eyes off Trick to look around. I don't take my eyes off him for a second. And I'm still looking at him, gunning my eyes into his, when the ambulance arrives a few minutes later.

I pace up and down the waiting room for an hour before a tiny doctor in a green shower cap sticks his head through the door and says, "Is someone here about the police officer?" and the six or eight people sitting in plastic chairs glance up from their magazines and look from him to me as I step forward and say, "Yeah, me."

I follow him out to the hall, and he leads me down near a water fountain where nobody is. He turns and looks up at me and says, "May I see your identification, please?"

I produce my badge. "Detective Sergeant Young, Homicide. I'm Detective Trick's senior officer."

The doctor nods. "I'm Dr. Herman." He pauses and takes a breath. "The prognosis, I'm afraid, isn't very good at this point. The bullet entered the left side of his neck and exited the right, but struck the neck spine on its way. Although he's stable and out of danger, there may be permanent damage."

"You mean he might be paralysed."

"Yes."

"How bad? From the neck down?"

"We won't know until the internal swelling diminishes and the wound heals enough so that we can run some tests."

"How long will that take?"

"I can't be sure, but – what's today, Tuesday? – probably Saturday or Sunday."

"Can I talk to him?"

Dr. Herman shakes his head. "He's sedated. Maybe tomorrow."

"Can I see him at least?"

"I'm sorry." He gives me a small sad smile, reaches up and pats my arm, then turns and hurries away. He leaves me standing there huge and useless beside the water fountain.

I walk outside to the parking lot and unlock the front door of the Volare. Inside, I stick the key in the ignition, but I don't start the car. I feel weird, shaky. I put my hands on the steering wheel and take a deep breath, but all of a sudden I'm bawling like a baby. "My poor friend," I say through my sobs, and I keep saying it. "My poor friend."

It lasts about five minutes. I can't remember the last time I cried like this. Sometimes a few tears if someone dies in a movie. But not like this. I thought I was okay. It was rough seeing him like that in the cruiser, and him trying to talk, but I thought I was okay. I thought I'd handled it. I've seen a lot worse. I guess it was because it was Trick. It just snuck up on me. It's like when you're lying in bed and your stomach's upset, and you wonder if you're going to puke, then all of a sudden you *know* you're going to puke, and you make tracks for the john. It was like that, only different.

There's some Subway napkins on the passenger seat. I use them to blow my nose and clean myself up.

I can hardly drive, but the Volare knows the way, and before I know it I'm pulling into McCully's.

"She's not in till four," Dexter tells me when I ask where Jessy is. He gives me a double Jack. I smoke a cigarette.

When I phone in, my hands are still shaking so much I drop the quarter. "How'd he know?" I ask Bateman. "How'd the fucker know?"

"Wheeler just came in. Ask her."

Wheeler comes on. "How's Trick?"

"Not so good. How'd he know, Wheeler?"

"How'd who know what? Where are you?"

"How'd the fucker know? Just answer me that."

"Are you talking about Woolley?"

"*Who the fuck do you think I'm talking about?*"

"Take it easy! I'm not the enemy. It was his mother. She phoned an hour ago. I just came back from her apartment."

"His mother?"

"She feels terrible . . ."

"For fucksake, Wheeler!"

"She told her daughter we were going to ambush Lawrence. When we were in her apartment she overheard your conversation on the phone – you were talking to Daniel, right? – and she told Mary."

I study the messages people have scratched into the wall in front of me. EAT SHIT, says one. FUCK YOU, says another. "And Mary warned him."

"She must have."

"How?"

"I don't know. Neither does Mrs. Woolley. But Mary went missing sometime last night. When Mrs. Woolley got up this morning she found a note from Mary saying she'd left home. She waited awhile hoping she'd hear something, but she finally gave up and phoned in a missing-person report about one-thirty. You were at the hospital, I guess."

"Why did she tell her?"

"I don't know. She's vindictive. She knows Mary loves her brother. Maybe she wanted to hurt her."

I think for a few seconds. "Where'd Woolley get a gun? He's never used a gun before."

"He's never done a lot of things before, but he's doing them now."

Then I see Joanne Stevenson's face again – low-angle camera from inside the toilet bowl, looking up at her swollen green face, eyes open and empty, hair floating and shifting slightly in whatever current can be found in a toilet bowl. Then Trick's face appears – his forehead against the steering wheel, one eye staring, his jaw convulsing like a pike's in the bottom of a boat.

Wheeler says, "That reporter's been trying to get in touch with you. Andy Bartle? Staff Inspector Bateman talked to him, but he phoned right back, so I talked to him. He said he wanted to talk to you. He said he knows you and Trick are close, that he wanted to get your reaction. I told him you were unavailable for comment. He said the phones over at *The Standard* were ringing off their hooks, concerned citizens worried about the wounded officer. Wondering if any headway's been made. Wondering when the killer will be caught. That sort of thing." She stops. "Are you still there?"

"Yeah, I'm still here. Why are you telling me this?"

She's quiet for a few seconds. "Oh, I'm so tired."

I don't say anything.

"Staff Inspector Bateman wants you to come in. Where are you?"

I hang up the phone and walk back to the bar. I tap the polished wood beside my empty shot glass, and Dexter pours me another double. I knock it back.

"Big game tonight," Dexter says. "Can I expect you and Brother Trick?"

He begins sliding stemmed glasses, clean from the dishwasher, into racks above the bar. Upside down.

I find my jacket and walk towards the door.

"Sarge?" says Dexter.

Reg whines for a long time. Finally, she just pisses on the carpet.

I'm staring at the TV. I've got the sound off. There's a picture of a diamond ring on the screen. Earlier, it was a child's doll. In the corner they show you the price and tell you how many of each item are still available. There's only eleven rings left. A few minutes ago there were twenty-five.

The phone has been ringing constantly. I listen to my taped voice tell whoever it is I'm out and to leave a message, and then I listen to what they say. Jessy, from McCully's. "Daniel told us what happened. It's awful. Poor Trick. Is there anything I can do? Want me to come over?"

Daniel himself. "Lynn Wheeler phoned me looking for you. She told me about Trick. We're all devastated. I phoned the hospital, they told me to check back in the morning. I read the poems. More on that later. Where are you? I'm down here watching the game. I figured you'd be here. I'll wait for you. It's one–all after six. Carter homered in the fourth. Give me a call, or if you don't make it I'll call you in the morning and we can go check on Trick together."

Staff Inspector Bateman. "Look, Camp, I know he's your best friend, but just take it easy. Don't knock any lockers around or do anything crazy. Please. I need you here tomorrow. I'll give you the weekend if you want it."

Somebody knocks on the door. Reg barks her brains out. The knocking keeps up, but I ignore it. After a while it stops.

Then two more phone calls.

Wheeler. "I'm worried about you. Give me a call at home. It's about eleven-fifteen. Call any time."

Lawrence Woolley. "Good evening, Detective Sergeant. How are you? And how is Mistah Trick? Fine, I hope. Miriam would like to say hello, but she's tied up at the moment. Tongue-tied, too, if you take my meaning. She wanted to dial herself, but the poor girl's running out of fingers. Imagine misplacing one's digits. So careless. So, tit for tat, eh, Detective Sergeant? Much like chess: you protect Monique Zimbabwe Farmer; I take your rook, the lyrically named Arthur Trick. One nigger for another, I guess. But seriously, I'm disappointed, Detective Sergeant. And irritated, too. I wanted the little, black, ball-busting bitch as a bookend for Miriam here. But hey, there's other fish in the sea, and as a matter of fact, I already have someone in mind."

CHAPTER 16

Wednesday, October 21

"WE KNOW YOU'RE IN there," Daniel says, "and we think it's a pretty low trick you're playing – no pun intended – just to get a few days off work."

But there's no reaction. Trick lies on his back with his eyes closed. His right arm is bent at the elbow with his fist clenched in the air, like he's making a muscle. He has a tube up each nostril, bandages on both sides of his neck, and another hole – doctor-made – just below his Adam's apple. A metal tube and respirator are attached there like a Texas string-tie. We can hear the hollow rasping of his breathing.

"The Jays won last night," Daniel says. "Three–two. Gruber homered in the eighth and Candy singled in the ninth to win it. We're up two games to one."

I'm holding Trick's left hand in my right. It's warm and dry, but there's no response when I squeeze.

When Dr. Herman came in earlier he explained that even though Trick was stable, he'd become semi-comatose. Most likely he'll come out of it – gradually, not suddenly like in the movies – but there's also a slim chance he'll go the other way and lapse into a full coma, which he might never recover from. As if to argue against what Dr. Herman was saying, Trick's eyelids fluttered half-open. Daniel said, "Doctor!" But Dr. Herman shook his head and said, "Watch." Trick's left eye was staring way to the left and the right eye way to the right, as if gravity was dragging them down either side of his head. Neither eye was focused. He wasn't seeing anything.

I remembered a car accident I saw years ago at Bloor and Parliament – a big old station wagon ploughed into a Volkswagen with two men in it. The whole thing happened in front of us; Tanya was beside me and Debi was in the back seat, about eight or nine years old. I pulled over to see if there was anything I could do. Tanya said, "It's not like it's a *bad* accident. I wish you wouldn't get involved. Why can't we just go home?" The woman who had been driving the station wagon was sitting on the sidewalk crying. Some kid in a Chicago Cubs ballcap – blue with a red C – was directing traffic. The two men were sitting stunned in the front seats of the Volkswagen. There was a deep gouge in the passenger's right hand with a bright blob of blood balanced on it like a cherry. A small blue teddy bear sat on his lap – facing forward, like the two men – which only later I understood had broken loose from the rearview mirror. The windshield was cobwebbed in front of the driver, and when I went around to his side and spoke to him, he turned to face me, and his eyes were splayed – one left, one right – just like Trick's.

Daniel asked the doctor about Trick's arm.

"Flexor tension," he said. "The damaged part of his brain has sent a message to his arm to flex the biceps, and it's stuck like that. Here, feel."

Daniel stepped forward and squeezed Trick's biceps. Then I did. It was hard as rock.

"The other problem," Dr. Herman said, "is that the swelling caused by the wound is still preventing us from determining the extent of the spinal-cord damage. It will be a few days yet before we know anything definite."

"Can we do anything?" Daniel asked.

"Yes," said Dr. Herman, "you can visit, talk to him, hold his hand. Maybe he can hear you. Maybe he can feel your hand. I don't know. Maybe you'll be here to comfort him when he wakes up. *If* he wakes up. Remember, don't expect him to just suddenly snap out of it. That's not the way it happens. If it happens at all, and there are no guarantees about things like this, it'll be slow, like he's coming out of a deep sleep."

"It's Key against Glavine tonight," Daniel says to Trick. "Classic. Maybe we can get a TV in here, and Campbell and I can watch the game with you." He looks at me and raises his eyebrows to ask if this sounds good to me. I nod.

As we're walking down the hall towards the elevators, Daniel says, "I read the poems you sent me."

"And?"

"And they're interesting all right. The names of Indians from Custer's Last Stand. Whitey Ford's pitching record. Card games and fireworks." He pauses. "But what intrigues me is that even though he has a poet's eye and a poet's fussiness – the way he orders the words, for example – he has no voice of his own. He has nothing to say."

"Don't a lot of poets write because they're angry with the world?" I ask.

"I suppose."

"Well, he's angry with the world. Why doesn't he write about that instead of just making lists. Or instead of killing people?"

Daniel shakes his head. "I don't know. Maybe he will."

In the parking lot he says, "We were worried about you last night. At McCully's."

"Who's 'we'?"

"Me, Dexter. Jessy asked after you. Where were you?"

"At home."

"I thought so. Why didn't you answer the door when I knocked?"

I think about it for a moment. "It was nothing personal. I didn't want to see anybody."

"Are you okay now?"

"I'm fine."

"You don't seem fine. You seem sort of out of it."

I look at him. "I'm fine, Daniel."

"Will I see you at the hospital tonight? Say around eight? Later we could go back to McCully's. Catch the rest of the game. Sound like a plan?"

Again, I nod.

Debi's not in the stable or the tack room when I phone the track, but I get a hold of Shorty Rogers, and after a minute or two of bull-shit, I ask him to write down a message and pass it along to Debi: *Your Uncle Artie is in intensive care at Toronto East General. Please visit him. He's going to be all right, but right now he's unconscious so hold his hand and talk to him. I'll see you Sunday. Love, Daddy.*

Then I phone Dr. Manning in Penetanguishene. I have to hold for at least ten minutes, but that's okay, I'm in no hurry.

When he finally comes on, I say, "Doctor, it's Detective Sergeant Campbell Young."

"Ah yes, you were the one who was interested in Larry Woolley, weren't you? Nice to hear from you again. How goes the investigation?"

"He's killed another woman since I last spoke to you, Doctor. That makes three. And he's abducted a fourth. If she's not dead yet, she will be soon. And he's critically injured a cop. Happens the cop's a friend of mine. Are you aware of any of this?"

Dr. Manning pauses. It sounds like he's lighting one of his pipes.

"Actually no, Detective Sergeant. We're fortunate here at Poplar Bluff in that we're insulated from the news of the world. It takes a little while to reach us. But I'm sorry to hear all of this."

"Remember sending me copies of those pieces of writing Woolley wrote for you?"

"Yes, of course."

"Did you send me *all* of them?"

"All the pieces he wrote?" There's a short silence. "No, no, as I recall, I sent you just those pieces I considered relevant."

"Which ones did you consider *un*relevant?"

Dr. Manning chuckles. Then he says, "I'm not sure. I'd have to check."

"Did he ever write one about going duck hunting with you?"

He stops chuckling. "No. I would remember if he had. Why?"

"Why? Because he *shot* my friend, that's why. I just wondered if you were the one that taught him how to use a gun."

Dr. Manning puffs away on his pipe.

"Well, were you?"

"I won't answer that. What are my rights here?"

"One more question, Doctor. Do you remember one of his pieces called 'Hard Times'?"

"No, I can't say that I do. There were so many –"

"Let me refresh your memory. He talks about some woman named Gloria that lives in B.C. She's always sending him stuff – socks, dirty pictures of herself."

"Yes, I remember now. What about her?"

"Well, she told him in one of her letters that she had needs, but she'd never had the guts to satisfy them."

"Did she say what kind of needs?"

"No, she didn't, but I'll bet they weren't very nice ones."

"What are you getting at? I have rounds to make."

"What I'm getting at, you asshole, you cocksucker, is that Woolley finished off the piece by saying he had needs, too, and if he ever got out – of Poplar Bluff, he meant – he'd be sure to satisfy them."

"And I told *you*," Dr. Manning says, his voice shaking, "that we kept Larry here as long as we could – he served his entire sentence. There was nothing we could do."

"My best friend's been shot, you piece of shit. You fucking asshole. He's paralysed. He's in a coma. Three women are dead. Another one's missing. *Larry* is responsible for this. He did all of it. So smoke your fucking pipe and make your fucking rounds!"

I'm sitting in a bar called Buster's. East end of the city where nobody knows me. There's a TV right above me, and I watched enough of the game to know Jimmy Key went seven and change, Duane Ward set it up for Henke, and it was a done deal. 2–1 Jays. Three games to one. Chokehold.

But I don't seem to care.

I don't seem to care about anything. The phone call to Dr. Manning messed me up. It iced me. I drove home and got Reg and put her in the car and started driving. We ended up here.

I thought about phoning in and telling Gallagher to let Bateman know I was taking the rest of the day off, but I didn't do it. I didn't even leave a message for Daniel that I wouldn't be able to meet him at the hospital. I wasn't thinking ahead. I didn't know what my plans were.

Sherie, the barmaid – not Sherry or Cherie, as she explained to me earlier in the evening when we were still friends – is about to kick me out. I ran out of money hours ago. Remember buying drinks for a couple of Americans – one of them a guy with glasses and a Pawtucket ballcap who kept saying, "You such nice people up here."

Talked to Sherie for a while. Told her I used to be a pulling guard with the Saskatchewan Roughriders. Trying to impress her, I guess. I don't know if she bought it. She just raised her eyebrows and said, "Oh really? That's neat. What's a pulling guard?" She asked me what I do now. Told her I was a professor of English literature, specializing in Shakespearean studies. She didn't buy that one, I know that. Her mouth sort of twisted at one end, like she was telling me she wasn't born yesterday. "You don't believe me?" I said. "Listen, I'll prove it." And I started in on the dog list from *Macbeth*. I'd memorized it for Reg. Thought it might add a little class to our lonely conversations in the kitchenette. Anyway, I made it as far as "the valu'd file distinguishes the swift, the slow, the subtle . . ." and then the wheels fell off. For the life of me I couldn't remember what came next. And Sherie, who was only half-listening, what with people asking her for drinks and the general noise and clamour, nodded at me, no expression on her face, and turned away.

No hope there. Nobody to blame but myself. Big stupid jerk like me trying to impersonate a Shakespearean scholar. What a joke. My weakness for barmaids makes me do stupid things. It undoes me, as some character in *Macbeth* might say. I'm undone by barmaids. They undo me. I wouldn't mind undoing Sherie. Not that I was really hitting on her. I guess I was, at least she seemed to think so, so maybe I was, but it's not like I planned it. It just happened. I guess the other night with Jessy gave me a taste of what I'd been missing. It ended a long dry spell, but it just made me thirstier. This is what you call a metaphor. As Trick would say, Don't try to fool me on the subject of metaphors. But this Sherie's nice. Straight black hair. Like Cher in – what was it? – *Moonstruck*? Or was it *Mermaids*? Tough, no-nonsense kind of girl. The kind who can look after herself. The kind I like. She could take me home, no problem. I could lie on my back on her sofa, my head in her lap. Maybe she'd have some smoke, like Jessy did. Maybe she'd have some Hip. Maybe she'd stroke my forehead. What is it, big guy? she'd say. Why the long face? I'd tell her about Trick. I'd cry like a baby. Even if she offered to fuck me, I probably wouldn't want to, or I'd lose interest halfway through. Trick would be pissed off. Thanks to me, he'd say, you're about to get some pussy, and you turn it down. You say, Sorry, miss, but I'm too upset? If I could get out of this bed, I'd kick your sorry ass. Now go get some, he'd say. For me.

But now she wants me gone. She was nice to me earlier. Gave me a couple on the house after I ran out of money. But now she's getting antsy. Definitely wants me gone. Looking at me, then over at the clock. What time is it, anyway? I try to focus. I can see the clock okay, but I can't make out what time it is.

With the toe of my shoe I can feel Reg asleep under my stool. I lower my head onto my arms on the bar.

"Come on, mister," I hear Sherie say, "it's closing time." An hour ago she was calling me Camp.

I raise my head and look around at the blurred blond wood, the mirrors. I'm the only one left. "I don't think I should drive," I say.

"Sleep in your car," she says. "I'm sure it won't be the first time. And take that ugly fucking excuse of a dog with you."

CHAPTER 17

Thursday, October 22

REG SLOBBERING ON my face wakes me in Buster's parking lot about five-thirty this morning. I'm on my back in the back seat of the Volare with my knees buckled and the soles of my feet up against the window. I'm staring up at the beige ceiling material hanging down in shreds towards me, like ribbons of flesh. Half-frozen, I manage to sit up, and out of nowhere – like a big, looping curveball – my hangover appears. My mouth is dry and tastes like foot odour. I'm thirsty as hell. What I need is a couple of cold 7-Ups. Lots of ice.

I open the door and climb out, stagger like an old stiff-jointed drunk around behind the building, and take a long steaming piss beside a dumpster. Then Reg gets out of the car and waddles over to where I'm standing. I'm shivering like a bastard while she squats and pisses. Then we go back to the car. She hops up onto the back seat, I slam her door, climb in the front, start the engine, crank the heater full-blast, and start driving, and before I know it, I'm back in Trick's room at Toronto East General, holding his left hand in my right, and telling him about the Jays' big win in game four.

A tiny Filipina nurse comes in and asks me if I'm Detective Sergeant Campbell Young. No, I consider telling her, I'm a pulling guard, I'm a professor, a man of many talents. When I finally say yes, she tells me I'm to call my desk sergeant immediately.

I look back down at Trick, who hasn't changed, who hasn't improved, whose eyes are still half-mast and wonky. "How long will he be like this?"

"I don't know, sir," she says.

"There's snot in his mustache and white stuff in the corners of his mouth."

"I'll wash his face," the nurse says. "You'd better make that phone call. It sounded urgent."

"How long's his arm going to be flexed like this?"

"I don't know. If you want to speak to a doctor –"

"And would you please arrange to get a TV in here."

"But, sir, he's comatose, he can't –"

"The doctor said we should talk to him when we visit. While we're not here, the TV can do the talking."

"All right."

"And a telephone."

"But he can't –"

"When he wakes up, when he comes out of it, I want him to be able to call me."

"All right," she says again.

She steps over to the bedside table and pulls a Kleenex from the box. She hands it to me. I wipe my eyes. I blow my nose with it, too. A loud honking noise. Sometimes I can play the first few notes of "Basin Street Blues" when I'm blowing my nose. Trick's heard me do it a thousand times. *Buuuuuuuh . . . bum-bee-bum bum bum-bum.*

I turn towards the little nurse. "I'll pay for everything."

"Fine, sir. A TV and a phone."

I walk out of Trick's room and down the hall. I fish a quarter out of my pocket and find a pay phone and dial Homicide. Gallagher puts me through to Bateman.

"Camp! Where the hell have you been?"

"I went for a drive."

"A drive? Where?"

"It doesn't matter. Not far enough."

"Get your ass in here. We've got a situation. There's been a development. Where the hell are you?"

"At the hospital. What situation?"

"Mary Woolley. She ran away, right? Well, she came home. She'd been with her brother. He gave her some new poems and told her to bring them to us. To make sure *you* saw them. She dropped them off on her way back to her mother's."

"Why does he want me to see them?"

"Well, he seems to have it in for you."

"So why would a bunch of list poems –?"

"These aren't list poems, these are different."

This stops me. "How are they different?"

"Camp, brace yourself, but I think Wheeler's in trouble."

"Wheeler? What do you mean? Where is she?"

"That's just it. She's missing. When you didn't come back in yesterday afternoon, she went off on her own, chasing down a lead."

"What lead?"

"Some girl – a young woman, really, I guess – phoned in a tip, so Wheeler headed off to follow it up. She phoned in late last night, but I didn't get the message till this morning. She phoned from a hotel in Sutton."

"Sutton? What the hell was she doing in Sutton?"

"I don't know, but I'm worried. She was supposed to be in at eight this morning. She still hasn't shown up."

"I'll be right there. But what do these poems have to do with Wheeler?"

"That's just it. One of them's about her."

"What do you mean *about* her?"

"You'll see when you read it. I hate to say this, Camp, and I hope to hell I'm wrong, but I think the bastard's got her."

"Woolley's got Wheeler?"

"I don't know what else to think."

Before I leave the hospital I phone Daniel's receptionist at Seneca College. He's not in till this afternoon, she tells me. I phone his home. Alice answers. He's out looking at golf clubs, she says. There's a sale. She thinks he'll go straight to the college. If you hear from him, I tell her, tell him it's an emergency, to call Homicide right away, or better yet to come straight down if he can, I need his help. I hang up and phone Daniel's receptionist back and tell her the same thing.

Then I phone the Woolley residence. Mrs. Woolley answers. I ask to speak to Mary. Mrs. Woolley says she's not home. So I get tough. If you don't let me talk to her, Mrs. Woolley, I say, other girls are going to die, and not only will you be *morally* responsible for letting it happen, you'll be *criminally* responsible, and you'll go to prison, Mrs. Woolley, you'll do time, and then she goes and gets her daughter.

Mary is the key, the link, and this is the first time I've spoken to her.

"Yes?"

"Mary, this is Detective Sergeant Young of the Toronto Police Service. I need to ask you a few questions."

"Go ahead." There's a tone to her voice that worries me. She sounds beaten. Numb, almost.

"I understand your brother asked you to drop off some poems for me."

"That's right."

"Did you read them first yourself?"

She pauses. "He told me not to, but I did. I was the only person he could trust, and he didn't think I would disobey him. But I had to see for myself."

"See what, Mary?"

"I had to see whether they might prove anything . . . one way or the other."

"And did they?"

Her voice has been soft throughout, but now it's barely a whisper. "Yes. He's the killer."

I give her a moment, then I say, "Why did he contact you, Mary? Why didn't he just mail them in?"

"There was no time. He's going to attack another woman very soon, a policewoman, I think. And he needed money. He had me forge my mother's signature on a blank cheque. I took out two thousand dollars."

"Did you take it to him?"

"Yes."

"Where?"

"He told me to meet him at the Henry Moore sculpture in front of City Hall."

"When was this?"

She thinks for a moment. "Monday."

"What time Monday?"

"In the evening."

"Can you be more specific?"

"I don't know. I can't remember. Suppertime, I guess."

"How was he dressed? Was he wearing a disguise?"

At first she doesn't answer.

"Mary?"

"He was wearing cycling shorts. A yellow-and-black striped jersey. A black helmet. Like a courier. He had a Walkman and sunglasses. He rode up to me on a bicycle. I didn't recognize him at first, until he took the glasses off. He scared me."

"How much time did you spend with him?"

"Two or three minutes. I gave him the money. He gave me the envelope with the poems in it. He said he'd been tempted to deliver them himself, right to police headquarters, but he decided to let me do it when I brought the money down. He said he thought it would make a better impression if I brought the poems in. But don't look at them, he said. They're for Campbell Young's eyes only. Then I told him I'd left home. I asked him to let me stay with him. He laughed at me and said I wouldn't want to go where he was going."

"What did he mean?"

"I'm not sure, but maybe he thinks he's running out of time."

"Is that why he needed the money? To get away?"

"I don't think so. He said he had to buy some equipment. 'To record the final chapter,' he said."

"That's what he said, 'the final chapter'?"

"Those were his exact words."

"How did he contact you in the first place?"

"He phoned me here. While Mother was at work."

"But your phone's bugged. We should've picked up the call."

I can almost hear her smile. "He's too smart for that. On the phone he pretended he was a deliveryman. 'Package for Cordelia,' he said, so I knew it was him."

"Cordelia. Is that a pet name he has for you?"

"Yes, and he spoke in this phony British accent he likes to use. Very working-class. Cockney. So I told him he had the wrong number, and he hung up. When I went down to the lobby and checked our mailbox, there was a note in it. From him."

"Telling you where to meet him."

"And when. And to bring the money."

"Had he phoned you before?"

"No. I hadn't heard from him since he got out of Poplar Bluff."

"Did you ask him where he was living?"

"Yes, I did, as a matter of fact. He said he was staying in a golden palace with a beautiful East Indian princess. 'She's just like you,' he told me. 'Locked up in a tower.'"

Twenty minutes later I'm at HQ. I knock on the half-open door to Staff Inspector Bateman's office. He's on the phone, but he waves me in and points to the chair in front of his desk. He says something into the phone and hangs up. I ask him if Lawrence Woolley's phone calls to his sister and me were traced. They were. Woolley phoned Mary late Monday morning from a pay phone in Oshawa, forty miles east of Toronto, but Surveillance fell for his "Cordelia" trick, and the trace wasn't investigated till after she'd gone to meet him. He'd already planted the note in her mailbox. After she found it, she slipped out of her building unnoticed. The second phone call – the one he made to me – was made from a pay phone in Newmarket, twenty miles north of the city.

"We got the voice expert on the call to Cordelia," Bateman says, "but he couldn't tell us anything definite, except that the voice was faked."

"It was," I say. "It was Woolley faking a Cockney accent. But what I want to know is how's he getting around? He's making phone calls from all over the place. His sister says he's got a bicycle, but he's not riding it forty miles out of town to make phone calls."

"He must have a car, but there's been nothing registered under his name for the last seven years."

"Probably stolen. That's how he abducted Ms. Qureshi."

Bateman pats a manila envelope on the desk in front of him and says, "These are the poems. The new ones. Read them over and get back to me."

I stand up and reach for the envelope. "What's the news on Wheeler?"

He shakes his head. "Nothing yet."

"What have you got on the young woman who phoned in the tip?"

"Nothing. All Wheeler told Gallagher before she took off was that a young woman phoned in a tip and she was going to follow it up."

I leave his office and walk back to my cubicle. I've just sat down when Gallagher buzzes to tell me Daniel's arrived. Seconds later, an out-of-breath Daniel is leaning on my desk. "I got here as quickly as I could," he pants. "What's up?"

"Take a seat," I say. "I need your help."

He leans forward to catch his breath, his hands on his knees, just like in the huddle a hundred years ago. "Where did *you* get to last night?" he asks. "I'm glad I brought Alice along. She and I watched the whole game in Trick's room. I kept waiting for you to show up."

"It's a long story. I'll fill you in later. Take a seat."

THE GIRL IN 412

Sweatpants catch
on the stubble of its legs.

Its toenails are unadorned.
I could shave those legs.

I could paint those toenails
silver. It brushes a strand

of hair off its forehead.
Weekdays, it edits a magazine:

it should be behind a counter
at The Bay, painting the faces

of customers. They could admire
themselves in mirrors. Weekends,

it plays the harp: it should be
playing volleyball at the beach.

Nights, it kneads itself
to images of James Joyce

and Dante Gabriel Rossetti:
what it really needs is me.

"Well, it's about Joanne," Daniel says. "That's clear enough."

"It sounds like he wrote this before he killed her," I say. "He studied her."

"I'm not so sure," Daniel says. "Most amateur writers write *from* experience, not before it. He makes it *sound* as if it was written first – while he was stalking her – but how would he know about the harp, for instance, or the unpainted toenails? Or the sweatpants. Was she even wearing sweatpants?"

I try to think back. I reach behind me to the file cabinet and pull out her file. I spread the crime scene photos across my desk.

"Yes, she was," Daniel says in a tight voice. "Pink ones."

MY NEIGHBOUR'S WIFE

Old enough to be its father
he watches, sullen-eyed,

from his rocker on the verandah
as it prances through his azaleas,

legs shaven (or *nude*, to use
a word as crude as cunt),

in a halter top and the sort
of satin shorts that billow.

When men walk past his garden gate
(myself included), it turns and

dances. He grows gaunt
with worry. He would like

to lay his hoary head upon
the pillow of its buttocks;

I would like to carve
my initials in them.

"This one has a real *Lolita* feel to it," Daniel says grimly.

"You mean the movie with James Mason?"

"It was a novel before it was a movie. It's about a middle-aged man's obsession with a young girl."

"I know what it's about, but maybe he's talking about some neighbour when he was teaching in Peterborough."

"Could be. Assuming they were written recently, it backs up my theory that he wrote these poems after the event. And I think they *were* written recently. He's graduated from list poems to a more descriptive style. He's becoming more creative."

"That's not necessarily good news," I say.

"No, it's not."

"Which reminds me, he has a pretty creative nickname for his sister. He calls her Cordelia. He used it when he phoned her Monday."

"Really?" Daniel says. "It's from *King Lear*. Cordelia was one of the three sisters." Then he looks at me. "Interesting."

"What?"

"She was the good one. She was the only one who was loyal to the king. Near the end of the play, Lear says – how does it go? – 'Come,

let's away to prison: We two alone will sing like birds i' the cage . . .
And take upon's the mystery of things, As if we were God's spies.'"

LUCAYA

I sip burgundy at Naughty's,
on Grand Bahama Island, smile

at the scenes of mayhem my mind
creates, and ogle the buttocks

of barmaids I'd like
to carve my initials in.

"It goes back to his Bahamas trip when he raped the first
woman," I say. Again I reach into my file cabinet. This time I pull out
the file of creative pieces Woolley wrote for Dr. Manning. I turn to
the first one, "In the Bahamas," and hand it to Daniel.

He reads it quickly, and when he's done, he says, "Fascinating."
Then he rereads "Lucaya." "My guess is this was an unfinished
poem. A fragment, really, which he used in 'My Neighbour's Wife.'"

COP IT

Not only does it dress
like a man, it dresses

like a cop. At the moment,
however, it wears no clothes

at all, unless you consider
handcuffs clothes — its own

handcuffs, as a matter of fact.
Not a very good cop, this cop "it."

Lost its uniform and its cuffs
and its gun real quick.

Lost its dignity, too.
But what to do

with this cop "it"?
What a pretty dilemma,

what a fine mess,
what a pickle,

what a puzzle, what a stew.
What a rude situation.

Just the kind I like
to sink my teeth into.

I look at Daniel. His face is white. "Is this about Lynn?"

Then I tell him. "She went missing yesterday. We don't know where she is. If you're right about him writing *after* the event, we've got to move fast."

"But how? Where do we go?"

For starters, we phone Mary Woolley again to find out what else she knows, but there's no answer. I requisition an unmarked car, and using what Woolley said to his sister about living in a palace as a clue we start a random search: we drive out to the Palace Motel in the west end; ditto the King's Court on Lakeshore Boulevard; we try the Sushi Palace near High Park and two different Shoe Palaces in Mississauga strip malls. We come up empty on all of them.

Daniel rides around with me all afternoon, and while I'm chain-smoking and driving, he's flipping through the Yellow Pages and the white pages and making notes and asking questions. "He told Mary he was living in a golden palace with a beautiful East Indian princess," he says at one point. "We've been concentrating on the west end. Maybe she's in the *east* end."

So out to Riverdale we go, and then along the Danforth to East York and, eventually, Scarborough. We visit the Bombay Palace, the Burger Palace and Palace Lumber, the Castle Motel and the Palais d'Or, which Daniel's real optimistic about, but which turns out to have gone out of business as a massage parlour and is now a Jiffy Lube.

At five we give up and drive ourselves back to HQ. I say goodbye to Daniel at his car in the parking garage. We agree to meet at McCully's later.

I'm slowly climbing the two flights to Homicide when I hear shouting. I charge up the rest of the stairs, the old gridiron adrenalin kicking in, and burst through the double doors into the main office. Barkas is there and Estabrooks and Staff Inspector Bateman and Big Urmson and three or four others all cheering and hugging in a circle, and carrying on like they just won the lottery, and for a minute I think, Oh God, it was an afternoon game, and we won and I missed it, but when they see me they turn and separate, and that's when I see her. Standing in the middle of them all. Wheeler.

Bateman takes us into his office and tells us to sit down. He listens as me and Wheeler debrief.

"I just got back myself," she says, "about two minutes before you came in."

"From Sutton, right?"

"Right. I spent the night there."

"How did you end up in Sutton? Who was this mysterious young woman who gave you the tip?"

"Well, it's kind of complicated. A call came in yesterday from a woman named Andrea Sunstrum."

The name rings a bell, but I can't place it. "Who's she?"

"She was Woolley's student, the one he raped at the college he was teaching at in Peterborough. She was the one who got him arrested."

"Right," I say. "I remember."

"She saw his name in the paper or heard it on TV, phoned Staff Inspector Bateman, and said she wanted to talk to me."

"So? Did you talk to her?"

Wheeler sighs. "Not exactly. The message said she would only talk in person, and only to me."

"You're a popular girl," I say. "First, Ms. Qureshi's girlfriend will only talk to you, and now this one."

"The message said to meet her at the downtown Pizza Hut in Peterborough." Wheeler combs her fingers through her blonde hair.

"What happened?"

She shows me her brown eye. "She wasn't there. I waited twenty minutes, and then there was a phone call. From her. Telling me to meet her at a hotel called the Pines, up near Sutton."

I scratch my head. "Sutton's not even close to Peterborough."

"I know. It was another hour's drive. But she claimed she had information about Woolley's whereabouts, so I went up to Sutton, found the hotel, and there was another message waiting for me at the desk saying there was a room reserved in my name, and I was supposed to check in and wait for her to contact me."

"What time was this?"

"Oh gosh, it had to have been nine, nine-thirty."

"Go on."

"I phoned in, told Gallagher what was up. I waited in my room for Andrea to make contact, but she didn't, so at eleven I went down to the bar. Fought off a couple of swimming-pool salesmen from Ohio. Fought off the bartender." Wheeler shrugs. "She never showed."

"Then what?"

"I went back to my room. I had a Jacuzzi and went to bed. There was a Jacuzzi right in the room."

"You figured she might contact you in the morning?"

"Yes, but she didn't, so I headed back here about eight-thirty this morning. I guess I should have phoned in – I hear there was a bit of excitement – but I thought everybody knew where I was. I only found out a few minutes ago that my message got lost on Gallagher's desk."

Again I scratch my head. "I don't get it. Why didn't this Sunstrum woman show up?"

"I don't know. She sounded so . . . I don't know, *sincere*, on the phone."

"Sincere?"

"Yes, but worried, too. Nervous. Anxious."

"Well, who can blame her? She found out Woolley's been released and that he's a suspect in these sex murders. Maybe she's afraid he's gonna come looking for her. After all, it was her that put him away for six years."

Bateman tells us to go home and get some rest. "Meanwhile," he says, "we'll track down Andrea Sunstrum. Find out what she knows. I'll see the two of you at seven in the morning. Sharp."

But instead of going home, we go to the hospital.

When we get to Trick's room, the same little Filipina nurse I met earlier is there. Also, a woman in a lab coat, a tall white woman with big blonde hair. They both seem to be in a sweat about something.

"Is there any change?" I ask, and they turn to look at us. The tall one has something in her hands.

The little nurse says, "No, he's still comatose."

I look at Trick. He's still on his back, strapped down. His eyes are still half-open, the tubes are still up his nose, and the breathing gadget's still hooked to the hole in his throat. His right arm's still fully bent at the elbow, his biceps flexed, his fist clenched three or four inches above his shoulder.

I turn to the tall woman. "What's that?" I ask, nodding at the thing she's holding.

She holds it up for me to see. "It's a brace for his arm. For the flexor tension." It looks like an elbow pad for a hockey player. White plastic and foam rubber and Velcro straps. "We're having some difficulty getting it on. Perhaps you could help?"

I walk around to the other side of the bed where the tall woman's standing. "Why's he need it?"

The tall woman pulls the straps open with a ripping sound. "With his arm bent like this and his fist up near his shoulder, the tendons in his elbow will shorten. If we can extend his arm and put this brace on it to keep it straight, then the tendons won't shrink, and eventually, when he returns to consciousness and the flexor tension relaxes, he should have full use of his arm again."

From the other side of the bed, Wheeler says, "What do you want us to do?"

"The problem is we can't keep his arm straight long enough to get the brace on properly." She nods to me. "If you could just pull down on his arm – straighten it, that is – while I get this on, then we're in business."

I move in closer and take Trick's fist in my right hand and gently draw it towards me. It won't move. It's like he's arm-wrestling me. I pull harder, and his whole torso begins to rise up off the bed. I lower him back down. "Wheeler," I say, "hold him down by the shoulders."

Wheeler and the little nurse go to the head of the bed on opposite sides and press down on Trick's shoulders. I look at the tall woman again and she nods, the brace open and ready in her hands.

I start to pull on Trick's fist again. The resistance in his arm is scary. It's like I'm pulling on a giant wishbone. I look at Trick's face, but it tells me nothing. No expression. No confusion or pain or anger at what we're doing to him.

"Farther," the tall woman says. "Another six inches."

I pull harder. "I'm afraid his arm's going to snap," I tell her. I'm starting to feel queasy.

"A little farther," the woman says. I look at her. Her face is covered in sweat.

I close my eyes and pull. I can feel the woman move the brace into position and I can hear her attach the Velcro straps. "Okay," she says.

I open my eyes. She's nodding at me to let go. I look at Wheeler's face and the little nurse's, and then Trick's.

When I let go, Trick's fist jerks up with such force the brace pops off, flies across the room, and lands on the windowsill.

All four of us follow the path of the brace, and then we all look back at Trick. Then we look at each other. "Unco-operative bastard," I say, and wipe my forehead with the sleeve of my shirt.

It's half-price wing night at McCully's, and me and Wheeler are halfway through forty mediums when Daniel arrives. I'd phoned him with the news that Wheeler was back, and he throws open his arms and gives her a big hug. We tell him all about our visit to the hospital and what happened with the physiotherapist and Trick's elbow brace. When Jessy comes by to take his order, she lays a hand on my shoulder, and Wheeler sees it and looks at me funny and smiles. I know I'm turning red, so I get up and walk over to the bar and ask Dexter for a pickled egg.

When I get back to the table, Wheeler's filling Daniel in on how she spent the last twenty-four hours, and we fill her in on how we spent the afternoon.

"That's so sweet," she says. "The two of you beating the bushes for me."

Daniel takes out his copies of the new poems and shows them to her, and when she reads "Cop It," her jaw drops. "Wow," she says, "this guy really does have an active imagination." But she's not laughing when she says it. Then Daniel says he's never been so happy to see one of his theories go belly-up. When she asks what theory, he explains how he thought Woolley wrote all four poems after the fact – "*after* his trip to the Bahamas, *after* ogling his neighbour's wife, *after* murdering Joanne, *after* abducting you. Except he didn't abduct you. So my brainwave's a pleasant pile of bullshit."

"But he wanted you to see the poems, right?" Wheeler says, turning to me. "He had Mary deliver them."

"Right."

"So why did he write a poem about me if he didn't intend to abduct me, and then send the poems to you?"

Daniel says, "Woolley knows you're partners. He figures Campbell's fond of you, loyal to you." He turns to me, his eyes wide. "Now I get it! He wanted to distract *you*! He sent you on a wild goose chase."

"Today, you mean?"

"Yeah, you and me scouring the city."

Wheeler says, "But how did he know I'd actually be away?"

Daniel says, "Wait a minute, wait a minute."

We both look at him.

Then he says, "Campbell, remember how he faked a Cockney dialect so that he could make contact with his sister? How he fooled the guys on the wire tap?"

I nod.

"Lynn," he says, turning towards Wheeler, "you weren't talking to Andrea Sunstrum at all. You were talking to Lawrence Woolley."

The hairs on the back of my neck stand up.

"But that's impossible," says Wheeler. "I'm sure it was a woman's voice. It *had* to be."

"But think about it," Daniel persists. "If he can fool the wiretap boys, why shouldn't he be able to fool you?"

"Okay," I say, "supposing you're right. Why did he do it? Why did he go to such trouble to lead Wheeler off on a wild goose chase?"

"I told you. He knows you're fond of her. He did it to get at you. Don't you remember what he said after you saved Ms. Farmer? When he phoned you?"

"Yeah, he was pissed off that I'd messed up his plans – he wanted Ms. Farmer as a bookend for Ms. Qureshi. And he said something about other fish in the sea, that he already had someone else in mind."

"Me, from the sounds of it," says Wheeler. "But nothing happened at the Pines. I never heard from him again."

"Maybe he was just messing with us," I say.

"Or maybe," says Daniel, "something happened that we don't know about, and he had to change his plans. Maybe he did intend to . . . to do something."

"Yikes," says Wheeler.

"You'd better stay away from your apartment," I tell her.

"I'll stay at my sister's. Totally the other end of the city." She stands up. "I'll go and phone her now."

"Make sure you leave me her number."

As Wheeler goes off to phone, Daniel says, "I'd like to know what Woolley's up to. Maybe he was after Lynn and had to abort his plan, or maybe all that was just to distract you from something else he has up his sleeve."

"Okay," I say, "but tell me this. How did he know she'd go alone to Peterborough? How did he know I wouldn't be with her? He didn't know I'd taken the afternoon off."

Daniel frowns. "Maybe it would have been just fine with him if you'd both gone. If you had, maybe he would have gone after you both."

"But didn't Wheeler just tell us the hotel reservation was made in *her* name?"

"By that point he must have known it was just her. He phoned in, used the fake voice – Andrea's voice – got the information out of your desk sergeant, and then altered his plans."

It made sense. Gallagher likes to talk. He likes to lose messages and he likes to talk.

Daniel stands up to go to the washroom. At the same instant a massive groan goes up from the general population of McCully's. "Look," Daniel says, and I follow his pointing finger to the TV above the bar just in time to see Lonnie Smith round second base in a home-run trot. We watch as he touches third and then coasts the last ninety feet, crosses the plate, and high-fives three of his teammates.

"Grand slam," says Daniel.

"Listen to the clamour," I say, shaking my head.

Daniel looks at me. "What did you say?"

"Clamour." I look up at him, all innocence. "It's a noun. I'm surprised you're not familiar with it. It means a fuck of a lot of noise."

The score appears on the screen. Atlanta 7, Toronto 2. Top of five.

This is game five of the World Series, for crying out loud. We can win it all tonight. At home, no less. If we lose tonight, we have to go back to Atlanta. Where has my mind been? Why haven't I been concentrating? Psychic energy and all that. Beaming it down to the lakeshore, not three miles away, where our brave boys in blue are doing battle with the bad Braves of Georgia. Where have I been? "Let's go, you bums!" I yell. "Let's *go!*" And soon all of McCully's is chanting "Go Jays go! Go Jays go!"

But it doesn't help. It's still 7–2 after seven when Wheeler gives up and heads off to her sister's, and it's still 7–2 after nine.

Me and Daniel turn and look at each other across our little round table.

"Saturday in Atlanta, buddy," Daniel says. "Guess who's pitching?"

"The mighty David Cone," I say, brightening. "How much?"

"Let's make it a hundred."

"A C-note it is," I say. "But how can you bet against your own team in a game of this magnitude? What kind of man are you?"

Daniel stares at me. "First 'clamour,' then 'magnitude.' Since when has 'magnitude' been part of your vocabulary? I thought you were strictly a four-letter man."

"Eat me."

"Eat me. That's good. That's clever. A very clever rejoinder. *Two* words, and only *five* letters."

"Answer the question. How can you do it? How can you bet against your own team?"

"I'm not only a humble college professor, I'm also a businessman. If Toronto loses, I'm up a hundred dollars. 'There art thou happy.' If Toronto wins, we're World Series champs, and I will happily hand over a hundred dollars to you as my price of admission. 'There art thou happy.' See? I'm happy either way. Campbell, my son, it's what we call a win-win situation."

He gets up and heads off towards the john. A minute later, as I'm staring mindlessly at the TV, I feel a hand on the back of my neck. I twist my head around and look up. It's Jessy. She's got a green-and-white checkered tea towel over one shoulder. And of course she's got the green eyes. "What do you say, big guy? Give a girl a ride home?"

I look at her for a long time.

"Well, forget it then," she says, and starts to walk away, but I grab her hand and pull her back.

"I'd like to," I tell her. "I really would. But . . ."

"But what?"

"But you'll wear me out, and I need my wits about me tomorrow."

"What's so special about tomorrow?"

I'm still holding her hand. I rub my thumb across its freckled back. "I'll tell you what's so special. We're going to catch a killer."

I'm dozing in bed, my reading lamp on, a *Sports Illustrated* across my chest, when the phone rings. I hear Reggie snort in her sleep from the floor beside me. I glance at the clock radio on my bedside table; it's just past midnight.

It's Gallagher, at Homicide. "Sorry to call you so late, Camp, but I just got a call here. Guy says his name's Shorty Rogers."

"Sure, I know him."

"Says he's your daughter's boss."

"That's right. What's he want? Why's he calling so late?"

"Wants me to tell you he's not your daughter's boss any more. He fired her."

I struggle to a sitting position. "What? Why?"

"He phoned just now, eh, real pissed off. Drunk, too, from the sounds of it. Every second word's the F-word. Wanted your home number. I said no way, that's classified. Besides, I said, it's midnight. He said it was real important, he absolutely had to talk to you. He said he tried the phone book, but he couldn't find your number, and when he tried to get it off directory assistance, they told him it's unlisted."

"That's right."

"So he keeps telling me how you're old friends and how he hates to do this and how he wants to explain it to you personally, and by this time I'm convinced he's for real, so I tell him that even though I'm not supposed to give out any information, *I'd* phone you. Which is what I'm doing right now. Then if you want to, you can call him back. I've got his number right here. You got a pencil handy?"

"But why did he fire her? Did he say?"

"Well, all I know is he had a horse running this afternoon. He told me all about it. I was interested. I like the ponies just like you do, Camp, you know that. Grey filly, first-time starter. Glenora something. He told me her name."

"Glenora Ferry."

"That's it, Glenora Ferry. So anyway, this Shorty fella had to go to Montreal yesterday to meet the new owners, a Japanese couple. They have some kind of business down there. Importing glass. Or exporting it. I can't remember what he said. Anyway, he just flew back this afternoon with these Japanese people, and the long and the short of it is your daughter never showed, the horse never showed, and so the track stewards had to scratch her. Very embarrassing. So this Shorty fella's real angry because your daughter knew this was a heavy-duty situation – them flying in from Montreal and all that – so later when he goes around to the barn to find out what the hell happened, he finds out from somebody that your daughter never even showed up for work *at all* today."

CHAPTER 18

Friday, October 23

THE PHONE RINGS at 11:54 a.m. The speaker asks for me, and as soon as we have everyone in place, he's transferred through. I've been here at Homicide all night and all morning. Wheeler, too. I phoned her at her sister's right after Gallagher talked to me, and she came right in. We've been poring over files, clues, evidence, patterns, but nothing's told us where Debi might be. And now, just when we're beginning to think our luck's run out, Woolley comes to us.

I put the receiver to my ear. "Young here."

"What a big, strong girl your daughter is."

If I hadn't already wanted to kill him, I do now.

"You probably want to know how I found her, or how I even knew you had a daughter at all." He laughs. "Do you want to know?"

Something tells me I'd better indulge him. "Sure," I say. "Tell me."

"Well, okay, if you insist. It was an easy trick, really. A few days ago I phoned Homicide – just as I am now – and spoke to your desk sergeant, who proved most helpful. I took a bit of a gamble and asked for you, and when he told me you weren't available – I would have hung up if you *were* available – I told him I was an old school-mate of your kid. It was another gamble, but I figured you for the fatherly type. So he said, 'You're an old schoolmate of Debi's?' and I said, 'Yes, that's right, Debi, and I'm just in town for a few days, and I thought I'd try to look her up, but I don't know where she's living,' and he said, 'Well, all I know is she works out at Caledonia Downs.' So I said, "Thank you very much," and phoned the racetrack and repeated my story, and in no time I had her address, her phone number, her work schedule, even her baby's name. Jamal. That's quite the moniker. Anyway, I made some other arrangements, and when all the stars were aligned I drove to her building very early yesterday morning, waited for one of the tenants to activate the door to the underground garage, drove in and parked my car, a brand-new Mercury someone foolishly left running outside a dry cleaner's, in an empty space near hers. Do you want to know how I knew which space was hers?" He waited. "Well, do you?"

"Yes."

"I used the intercom beside the elevator and buzzed the super: 'Bill Dunphy of CAA,' I said. 'Debi Young in 1603 needs a boost, but she didn't tell me where to find her car. Same number parking space as her apartment? Right, chief, thanks.' Then I waited for her. When she showed up, I pretended *I* needed a boost. Hood open. Cables in hand. 'Excuse me, miss,' I said, when she was close enough. She had the little mulatto whelp in one arm and a diaper bag in the other. I took the .22 out from behind me – the same .22 I shot your partner with, as a matter of fact – and in two beats of your heart I had little Café au Lait snuggled up beside me in the back seat of my sparkling silver Sable. Debi drove. I kept the barrel of the gun pressed against the back of her seat." He stops and takes a breath. "You'll be interested to know that I also have a single-barrel, twelve-gauge, pump-action Winchester, a duck gun I acquired from a friend of a friend inside, the same friend of a friend, incidentally, who provided me with the .22 I used to maim your partner, and you'll *never* guess, Detective Sergeant, who taught me how to use a shotgun. My shrink did. Can you believe it? My shrink taught me how to use a shotgun. What a world. And I have to tell you, I'm just dying to try it out. Are you still there?"

I can't trust myself to speak.

"Would you like to speak to Debi?"

Then I can. "Yes," I tell him.

"Say please."

"Please."

He giggles. "Yes please, Professor Woolley, I would like to speak to my daughter."

"Yes please, Professor Woolley, I would like to speak to my daughter."

"Just a moment."

I wait, my hand trembling on the receiver.

"Daddy!"

"Debi! Are you all right?"

"There's a dead woman here." Her voice high, screeching.

"What's he done to you? Are you all right?"

"She's dead. He says –"

"Has he hurt you?"

"He says if I don't –"

"Do you know where you are?"

"No. No, it's like a . . . it's just a room."

"Do you remember any street signs?"

But she starts to cry.

"Is Jamal all right?"

"Yes," she sobs.

"It's okay, Sweetie. I'm coming. I'm going to get you out of there. You just –"

"That's enough for now," Woolley interrupts. "We don't want to give Daddy too much to go on. There's still some fun to be had before the nasty old policemen arrive and spoil the party. Right, Debi? Say, you're almost as broad back there as a Percheron. You're a big, *big* girl!"

"Woolley!" I scream. "If you touch her, I'll kill you. You fucking scum! I'll kill you myself, you –"

"Good gracious, Detective Sergeant! Such passion. But what did you expect? When you ruined my plans for Monique Mozambique Farmer, I had to find a replacement, someone near and dear. Did you enjoy the little diversion I created? You must have; you went for it like a moth to the flame. A fish to the bait. Your precious partner. Except it was never her I was after. She was too obvious a choice. But your daughter, now that was inspired. And Detective Wheeler provided the perfect decoy. All I had to do was get her out of town, make her disappear for a little while. And then you conveniently disappeared, too. I didn't know how I was going to get her off on her own, away from you, and then poof! you were gone, too. You helped me out. I'm obliged, Detective Sergeant. Someday you'll have to tell me where you went and what you were up to, but now's not the time, time being of the essence."

"Woolley, what do you want? Is there something you want?"

He laughs. "Just your attention, Detective Sergeant. Say, I hope you enjoyed the poem I wrote about your little partner. A bit of a departure for me, as I'm sure you noted, as are the others in that package. More expressive, I feel. Less clinical. Less – I don't know – antiseptic. And although I didn't use it in the poem about your partner, there is one line I'm especially fond of, so fond in fact that I used it twice, in other poems, the line about carving my initials in somebody's buttocks. I'm sure you took note of it. Chances are, you're thinking about it right now. Anyway, I certainly hope Detective Wheeler enjoyed her stay at the Pines. I was hoping I might have an opportunity to dash up there and pay her a visit. Sadly, however, time did not permit. But listen, I can't natter on forever. I've got work to do. Not to worry, though. You'll find me soon – whether or not you find me soon *enough* depends entirely on you. If you're any good, you'll find me this afternoon. I've given you plenty of time to trace this call. We'll be expecting you shortly – Debi and myself, little Kareem Abdul Shaquille, the mocha miracle, and of course our poor old tuckered-out Aunty Miriam over there in the chair, a little the worse for wear."

"Do you want money? What do you want, Woolley? What –?"

"I lack for nothing, my friend. Just an hour of bliss with this, my blushing bride. Say Debi, we'd better get started! Our guests will be here before we know it. Oh, I forgot to tell you, darling. I've pre-pared a special treat for our guests. Won't they be surprised when they see it!"

He hangs up before I can say another word.

I turn to Wheeler. My heart's pounding, and the sweat's pouring off my forehead. "What did we get?"

She has a phone to her ear. "It's coming. They've got the phone number. They're working on the address. Here it is, here it is," she says, scribbling it down. "All right. The Camelot Arms Apartments, Annette Street. It's in Etobicoke."

About a dozen of us are heading for the doors when Staff Inspector Bateman pulls up alongside me. "I've called in the Emergency Task Force, Camp. Just so you know."

I shake my head. "Let me handle this one, boss." We push through the doorway and start down the stairs. "We don't want those guys in on this. They barge in like fucking Marines, and they're too fucking trigger-happy, and it's my daughter we're talking about, it's my daughter in there."

"That's just it, Camp. Because it's Debi in there, you can't go in."

I stop midway down the stairs. "What are you talking about? I *have* to go in."

Bateman shakes his head. "You know the rules. If a cop's got a relative or a friend in a high-risk situation, he can't go in."

I look at him for a minute, then start down the stairs again.

"And furthermore," Bateman says, hurrying after me, "it's procedure when there's a hostage-taking to bring in the ETF. You know that. We have to call them in."

"Just let me go in first and size things up. Give me that much."

"I can't –"

"Who's got authority, you or the ETF?"

"I do, but –"

"Well, there you go. Just let me go in and size up the situation."

"Camp, I can't break procedure."

We're outside and heading for the cars. I turn and face him. "If it was your daughter in there you would."

He looks at me silently. "Okay, I'll give you five minutes. You can go in and size things up. But then you come right back out. Five minutes inside, and that's it."

I nod at him and turn to go, but he puts his hand on my arm.

"What?" I say.

"There's something else."

I look at him. "So tell me."

"We found Andrea Sunstrum."

"No kidding. What did she have to say?"

He pauses. "Nothing, I'm afraid. She didn't have anything to say."

"What do you mean?"

"She's dead. She committed suicide four years ago."

Etobicoke is in the west end. Barkas drives, siren wailing. I'm beside him. Big Urmson and Wheeler are in back. Bateman and Estabrooks and a dozen others are in the rest of the cruisers racing along the Gardiner Expressway. We take the South Kingsway exit, then Jane Street, and then we race east along Annette and squeal to a stop in front of an old yellow low-rise – four or five floors of cheap furnished apartments. From the back seat Wheeler says, "The Camelot Arms. There's your 'golden palace.'"

As I'm climbing out, I can see the ETF boys – about a dozen of them – trotting towards us along the sidewalk in their helmets and masks, with their weapons across their chests.

"Keep those bastards out here!" I yell at Bateman. "Five minutes! I'll be in radio contact or I'll come back outside, but don't send them in."

And in we go: me and Barkas and Wheeler and Big Urmson. We buzz the landlord and identify ourselves. He tells us to come along the hall to number 11, and the door into the foyer unlocks.

He meets us at the door to his apartment, and we push right past him into his living room. He's a skinny man in a stained T-shirt and Coke-bottle glasses whose beer lunch we've interrupted. His apartment smells like cat shit.

"We're looking for a man named Lawrence Woolley," I tell him.

He shakes his head. "Name don't ring a bell. Let me check my ledger." He goes to an open binder on his coffee table. There's an ashtray and a Budweiser can on top of it. "Most of the people we get are transients, eh," he says, clearing off the binder and turning a page. "Most of them only stay a few days. A few weeks at most."

"Hurry up," I say.

"Nobody here named Woolley," he says. He looks up at me. "Don't mean he's not here, though. Some of 'em uses fake names."

"Tall guy," I say. "Skinny face. Dark hair."

"How old you figure?"

"He's thirty-five years old."

He nods. "Could be the guy in number forty-eight." He runs his finger down a page in the ledger. "Here it is. Number forty-eight. Lennox Ross."

"Let's go," I say to the others.

As we make our way towards the door, the landlord follows us. "Said he wanted solitude, so I give him the farthest room I got. Has the whole top floor to himself. Hasn't give me no trouble, paid a month in advance, which is seldom around here, let me tell you. There *was* a noise up there about twenty minutes ago."

I stop at the door and face him. "What kind of noise?"

He laughs and lets me see his crooked dirty teeth. "Prolly nothin'." Then he frowns and says, "Two of 'em actually. Like thuds, I guess is how you'd describe it. I was just about to go up myself and investigate, eh, soon's I finished my lunch."

I drag him down the hall to the foyer of the building. I tell Big Urmson to go outside and tell Bateman I need five more minutes, and make sure he's posted ETF men at every exit. Also, make sure the street's cordoned off, and whatever onlookers have gathered are a safe distance away. "Then I want you back in here."

"Right, Sarge," he says, and off he goes.

"Where's his room?" I ask the landlord.

"Fourth floor. End of the hall."

I start off. Barkas and Wheeler hurry after me.

Wheeler says, "Sarge, you're not supposed to go up there."

"You're not going to try and stop me, are you," I say.

Four flights up and my heart's kicking like a piston. The hallway's badly lit: two or three bare bulbs, a FIRE EXIT sign. There's a burnt smell in the air. Gunpowder. As we get near the last door, I see something on the floor in front of it. A package. I wave Barkas to the far side of the door. We all have our guns drawn. I kneel down. It's a manila envelope, the kind Woolley's used before. Something bulky inside. On the outside in black marker he's printed

IF YOU'RE EVER TO GAZE AGAIN
INTO LITTLE BLACK SAMBO'S BIG BROWN EYES,
YOU'LL TAKE A MOMENT – OR FIVE OR TEN –
TO VIEW MY SPECIAL SURPRISE

I unwind the red string that holds the envelope closed. Inside there's a videotape. I kneel there for a moment, thinking. One of the things I'm thinking is my daughter's only a few feet behind the door I'm kneeling in front of.

I stand up. I look at Barkas and then at Wheeler. They're staring at me. Waiting. I shake my head. I make a T with my hands and point back down the hall. At first they don't move. I can read it on their faces: they can't believe we're not going in.

I keep pointing back down the hall until they begin to move.

We find the landlord in the foyer. I ask him if he's got a VCR. He says yes, and we hurry down the hall to his apartment. We go into his living room, and he turns on the TV and the VCR. He sticks out his hand for the videotape. "Wait outside in the hall, please," I tell him.

"Wait a minute," he says. "This is my apartment. I was nice enough to let youse in here."

He wants to watch the video. He figures maybe somebody dies in it. But I'm not about to share my daughter's murder with the likes of him.

"Barkas," I say, "take him out in the hall. And stay with him."

Barkas steps towards the landlord.

"Okay, okay," says the landlord, "I'm goin'."

Big Urmson comes back. "Staff Inspector's getting kind of antsy, Sarge. He wants to know what's going on."

"Tell him it's under control. Five more minutes. Go back out there and tell him, then come back in."

When it's just me and Wheeler in the landlord's apartment, she turns on me. "First you break procedure and go up there when you're not supposed to, then when you get there you quit on it. Why did you stop us? Debi's in there."

I look at her hard. "You need to tell me that?"

She shouts at me, "Your daughter and your grandson are in there!"

"For fucksake, Wheeler —"

"It's like Tim Hortons all over again. It's like Parliament Street. I can't believe —"

"This is different!" I shout back. "We have to play by *his* rules. At least for now. We didn't go in because I want to see my grandson again. I don't know if Debi's still alive, but the note says Jamal is. I have to do it this way."

She just stares at me.

Then I say, "I know what equipment Woolley bought. For the final chapter. What he meant when he was talking to his sister."

"What? What did he buy?"

I hold up the videotape. "A video camera. Now shut up and let me watch this." I slide the tape into the VCR and push play. We don't sit down; we stand in front of the television. The image is scrambled at first and then straightens out, and there's Debi lying on her side on the floor in a corner of a room. She's facing the camera. She's fully dressed. The way her arms are, her hands must be tied behind her, and Jamal, who seems to be asleep, is beside her. The camera zooms in shakily on her face. "Watch the birdie," Lawrence Woolley's voice says. Her eyes are open but they don't move. They're blank. They're looking straight ahead at nothing. The camera backs off and starts to pan around the room. "What have we got here?" says Woolley, and it's the naked corpse of Miriam Qureshi, still seated on a chair, still tied up. Her head's thrown back, her mouth's open. "Aunty Miriam looks a little worn out." He zooms in on her face. He's done something to her eyes. Beside me, Wheeler grunts. Woolley turns the camera on himself. We're looking up his long arms. His huge chin is blue with whiskers, but the rest of his face is white as a sheet. He looks down at us. "*I* wore her out. Perfect fit. Just like an old shoe. Snug. Hated to throw it away." He pulls the camera up close to his face. His lips are red and wet. "More to come, Detective Sergeant. Don't touch that dial!"

The screen goes blank. Wheeler's holding my arm. I look at her, the anger and pain in her eyes. I turn back to the television. An image appears. It's Woolley, sitting on a kitchen chair in front of a refrigerator, some distance from the camera, which must be on a tripod. After about twenty seconds of staring at us, his long narrow weasel face breaks into a smile. "First, a little something from the bard." He clears his throat. "*Othello*. Act three, scene three. Our hero has just heard the bad news. His wife's a whore! He had no idea; he wishes Iago had kept his mouth shut. 'He that is robb'd, not wanting what is stol'n, Let him not know't, and he's not robb'd at all.'" Woolley shakes his head, still smiling. "Such simple wisdom. He goes on to say, 'I had been happy, if the general camp, Pioners and all, had tasted her sweet body, So I had nothing known.' Oh, if we could only be ignorant of the evil around us. Don't you agree, Detective Sergeant?" He looks down at something on the floor. "Once he understood his wife was corrupt – as all women are – his life was forever changed, and it is here that Willie the Shake furnishes us with one last list." Woolley clears his throat.

> "'O now for ever
> Farewell the tranquil mind! farewell content!
> Farewell the plumed troop, and the big wars,
> That makes ambition virtue! O, farewell!
> Farewell the neighing steed, and the shrill trump,
> The spirit-stirring drum, the ear-piercing fife,
> The royal banner, and all quality,
> Pride, pomp and circumstance of glorious war!'"

He reaches to his left and brings back a wineglass, half-filled with a light, almost clear liquid. "Mumm's," he says, looking at the camera, and raises the glass. "Only the best for so auspicious an occasion." He takes a sip, swirls it around inside his mouth, and smacks his lips. He makes a sound that could be a chuckle or a sob. Then he collects himself. "So, anyway, just as Othello had to say goodbye to the things he loved – peace of mind, happiness, but most of all 'glorious war' – so I must bid farewell to the things *I* love – poetry, murder, mayhem." He takes another sip. "By the way, my original plan was to use this quotation on the slant. She was next. Megan Wong-Whatthefuck. Editor of *Bugle*. Bugle, 'Shrill trump,' get it? And they sure are shrill, the womenfolks, don't you agree, Detective Sergeant? I also had a new list poem I wanted to send you. It's called 'Catch My Death.' I was going to use it with this videotape, to accompany my final moments, hence the not-to-be-unappreciated pun in the title. But the truth is it's not quite ready. You can't rush great art, and I'm not about to serve anything before its time, not even at my farewell feast." His expression has been serious for the last few seconds, but now he smiles again. "It has some great stuff in it, though:

Curtains
Croak
Give up the ghost

Last legs
Last roundup
Last gasp

Death rattle
Death's door
Done for

Great stuff. But unfortunately the last grains of sand are soon to slip from the top to the bottom of my hourglass. No more time for revision, as I must expeditiously exit this vale of tears." He reaches beneath him. When we see his hand again, it's holding a shotgun by the barrel. He opens the breech, leans down out of sight again, reappears and holds up a shell between his thumb and index finger, and he's smiling like he wants us to admire it, like a kid who's brought something in for show and tell, then he slides it into the chamber and snaps the gun shut. "In a moment or two I'm going to turn off the camera. I will then leave this videotape outside the door for you to find. And while you're watching it – as you're listening to these very words, perhaps – I'll have loaded a fresh videotape into the camera and I will be recording the tragic event of my death. As you are no doubt aware, most of us – and by us I mean the select members of that secret society known as the Serial Killers Club – kill ourselves. We commit suicide. We kick the stool out from under us, take a long walk off a short pier. The general public thinks we self-destruct because we have finally disgusted ourselves so much that even *we* can't abide ourselves any more. But that's not the case." Woolley leans towards the camera. "The real reason we 'off' ourselves, Detective Sergeant, is because we want the last laugh. We want to die unapprehended and unrepentant. We want to die according to our own rules and by our own design. We want to die unapprehended and un*com*prehended." He leans back again and glances from side to side. "Well, as the film director might say, I think we're about ready! Only one question remains, and I think you know what that question is, Detective Sergeant." My breath catches. I can feel Wheeler's grip tighten on my arm. "Will I take the broad-of-beam Miss Debi with me? Will I or won't I? And Mudpie Baby, what about him? *Eeny meeny miney moe, catch a nigger by the toe.* How apropos, don't you agree, Detective Sergeant? What to do, what to do?" Woolley leans his face right into the lens, his nose and eyes huge. "So many decisions, so little time." Then he moves his face back, but as his hand reaches towards us, towards the camera, so that we can't see his face any more, we can hear his voice say, "Of course, maybe they're already dead." Then the TV screen goes black.

"Get the tape out of the machine," I say to Wheeler.

Big Urmson's at the door. "Staff Inspector wants you outside. He says it's an order. I'm supposed to bring you out myself."

I push him back into the hall. "We're going back up there," I tell him. "Me and Barkas and Wheeler. You can come with us, or you can go back outside and tell Bateman to leave me alone. What's it going to be?"

He doesn't even hesitate. "I'm with you, Sarge."

"Good," I say. "Good man." I turn to the landlord, who's standing there with Barkas. "Get outside and ask for Staff Inspector

Bateman. Tell him I need two more minutes." I turn him by the shoulders and propel him down the hall towards the foyer. Then I look at the others. "Ready?"

They're so ready they can't stand still, like football players in the dressing room minutes before kickoff. Barkas's expression is scary – his olive complexion's gone white as paste. Big Urmson is red-faced and sweating, bouncing from one foot to the other. Wheeler's brown eye is sparking like a fuse.

"When we go in," I tell them, "we'll find Ms. Qureshi dead in a chair in the first room, probably on our left. Debi and my grandson will be in the bedroom" – I pause – "or the bathroom. Woolley may be dead in the kitchen. Debi and my grandson . . . ," I stumble, ". . . may be dead, too. If Woolley's still alive, he may initiate or return fire. He's got a single-barrel twelve-gauge shotgun. We go in hard, and if he's still alive and fighting, we take him down."

We run single file back down the hall and thunder up the stairs. As we stride along the fourth-floor corridor towards room 48, the gunpowder stink still hangs in the air. I wave Barkas and Big Urmson to the far side of the door. Holding my Glock in my left hand, I test the doorknob with my right. It's unlocked. I shove the door open. We wait, listening. Nothing. With a tilt of my head I motion Barkas in, then I follow, then Urmson and Wheeler.

Inside the first room the smell of gunpowder's overpowered by the sweet sickening stench of rotting flesh. It's so quiet I can hear a tap dripping somewhere. The drapes are drawn across the only window, and it's so dark we can barely see. "Use your flashlight," I whisper to Urmson. He turns it on and shines it on Ms. Qureshi's body. She's still tied to her chair – head tipped back, mouth open, body bloated with gases, brown skin gone black. "Shine it around the room." In the corner there's a TV on a stand with its screen smashed in and damage to the wall behind it.

"That explains the shotgun blasts," Wheeler whispers.

"Okay," I tell Urmson, "switch it off."

The light in the kitchen is on and I move towards it, both hands on my gun, swinging left and right, ready for whatever's waiting. As I step into the light I see the video camera on its tripod pointing to my right.

Knees bent, I pivot hard into the kitchen.

Woolley's still sitting on the chair in front of the refrigerator, four feet from me. His shotgun is levelled at my gut.

"Face to face," he says, "at last." His uncombed black hair looks greasy and his skin's the colour of bread dough. He looks like he's about to die. "I decided to hang around a little longer before I took my leave," he says. "It seemed the polite thing to do, to wait for your arrival. I hope you're not angry." He nods towards the camera on its tripod. "It's rolling, Detective Sergeant. Anyone you'd care to say goodbye to?"

"Where's Debi?" I still have both hands on my gun, the barrel aimed at his head.

"Where do you *think* she is?" he says, his voice suddenly cold. "Where do I *always* put them?"

I take a step back, my gun trained on his forehead.

"Easy," he says, his shotgun moving with me.

"Where is it?" I ask.

"Where is what?"

"The bathroom."

He smiles. "See the door to my left?"

My eyes swivel. The door's partway open. It's dark inside.

"Debi!" I yell.

No answer.

"Curious layout, don't you agree, Detective Sergeant? Bathroom right off the kitchen. Unusual. Proximity of odours, and all that. Unsanitary, if you ask me. So near, in one sense, and yet – what with me so cleverly positioned midway between you and her – still so damned far."

I take a step towards the bathroom. Woolley raises the barrel of the shotgun to my chest. I stop. I close my eyes and breathe quick a few times. Quick and shallow. I take my right hand from my gun and reach towards the knob of the bathroom door. My gun's still in my left hand. "Are they dead?" I ask.

Woolley smiles. "Maybe, maybe not," he says, and again his voice turns to ice, "but one thing's for sure. *You are.*" The muzzle of the shotgun lifts slightly.

Behind me in the other room, a voice – Wheeler's – shouts, "Mary! Get back, Mary!"

As Woolley's head jerks, I fire. It's like a rope yanks him backwards off the chair; he hits the fridge, seems to hang there a second in the loud crack of the gunshot, then does a slow-motion slide to the floor. His feet move forward and bump into the overturned chair, which scrapes on the linoleum. When he comes to a stop, he's on his back, head pushed forward by the fridge, chin jammed into his collar bone, small smoking hole in his forehead. Shotgun still in his hands. Eyes wide open. Smug red mouth. Red smear up the white fridge door.

"Debi!" I yell. I wait one, two seconds, kick the shotgun out of Woolley's hands, and as it clatters across the kitchen floor, I step past him and towards the half-open door of the bathroom. I push it the rest of the way.

The light's off, and despite the light from the kitchen, all I can make out are shadows. Woolley must have put something over the window to keep the room dark. Then I make out a shape. I feel along the wall for the switch and find it, and there's Debi suddenly flooded with light, duct-taped to the toilet tank, eyes shut tight against the brightness, her mouth duct-taped. She's not naked; she's fully dressed, struggling to get free. You're alive, I say to myself. You're alive and safe.

She opens her eyes and rolls them wildly, like a thoroughbred's in the starting gate, towards the bathtub. I step in, snap back the shower curtain, and there's Jamal in the tub. On a towel, eyes blinking, head twisting. Silver tape across his mouth.

I turn back. Wheeler's come in behind me. She goes to Debi.

I hear people running in the hall. I hear Bateman's voice in the other room.

I look back down at Jamal. He's terrified. His little arms are stretching up at me. Under the tape he's screaming. I reach down and scoop him up and press him to my shoulder. I turn back again.

In one movement, Wheeler pulls the tape off Debi's mouth.

"Owwww!" she screams. "Owwwwwwwww! The bastard! The dirty fucking goddamn bastard! Give me my baby!"

CHAPTER 19

Saturday, October 24

I EXPECT TO SEE my clock radio when I open my eyes, the time digitally displayed, and then Debi's picture in its frame on the dresser. Instead I see the TV across from me and I realize I'm on the sofa. Why am I on the sofa? I can hear Reg, wedged between the sofa and the coffee table, idling like a Harley. Poor old dog smells like dirty socks. I roll on my side. The coffee table looks like it usually does: an empty Hawkins Cheezies bag; a stinking ashtray; a capless, half-gone twenty-sixer of Jack Daniel's.

I sit up and suddenly – as everything comes flooding back – my heart double-clutches. I stand up and hurry into the hallway. I nudge open my bedroom door, and there's my big brave sleeping daughter.

Just before we said goodnight last night she asked me what I thought about her and Jamal moving into my neighbourhood. Great idea, I told her. You can stay here until you find a place of your own. Thanks, Daddy, she said. Long way to go to work, though, I said. That's okay, she said. As long as I'm up by four-thirty. The daycare near the track opens at five. I can drop Jamal off there. If Shorty will give me my job back. Of course he will, Sweetie, once he hears what happened. I'll give him a call.

I stand there watching my big, brave, sleeping girl, curled up like a baby, one arm choking the life out of my Obusforme. I stand there for a good five minutes – even though I've got to piss so bad I can taste it – until she stirs, rolls over, sits up, and rubs her eyes. "Goddamn," she says. "Where the fuck am I?"

Wheeler phones around noon. Debi's in the shower, and I'm making sandwiches for lunch – mustardseed salami on caraway rye. Alfalfa sprouts.

"How are you?" she says.

"Good. How about you?"

"I'm good, too. How's Debi?"

"She's great. She came through it with flying colours."

"She's a trooper. How's Jamal?"

"Fine. He's in the living room watching TV. He's chewing on one of Reggie's Milk-Bones. He prefers the mint-flavoured to the charcoal."

Wheeler laughs. "Well, I just thought I'd see how you're doing."

"We're doing just fine. Never better. See you at McCully's later on? Game six, you know. We can win it all tonight."

"I'll be there."

"Good. Listen, Wheeler, you were great yesterday. Yelling out Mary's name like that – where did that come from? Saved my life."

At first she doesn't reply. Then she says, "When you asked him if Debi and Jamal were dead, and he said, 'Maybe, maybe not, but you are,' I knew he was ready to kill you." Wheeler's voice has turned serious. She'd be showing the brown eye. "It just kind of came to me in a flash. The only person he cared about in the world was his sister. So I called her name."

"I'm not sure he even cared about her, but you sure got his attention. Like I say, you were great. I'll never forget it."

"You were great, too," she says, brightly, and I can picture the blue eye, like diving into the ocean. "I'm sorry about doubting you, you know, when you insisted on looking at the video."

"It's all right. I felt like we had to do it the way he wanted. Not that it mattered in the long run, but I felt like if we did it the way he wanted, everything might turn out."

"Well, it did."

"Do you think Bateman's going to have me up before the board?"

She laughed. "What do you think? You disobeyed him. You broke procedure. You were unprofessional. There's no question you're going to be disciplined. It's only a matter of how much."

"Do you think I was unprofessional?"

"I thought you were spectacular, and I'll say so if I'm called in as a witness."

"Thanks, Wheeler."

"That's okay, Sarge. I love you. I'll see you this evening."

"Wait!" I say. Then I clear my throat and tell her what I've been wanting to tell her for a long time. "I know you probably won't think it's a very smart idea, and you can say no if you want to, and I sure wouldn't blame you if you did, I know I would if I were you, but I was wondering if sometime you might want to, uh . . . go out with me . . . like to dinner or a movie or something. Bowling, maybe. Do you bowl? Myself, I've never bowled, but I –"

"Wait a minute, wait a minute. You mean like a date?"

"Yeah, like a date. Well, sort of. I know I'm too old, and I know I've let you down in the past –"

"I love you, Sarge –"

"Well, I thought that's what you said, and that's why –"

"But not like *that*. More like an older brother, or a big old uncle."

"A big old uncle?"

"Besides, that waitress at McCully's is more your type."

"Jessy? Nah, we're just friends."

"Don't be so modest. She likes you big time. Big guy."

"Ah, well . . ."

"And anyway, there's something I should tell you."

"You're in love with someone else?"

"No, that's not it."

"Who is it? Barkas? Big Urmson? No, no, don't tell me you've fallen in love with Estabrooks!"

"No, Sarge, it's nothing like that."

"Well, what is it? Tell me."

"I'm trying to tell you. Just be quiet. You remember Sandra Mulligan?"

"Sandra Mulligan?" I have to think for a minute. "The butch? Ms. Qureshi's girlfriend? What about her?"

"Well, she's more *my* type. Not her, in particular, but, well . . . her type."

This stops me. "Say again?"

"She's more *my* type."

"You're a . . ."

"That's right."

"Wheeler, don't fuck around. This isn't funny. Besides, I would've noticed."

"Noticed what?"

"Well, you know what I mean. Those women have certain characteristics that, um, most of those women have."

"Really." Her tone of voice changes. It turns sort of brown-eyed. "Maybe you'd like to tell me what those characteristics are."

"Well, um, you don't roll your shoulders when you walk, or hike up your pants like a man does."

"I don't have the haircut, either –"

"Exactly."

"– but it's still true, Sarge. Surprise, surprise. I'm that way."

"You're really not kidding? Please tell me you're kidding."

"Sarge."

"You're not kidding."

"Sarge!"

"I mean, Christ, I don't know what to say."

"*Sarge!*"

"What?"

"I know what you could say. You could say you love me, too."

Everyone's here.

It's crowded and noisy and smoky and wonderful. Behind the bar Dexter's in a total sweat, and Jessy's run off her feet slinging pitchers of beer and baskets of wings. Debi's sitting beside me, and Barkas and Estabrooks are right across. Staff Inspector Bateman, who so far hasn't said diddly about a disciplinary hearing, is sitting on my other side, and next to him is Big Urmson and across from them is Gallagher and even Wicary from Fingerprinting in his line-dancing outfit – cowboy boots and Stetson, little black vest over a yellow shirt. Silliphant's here and the black guy with red hair whose name I can never remember. Daniel, wearing his professor's uniform – his tweed jacket with the leather elbow patches – and puffing on his pipe, is sitting next to Debi. She's got one hand on the top of the waiter's cart behind her, moving it slowly backwards and forwards. On the top shelf there are bottles of ketchup and mustard and vinegar. Jamal's on the bottom shelf on a bed of paper napkins, sound asleep. He was awake earlier, running around, everyone picking him up and squeezing him. Time of his life.

Wheeler's next to Daniel. When she came in she looked at me sort of shyly, but I went right over to her. "Yeah," I said into her ear, "I love you, too." She had tears in her eyes – or maybe it was me.

Even this guy Priam Harvey that I used to drink with that I haven't seen in over a year is here. I was at the bar trying to get a pickled egg when he squeezes through the crowd and lifts a hand to my shoulder. He used to write about horseracing for *Sport of Kings* magazine. In fact, it was him that I asked two years ago about a job at the track for Debi, and it was him that suggested I talk to Shorty

Rogers, another old drinking buddy, and that's how she got her job.

"How's it going, Young?" he says.

"Priam Harvey," I say, "Haven't seen you in a month of Sundays."

"On the wagon," he says.

"On the wagon? Well, what're you doing here?"

"Fell off. About two weeks ago. Pennant stress followed by World Series stress. As well as certain gambling setbacks."

I'm patting myself down for cigarettes. Must have left them at the table. But Priam's got Player's Light in his shirt pocket. " Pry," I say, "spot me a smoke?"

"Be my guest." Then he leans forward and calls down the bar, "Dexter, a shot of Bushmills, please."

But a minute later, as I'm tapping the first ash off my cigarette, it's Jessy who brings him his drink. "Here you go, Mr. Harvey," she says, and puts the glass of whiskey down on a coaster in front of him. Then she turns to me. "What do you say, big guy?"

"Hey, Jessy," I say.

She's working her butt off. Dark red curls are plastered to her forehead, and there's tiny beads of sweat, like a necklace, along her upper lip. She's busy, but she's smiling. And she's got the eyes working. The big green eyes. In the background, over the noise of the ballgame, I can hear Bob Seger on the jukebox. *Out past the corn-fields where the woods got heavy. Out in the back of my '60 Chevy.* I wink at her, and she flicks her tea towel at my ear.

Yes sir, everyone's here.

After four innings it's 2–1 Toronto. "Come on," I say to Debi.

"Where're we going?"

"Pay a visit. We'll be back in an hour."

"What about Jamal?"

"I'll ask Jessy to look after him. She can put him behind the bar."

"Goddamn it, Daddy! Somebody'll spill beer on him or puke on him or something."

"Well, maybe Wheeler'll keep an eye on him. Come on."

As we're standing up Barkas yells, "Where are you guys going? The game's just heating up!"

"You can't leave now," Daniel calls out. "We're on the doorstep, we're on the *threshold* of the World Series!"

I lean down to his ear. "We'll be back soon. Come with us if you want."

Over the noise he yells, "No, you two go. I want to be here when they get to Cone. Just make sure you come back. Hunna dolla now!"

"We'll be back." I turn to Wheeler. "Come on with us," I say.

"No," she says. "I'll go tomorrow. You and Debi go."

"In that case," I say, leaning down near *her* ear, "would you do us a small favour and babysit the kid? It's only for an hour."

She smiles up at me. "Send him over." And I roll the waiter's cart over behind Wheeler's chair.

Me and Debi walk out into the cool night air, leaving the smoke and noise behind. I unlock the driver's door of the Volare and lean across and unlock Debi's door.

"That Barry," she says, sliding in. "What a dork."

"Barry? Oh, you mean Estabrooks."

"Estabrooks, whatever. He keeps trying to hit on me. 'So you're Camp's daughter, eh?' he says to me. 'He's a mean mother at work, but I'll bet he's gentle as a lamb at home.' What a dork. What a fool."

I shake my head. "Thinks he's pretty hot with the ladies."

"So I said to him, 'Listen, fuckhead, you think my dad's gentle as a lamb? I'll just pass that message along to him.' He didn't like that very goddamn much. Shut him up like a goddamn clam."

She's a cop's daughter, that's for sure, I think to myself, and that's when I remember Woolley's last note. The crime-site boys found it yesterday afternoon, after all the excitement was over. Back at Homicide, after I'd finished my paperwork and made my 'discharge of weapon' statement, Bateman brought it to me in a plastic evidence bag and let me read it:

Dear Whoever,

When you read this, not only will I be dead, but so will Detective Sergeant Campbell Young, whose intrusion into my affairs has been unforgivable.

He must pay. The child, however, will live – despite its bastardy and its tainted blood. I draw the line at murdering babies. Like many people – not all, certainly, only the most honourable – I have my standards.

Unhappily, the child needs its mother, if only temporarily. Therefore, I will also spare the punctured, branded, big-butted whore-daughter of the policeman.

But he dies.

Professor L. C. Woolley

I asked Bateman where they found the note. It came as no surprise when he told me Woolley had stuffed it in the open mouth of Ms. Qureshi's corpse. In the dark, I'd walked right past it. But I guess I wasn't intended to read it anyway.

The little TV above Trick's bed is on, but it's tuned to "Dr. Quinn, Medicine Woman." "Uncle Artie," Debi says loudly, like Trick's deaf, "you've got the worst goddamn taste in television I ever seen."

While I'm switching the channel to the ballgame, Debi sits down beside him. When I turn and look at him closely, I can see there's no change. His eyes are still half-open and looking in different directions. His right arm's still fully flexed and his hand's still making a fist. There's no sign of the elbow brace. His moustache is full of snot again. I go into the bathroom to get a facecloth, and while I'm there I have to lean on the basin a minute.

Last Wednesday evening while I was getting drunk and generally making a fool of myself at Buster's, Daniel – as he made a point of telling me the next day – watched game four with Trick. Daniel brought his wife with him. She'd never met Trick before. Of course, they couldn't tell if Trick was listening or able to take in anything they were saying, or even if he was aware they were there, but they kept on talking anyway. While they watched the game, they just gabbed on about their kids, his job, whatever. When I phoned Daniel's place this afternoon to make sure he'd be at McCully's tonight, Alice answered, and I asked her about their visit with Trick. "Dan wanted me to go along," she said, "either for moral support or to make it seem like a social call, I don't know which." "Do *you* think he's in there?" I asked her. "Oh yes," she said, "I'm sure of it. I was holding his hand when Dan recited that old Dylan Thomas poem to him, and when he said, 'Rage, rage against the dying of the light,' your friend squeezed my hand." "Really?" I said. "Oh yes," she said, "no question about it."

I hold the facecloth under the cold tap. Then I wipe it over my own face – my forehead and my eyes. I dampen it again and go back out into the room and wipe Trick's face. Debi's sitting on the bed beside him, holding his left hand in both of hers. "Let me know if he squeezes," I say to Debi.

"What, now?"

"Whenever."

I pull a chair up near the head of the bed beside Debi, and we settle down to watch the rest of the game. The score's still 2–1. And that's the score after six, when David Cone gets the hook. For two more innings, the relievers do the job, and incredibly, as Atlanta comes up in the bottom of the ninth inning, it's still 2–1. But with a man on and two out and two strikes on Otis Nixon, Tom Henke, our closer, our stopper, our main man – the Terminator – one pitch away from all the marbles, *the World Series, for fucksake*, coughs up a single and the game's tied. I'm stunned. I'm speechless. Seconds ago, it was in the bag. Now I'm sitting here like a dead man. I have to leave the room. My heart's pounding in my throat. I need a drink. Where am I going to find a drink in a hospital? I take the elevator down to the underground parking and find the Volare and chug a warm Blue out of the trunk.

By the time I get back to Trick's room with the rest of the six-pack under my jacket, it's the bottom of the tenth, and the Braves are up again. I put the beers in the wash basin in the bathroom and turn the cold tap on. When I come out, there's a commercial on. "What happened? Is it over? Did they score?"

"No, we got them out," Debi says, big smile on her face. She's still sitting on the bed next to Trick. "Top of the eleventh coming up."

"Has he squeezed your hand yet?"

She shakes her head. "There was a twitch, but I think it was just nerves."

I look closely at Trick's face. I feel his forehead with my hand. He's hot, so I take the cloth and go back into the bathroom. I rinse it under the cold tap and come back out with two beers and the face-cloth. I pass one beer to Debi, open the other for myself, and cool off Trick's forehead with the cloth. Then I sit back down in the chair.

And then it happens.

With one out in the top of the eleventh inning, Devon White is hit by a pitch.

Roberto Alomar follows with a single.

Men on first and second.

One out.

Joe Carter flies to centre.

Two out.

Runners still on first and second.

Dave Winfield works the count full, then smacks the ball down the left-field line. All the way to the wall.

I'm jumping up and down and bellowing. White scores. Right behind him, Alomar scores. The little Filipina nurse, frowning, sticks her head into the room. I dance over to her and take her arm and pull her inside. "Baseball!" I shout at her. She looks at the score on the screen. Toronto 4, Atlanta 2.

"Oh, Jesus," she says, "we're winning!" Then she looks up at me with a worried look in her eyes. "But they've got last ups."

I get one of the beers from the bathroom, crack it, thrust it into her hands and sit her in the chair beside Trick. "What's your name?" I ask her.

"Lizzie," she says

"Do you mind holding his hand for a minute, Lizzie?"

"No, but I –"

"Good. Let me know if he squeezes."

Debi lets Lizzie take over holding Trick's hand and stands up beside me. Now she's holding my hand.

Atlanta gets the third out, and a commercial comes on.

I go into the bathroom. Two beers left. I crack one.

I go back into the room. Debi's standing at the head of the bed, behind Lizzie. Lizzie's holding Trick's hand. Their eyes are glued to the TV screen.

Jeff Blauser leads off the home half of the eleventh with a single. My guts twist.

Then Damon Berryhill – he of the three-run homer in game one – hits a tough grounder to short, and Alfredo Griffin boots it.

Men on first and third.

Nobody out.

Toronto 4, Atlanta 2.

John Smoltz, a pitcher, comes in to run for Berryhill.

Rafael Belliard sac bunts Smoltz to second. Blauser thinks about trying for home, but decides against it. Stays put at third.

One out. Men on second and third.

Pinch-hitter Brian Hunter grounds out to first.

Blauser scores from third.

Smoltz advances to third.

Toronto 4, Atlanta 3.

Two out.

Runner on third.

Otis Nixon – he of the run-scoring single in the bottom of the ninth – makes his way to the batter's box.

Toronto manager Cito Gaston walks slowly out to the mound. He takes the ball from Jimmy Key and waves for Mike Timlin.

Otis Nixon retires to the on-deck circle.

Two out.

Runner on third.

Timlin trots in from the bullpen.

The batboy comes out of the dugout to get Timlin's jacket.

Timlin begins his warm-ups.

I walk out into the hall, pulling my hair.

I take some deep breaths and walk back into the room. Nobody's moved. Lizzie's still sitting beside the bed, bottle of Blue in one hand, Trick's left hand in her other. Debi's still standing behind Lizzie, except now she has both hands balled up into fists at her cheeks.

Timlin finishes his warm-ups.

Otis Nixon steps up to the plate.

Two out.

Runner on third.

Bottom of the eleventh.

Toronto 4, Atlanta 3.

The World Series on the line.

The World Series.

Timlin winds and delivers his first pitch to Nixon.

Swing and a miss.

A national sigh of relief.

Timlin takes his cap off and wipes the sweat from his forehead.

He puts his cap back on.

He bends at the waist to get the signal from Pat Borders, his catcher.

He goes into his wind-up.

Second pitch to Nixon.

Nixon *bunts*. He bunts the ball to the first-base side.

Timlin's shocked. He didn't expect a bunt. He stumbles off the mound, chases the rolling ball, picks it up, and lobs it – *lobs it!* – towards Joe Carter at first as Nixon sprints down the baseline.

It takes an eternity, it seems to take an eternity, but the ball gets there *just* before Nixon does.

Otis Nixon is out.

Me and Lizzie and Debi are jumping up and down and hugging each other. And we bounce out into the hall, and the hall is suddenly full of cheering patients and nurses and orderlies and cleaners and interns and doctors.

"Did he squeeze?" I shout in Lizzie's ear.

"What?" she yells.

"Did he squeeze?"

"Yeah, a squeeze bunt, but they got him out!"

"No, not him. Trick! Arthur Trick! The patient!"

"Oh," she laughs, "I don't know. He might've. I certainly squeezed *him*!"

I break away from Lizzie and Debi and run back into Trick's room. On TV, the Blue Jays are heaped on top of each other near the pitcher's mound, shouting and laughing and crying. I reach for Trick's good hand, his left hand. "Squeeze, buddy," I say into his ear, but there's nothing, not a goddamn thing.

I walk into the bathroom and flick on the light. I crack the last beer and drain it in one swallow. I stand in front of the toilet. We aim to please. I'm trembling, I know that. I zip up and go back into the room and pick up the phone and dial McCully's. Someone answers, I don't know who, probably Dexter, but all I can hear is noise. Screaming, shouting, cheering. I lean over the bed and hold the receiver to Trick's ear. "Listen, Trick," I say. I lie down on my back beside him and put my head on the pillow beside his, with the receiver between us, and we're both listening to the wall of noise. "That's McCully's," I tell him. "We won. We won the World Series." I take his left hand in my right. Through the open door of the room I can see people in white coats running back and forth yelling "Blue Jays, Blue Jays!" Debi and Lizzie dance by, arm in arm, kicking like a chorus line. I squeeze Trick's hand tightly. "Squeeze back, buddy," I tell him. "Squeeze as hard as you can."

ACKNOWLEDGEMENTS

For her wise and tireless counsel, my thanks go to my editor, Dinah Forbes. For her confidence in me, I am indebted to my agent, Shawna McCarthy. I would also like to thank my copy editor, Peter Buck.

As well, for their help and encouragement, my thanks go to John Bemrose, Bob Bullen, Peter Carpenter, Carey Crockford, Cliff Donaldson, Janis Fertuck, Margaret Gilroy, Brian L. Flack, Anna Gard, Terence M. Green, David Hutchison, Roderick Jamer, Nicholas Mitchell, Dr. Bonnie Robson, Lawrence Scanlan, Barbara Simmons, Bob Simmons, and Jim Trempe.

Finally, I am most indebted to my son, Hadley, and my daughter, Reeves, and especially to my wife, Claudine, for their indulgence, support, and love.